Gillian woke and lay still.

Quickly, and in order, the events of the previous day came back to her. The flight to Mérida. The fear and fatigue. The frustrating search. The dingy little cantina where she'd found the man she had to believe would save her brother.

This was his room. This was his bed. Cautiously she turned her head—and let out a small groan. He was sleeping beside her, and in all probability he was as naked as the day he was born. His face, a little less harsh, a little less forbidding in sleep, was inches from hers. She felt then, as she'd felt when she'd first seen him, that it was the face of a man a woman would never be safe with.

Yet she'd spent the night with him and had been safe—safe from him, and from whatever forces were after her. Sighing, she shifted in bed, preparing to get up. His hand shot out. His eyes opened. Gillian froze.

Perhaps she wasn't as safe as she'd thought....

Dear Reader,

The Silhouette **Special Edition** selection has seldom been more satisfying than it is this month. For starters, beloved **Nora Roberts** delivers her long-awaited fourth volume of THE O'HURLEYS! *Without a Trace* joins its "sister" books, the first three O'Hurley stories, all now reissued with a distinctive new cover look. Award-winning novelist **Cheryl Reavis** also graces the Silhouette **Special Edition** list with a gritty, witty look into the ironclad heart of one of romance's most memorable heroes as he reluctantly pursues *Patrick Gallagher's Widow*. Another award-winner, **Mary Kirk**, returns with a unique twist on a universal theme drawn from the very furthest reaches of human experience in *Miracles*, while ever-popular **Debbie Macomber** brings her endearing characteristic touch to a wonderfully infuriating traditional male in *The Cowboy's Lady*. Well-known historical and contemporary writer **Victoria Pade** pulls out all the stops (including the f-stop) to get your heart *Out on a Limb*, and stylish, sophisticated **Brooke Hastings** gives new meaning to continental charm in an unforgettable *Seduction*. I hope you'll agree that, this month, these six stellar Silhouette authors bring new meaning to the words **Special Edition**!

Our best wishes,

Leslie Kazanjian
Senior Editor

NORA ROBERTS
Without a Trace

Silhouette Special Edition

Published by Silhouette Books New York

America's Publisher of Contemporary Romance

To black sheep

SILHOUETTE BOOKS
300 East 42nd St., New York, N.Y. 10017

ISBN: 0-373-09625-9

First Silhouette Books printing October 1990

Printed in the U.S.A.

Series by Nora Roberts

Silhouette Special Edition

MacGregor Series:

Playing the Odds #225
Tempting Fate #235
All the Possibilities #247
One Man's Art #259
For Now, Forever #361

THE O'HURLEYS!

The Last Honest Woman #451
Dance to the Piper #463
Skin Deep #475
Without a Trace #625

Silhouette Intimate Moments

Cordina's Royal Family:

Affaire Royale #142
Command Performance #198
The Playboy Prince #212

NORA ROBERTS

is one of Silhouette Books' most popular and prolific authors. She has written for the Silhouette Romance, Silhouette Special Edition and Silhouette Intimate Moments lines, as well as contributing stories to *Silhouette Christmas Stories 1986* and to the 1989 *Silhouette Summer Sizzler*.

When we published the four-book MacGregor Series, readers wrote in requesting the parents' story—and Nora Roberts responded by writing *For Now, Forever*. When we published the fifth MacGregor book, we reissued the first four. When Nora Roberts wrote THE O'HURLEYS! about triplet sisters, readers clamored for the story of their elusive older brother. Silhouette Books is pleased to present *Without a Trace*, along with reissuing *The Last Honest Woman*, *Dance to the Piper* and *Skin Deep*. When Silhouette asked Nora to comment on the miniseries, she said:

"Writing interlocking stories is always a pleasure. I get such a kick out of discovering what happened to the characters once their particular book closed! With the O'Hurleys, I discovered a family I could admire, a family I could laugh with and hurt for. I'm glad I had the chance to know them, and I hope that you'll feel the same way."

And for MacGregor fans, watch for a collection of historical Christmas stories in November for a look at the early MacGregor clan.

THE O'HURLEYS!
Book Four: Trace's Tale

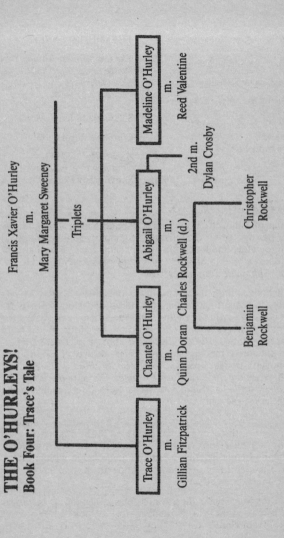

Francis Xavier O'Hurley
m.
Mary Margaret Sweeney

Triplets

Trace O'Hurley
m.
Gillian Fitzpatrick

Chantel O'Hurley
m.
Quinn Doran

Abigail O'Hurley
m.
Charles Rockwell (d.)
2nd m.
Dylan Crosby

Madeline O'Hurley
m.
Reed Valentine

Benjamin Rockwell

Christopher Rockwell

Prologue

Pick up the beat on the intro, Tracey boy, you're dragging it.''

Frank O'Hurley stood on his mark, stage right, and prepared to go through his opening routine again. The three-night run in Terre Haute might not be the highlight of his career, and it certainly wasn't the apex of his dreams, but he was going to give the audience their money's worth. Every two-bit gig was a dress rehearsal for the big break.

He counted off the beat, then swung into the routine with the enthusiasm of a man half his age. The calendar might put Frank's age at forty, but his feet would always be sixteen.

He'd written the little novelty number himself, with the wide-eyed hope that it would become the O'Hurley trademark. At the piano, his oldest child and only son tried to put some life into a melody he'd played too many times to count—and dreamed of other things and other places.

On cue, his mother spun onstage with his father. Even after endless routines, endless theaters, Trace still felt a tug of affection for them. Just as, after endless routines, endless theaters, he felt what had become a familiar tug of frustration.

Would he always be here, beating out a second rate tune on a second-rate piano, trying to fill his father's big dreams that hadn't a hope in hell of coming true?

As she'd been doing most of her life, Molly matched her steps to Frank's. She could have done the number blindfold. As it was, while she dipped, spun and doubledstepped, her mind was more on her son than her timing.

The boy wasn't happy, she thought. And he wasn't a child any longer. He was on the brink of manhood and straining to go his own way. It was that single fact, she knew, that terrified Frank to the point that he refused to acknowledge it.

The arguments had become more frequent, more heated. Soon, she thought, all too soon, something was going to explode, and she might not be able to pick up all the pieces.

Kick, ball change, dip, and her three daughters tapped onto the stage. With her heart close to Frank's, Molly could feel him swell with pride. She would hate for him to lose that pride or the hope that kept him the youthful dreamer she'd fallen in love with.

As Molly and Frank moved offstage, the routine eased smoothly into the opening song. The O'Hurley Triplets—Chantel, Abby and Maddy—launched into three-part harmony as if they'd been born singing.

They practically had, Molly thought. But, like Trace, they weren't children any longer. Chantel was already using her wit and her wiles to fascinate the men in the audience. Abby, steady and quiet, was just marking time. And it wouldn't be long before they lost Maddy. As a mother, Molly felt both pride and regret at the thought that her youngest had too much talent to remain part of a roving troupe for long.

Yet it was Trace who concerned her now. He sat at the scarred piano in the dingy little club, his mind a thousand miles away. She'd seen the brochures he collected. Pictures and stories on places like Zanzibar, New Guinea, Mazatlán. Sometimes, on the long train or bus rides from city to city, Trace would talk of the mosques and caverns and mountains he wanted to see.

And Frank would brush those dreams off like dust, desperately clinging to his own—and to his son.

"Not bad, darlings." Frank bounced back to center stage to give each of his daughters a hug. "Trace, your mind's not on the music. You need to pump some life into it."

"There hasn't been any life in that number since Des Moines."

A few months before, Frank would have chuckled and rubbed a hand over his son's hair. But now he felt the sting of criticism, man to man. His chin came up to a stubborn point. "Nothing wrong with the song and never has been. It's your playing that's lacking. You lost tempo twice. I'm tired of you sulking over the keys."

Playing peacemaker, Abby stepped between her father and brother. The growing tension had been keeping the family on edge for weeks. "We're all a little tired, I think."

"I can speak for myself, Abby." Trace pushed away from the piano. "No one's sulking at the keys."

"Hah!" Frank brushed Molly's restraining hand away. Lord, the boy was tall, Frank thought. Tall and straight and almost a stranger. But Frank O'Hurley was still in charge, and it was time his son remembered it. "You've been in a black mood since I told you I wouldn't have a son of mine harking off to Hong Kong or God knows where like some Gypsy. Your place is here, with your family. Your responsibility is to the troupe."

"It's not my damn responsibility."

Frank's eyes narrowed. "Watch your tone, boy-o, you're not so big I can't take you down."

"It's time somebody took that tone with you," Trace went on, spewing out everything he'd held back for too long. "Year after year we play second-rate songs in second-rate clubs."

"Trace." Maddy said it quietly, adding a pleading look. "Don't."

"Don't what?" he demanded. "Don't tell him the truth? God knows he won't hear it anyway, but I'll have my say. The three of you and Ma have protected him from it long enough."

"Temper tantrums are so boring," Chantel said lazily, though her nerves were strung tight. "Why don't we all break to neutral corners?"

"No." Quivering with indignation, Frank stepped away from his daughters. "Go on, then, have your say."

"I'm tired of riding a bus to nowhere, of pretending the next stop's the brass ring. You drag us from town to town, year after year."

"Drag you?" Frank's face flushed with fury. "Is that what I'm doing?"

"No." Molly stepped forward, her eyes on her son. "No, it's not. We've all of us gone willing, because it was what we wanted. If one of us doesn't want it, he has a right to say so, but not to be cruel."

"He doesn't listen!" Trace shouted. "He doesn't care what I want or don't want. I've told you. I've told you," he rounded on his father. "Every time I try to talk to you, all I get is how we have to keep the family together, how the big break is right around the corner, when there's nothing around the corner but another lousy one-night stand in another two-bit club."

It was too close to the truth, too close to what would make him feel like a failure when all he'd wanted was to give his family the best and the brightest. Temper was the only weapon Frank had, and he used it.

"You're ungrateful and selfish and stupid. All my life I've worked to pave the way for you. To open doors so you could step through. Now it's not good enough."

Trace felt tears of frustration burn his eyes, but didn't back down. "No, it's not good enough, because I don't want to walk through your doors. I want something else, I want something more, but you're so wrapped up in your own hopeless dream you can't see that I hate it. And that the more you push me to follow your dream instead of my own, the closer I come to hating you."

Trace hadn't meant to say that, and shocked himself speechless with his own bitter words. Before his stunned eyes, his father paled, aged and seemed to shrivel. If he could have taken the words back, he might have tried. But it was too late.

"Take your dream, then," Frank said in a voice rough with emotion. "Go where it takes you. But don't come back, Trace O'Hurley. Don't come back to me when it leaves you cold. There'll be no killing of the fatted calf for you."

He strode off, stage left.

"He didn't mean it," Abby said quickly, taking Trace's arm. "You know he didn't."

"Neither of them did." Her own eyes welling, Maddy looked helplessly at her mother.

"Everyone just needs to cool off." Even with her flair for the dramatic, Chantel was shaken. "Come on, Trace, we'll go for a walk."

"No." With a little sigh, Molly shook her head. "You girls go on now, let me talk to Trace." She waited until they were alone, then, feeling old and tired, sat on the piano bench. "I know you've been unhappy," she said quietly. "And that you've bottled things up. I should have done something about it."

"None of it's your fault."

"Mine as much as his, Trace. The things you said cut deep in him, and that won't heal for a while. I know some were said in temper, but others were true." She looked up, studying the face of her firstborn and only son. "I think it was true what you said about coming to hate him if he didn't let you go."

"Ma—"

"No. It was a hard thing to say, but harder if it came true. You want to go."

He opened his mouth, on the edge of caving in yet again. But the rage he had felt for his father was still too close, and it frightened him. "I have to go."

"Then do it." She stood again to put her hands on his shoulders. "And do it quick and clean, else he'll charm or shame you into staying and you'll never forgive him. Take your own road. We'll be here when you come back."

"I love you."

"I know. I want to keep it that way." She kissed him, then hurried away, knowing she had to hold off her own tears until she had comforted her husband.

That night, Trace packed his belongings—clothes, a harmonica, and dozens of brochures. He left a note that said simply, "I'll write." He had $327.00 in his pocket when he walked out of the motel and stuck out his thumb.

Chapter One

The whiskey was cheap and had the bite of an angry woman. Trace sucked air through his teeth and waited to die. When he didn't, he poured a second shot from the bottle, tipped back in his chair and watched the open expanse of the Gulf of Mexico. Behind him, the little cantina was gearing up for the evening's business. Frijoles and enchiladas were frying in the kitchen. The smell of onions was coming on strong, competing with the odors of liquor and stale tobacco. The conversations were in rapid-fire Spanish that Trace understood and ignored.

He didn't want company. He wanted the whiskey and the water.

The sun was a red ball over the Gulf. There were low-lying clouds shimmering with pinks and golds. The fire of the whiskey was settling into a nice, comfortable heat in the pit of his stomach. Trace O'Hurley was on vacation, and by God he was going to enjoy it.

The States was only a short plane ride away. He'd stopped thinking of them as home years before—or at least he'd convinced himself he had. It had been twelve years since he'd sailed out of San Francisco, a young, idealistic man riddled with guilt, driven by dreams. He'd seen Hong Kong, and Singapore. For a year he'd traveled the Orient, living by his wits and the talent he'd inherited from his parents. He'd played in hotel lounges and strip joints at night and soaked up the foreign sights and smells by day.

Then there had been Tokyo. He'd played American music in a seedy little club with the idea of making his way across Asia.

It had simply been a matter of being in the right place at the right time. Or, as Trace thought when he was feeling churlish, the wrong place at the wrong time. A barroom brawl was a common enough occurrence. Frank O'Hurley had taught his son more than how to keep the beat. Trace knew when to swing and when to retreat.

He hadn't started out with the intention of saving Charlie Forrester's life. And he certainly hadn't known that Forrester was an American agent.

Fate, Trace thought now as he watched the red sun sinking closer to the horizon. It was fate that had caused him to deflect the knife meant for Charlie's heart. And it was fate and its wily ways that had embroiled him in the grim game of espionage. Trace had indeed made his way across Asia, and beyond. But he'd been bankrolled by the International Security System.

Now Charlie was dead. Trace poured himself another shot and drank a toast to his friend and mentor. It wasn't an assassin's bullet or a knife in a dark alley that had gotten him, but a stroke. Charlie's body had simply decided his time was up.

So Trace O'Hurley sat in a little dive on the Mexican coast and held his own wake.

The funeral was in fourteen hours in Chicago. Because he wasn't ready to cross the Rio Grande, Trace would stay in Mexico, drink to his old friend and contemplate life. Charlie would understand, Trace decided as he stretched out long legs clad in dingy khaki. Charlie had never been one for ceremony. Just do the job, have a drink and get on with the next one.

Trace pulled out a crushed pack of cigarettes and searched in the pocket of his dirt-streaked shirt for a match. His hands were long and wide palmed. At ten he'd dreamed of becoming a concert pianist. But he'd dreamed of becoming many things. A battered bush hat shadowed his face as he struck the match and touched it to the end of the cigarette.

He was very tanned, because his last job had kept him outdoors. His hair was thick and, because he hadn't bothered to have it trimmed, long enough to curl beyond the hat in dark blond disarray. His face was damp from the heat, and lean. There was a scar, small and white, along the left side of his jaw—an encounter with a broken bottle. His nose had been slightly out of alignment ever since he'd been sixteen. A fight over a girl's honor—or lack thereof.

His body was on the lanky side at the moment, due to a prolonged hospital stay. The last bullet he'd taken had nearly killed him. Even without the whiskey and the grief, he had a dangerous look. The bones were prominent, the eyes intense. Even now, when he was on his own time, they made occasional sweeps of the room.

He hadn't shaved in three days, and his beard was rough enough to give his mouth a surly look. The waiter was happy to leave him with his bottle and his solitude.

As dusk fell, the sky became quieter, and the cantina noisier. A radio played Mexican music interrupted by occasional bursts of static. Someone broke a glass. Two men started to argue about fishing, politics and women. Trace poured another shot.

He saw her the minute she walked in. Old habits had his eye on the door. Training had him taking in the details without seeming to look at all. A tourist who'd made a wrong turn, he thought as he took in the ivory skin dashed with freckles that went with her red hair. She'd burn to a crisp after an hour under the Yucatán sun. A pity, he thought mildly, and went back to his drink.

He'd expected her to back out the moment she realized the type of place she'd wandered into. Instead, she went up to the bar. Trace crossed his ankles and whiled away the time by studying her.

Her white slacks were spotless despite the dusty heat of the day. She wore them with a purple shirt that was loose enough to be cool. Even so, he noted that she was slender, with enough curve to give the baggy slacks some style. Her hair, almost the color of the setting sun, was caught back in a braid, but her face was turned away, so he could see only her profile. Classic, he decided without much interest. Cameo style. The champagne-and-caviar type.

He tossed back the rest of the drink and decided to get very drunk—for Charlie's sake.

He'd just lifted the bottle when the woman turned and looked directly at him. From the shadow of his hat, Trace met the look. Tensed, he continued to pour as she crossed the room toward him.

"Mr. O'Hurley?"

His brow lifted only slightly at the accent. It had a trace of Ireland, the same trace his father's had taken on in anger or in joy. He sipped his whiskey and said nothing.

"You are Trace O'Hurley?"

There was a hint of nerves in the voice, as well, he noted. And, close up, he could see smudges of shadows under what were extraordinary green eyes. Her lips pressed together. Her fingers twisted on the handle of the canvas bag slung over her shoulder. Trace set the whiskey down and realized he was just a bit too drunk to be annoyed.

"Might be. Why?"

"I was told you'd be in Mérida. I've been looking for you for two days." And he was anything but what she'd expected. If she wasn't so desperate, she'd already have fled. His clothes were dirty, he smelled of whiskey, and he looked like a man who could peel the skin off you without drawing blood. She pulled in a deep breath and decided to take her chances. "May I sit down?"

With a shrug, Trace kicked a chair back from the table. An agent—from either side—would have approached him differently. "Suit yourself."

She wrapped her fingers around the back of the chair and wondered why her father believed this crude drunkard was the answer. But her legs weren't as steady as they might be, so she sat down. "It's very important that I speak with you. Privately."

Trace looked beyond her to the cantina. It was crowded now, and getting noisier by the minute. "This'll do. Now why don't you tell me who you are, how you knew I'd be in Mérida, and what the hell you want?"

She linked her fingers together because they were trembling. "I'm Dr. Fitzpatrick. Dr. Gillian Fitzpatrick. Charles Forrester told me where you were, and I want you to save my brother's life."

Trace kept his eyes on her as he lifted the bottle. His voice was quiet and flat. "Charlie's dead."

"I know." She thought she'd glimpsed something, some flash of humanity, in his eyes. It was gone now, but Gillian still responded to it. "I'm sorry. I understand you were close."

"I'd like to know how you understand anything or why you expect me to believe Charlie would have told you where to find me."

Gillian wiped a damp palm over the thigh of her slacks before reaching into her bag. In silence, she handed a sealed envelope to him.

Something told Trace he'd be better off not taking it. He should get up, walk out and lose himself in the warm Mexican night. It was only because she'd mentioned Charlie that he broke the seal and read the note inside.

Charlie had used the code they'd communicated with during their last assignment. As always, he'd kept the message brief: "Listen to the lady. No involvement with the organization at this time. Contact me."

Of course, there was no way to contact Charlie now, Trace thought as he folded the letter again. With the feeling that, even dead, Charlie was still guiding his moves, he looked at the woman again. "Explain."

"Mr. Forrester was a friend of my father's. I didn't know him well myself. I was away a lot. About fifteen years ago they worked together on a project known as Horizon."

Trace pushed the bottle aside. Vacation or not, he couldn't afford to dull his senses any further. "What's your father's name?"

"Sean. Dr. Sean Brady Fitzpatrick."

He knew the name. He knew the project. Fifteen years before, some of the top researchers and scientists in the world had been employed to develop a serum that would immunize man against the effects of ionizing radiation injury—one of the nastier side effects of nuclear war. The ISS had been in charge of security and had monitored and maintained the project. It had cost hundreds of millions, and it had been a whopping failure.

"You'd have been a kid."

"I was twelve." She jolted and turned around nervously when something crashed in the kitchen. "Of course, I didn't know about the project then, but later..." The smell of onions and liquor was overpowering. She wanted to get up, wanted to walk along the beach, where the air would be warm and clear, but she forced herself to continue. "The project was dropped, but my father continued to work on it. He had other obligations, but whenever possible he resumed experimenting."

"Why? He wouldn't have been funded for it."

"My father believed in Horizon. The concept fascinated him, not as a defense, but as an answer to the insanity we're all aware exists. As to the money—well, my father has reached a point where he can afford to indulge his beliefs."

Not only a scientist, but a rich scientist, Trace thought as he watched her from under the brim of his hat. And this one looked as if she'd gone to a tidy convent school in Switzerland. It was the posture that usually gave it away. No one taught proper posture like a nun.

"Go on."

"In any case, my father turned all his notes and findings over to my brother five years ago, after he suffered his first heart attack. For the past few years, my father has been too ill to continue intense laboratory work. And now..."

For a moment, Gillian closed her eyes. The terror and the traveling were taking their toll. As a scientist, she knew she needed food and rest. As a daughter, a sister, she had to finish. "Mr. O'Hurley, might I have a drink?"

Trace shoved both bottle and glass across the table. He was nibbling, but he wasn't ready to bite yet. She interested him, certainly, but he'd learned long ago that you could be interested and uninvolved.

She'd have preferred coffee or at the most, a snifter of warm brandy. She started to refuse the whiskey, but then caught the look in Trace's eye. So he was testing her. She was used to being tested. Her chin came up automatically. Her shoulders straightened. Steady, she poured a double shot and downed it in one swallow.

She drew in breath through a throat that felt as if it had been blowtorched. Blinking the moisture from her eyes, she let it out again. "Thank you."

The light of humor flashed in his eyes for the first time. "Don't mention it."

Hot and bitter though it was, the whiskey helped. "My father is very ill, Mr. O'Hurley. Too ill to travel. He contacted Mr. Forrester but was unable to fly to Chicago himself. I went to Mr. Forrester in his place, and Mr. Forrester sent me to you. I was told that you're the best man for the job."

Trace lit another cigarette. He figured he hadn't been the best man for anything since he'd lain bleeding in the dirt, a bullet two inches from his heart. "Which is?"

"About a week ago, my brother was taken, kidnapped by an organization known as Hammer. You've heard of them?"

It was training that kept his face blank over a mix of fear and rage. His association with that particular organization had nearly killed him.

"I've heard of them."

"All we know is that they took my brother from his home in Ireland, where he had continued, and nearly completed, his work on the Horizon project. They intend to hold him until he has perfected the serum. You understand what the repercussions could be if a group like that possessed the formula?''

Trace tapped the ash of his cigarette onto the wooden floor. ''I've been told I have a reasonably developed intelligence.''

Driven, she grabbed his wrist. Because she was a woman in a man's field, physical contact was usually reserved for family and loved ones. Now she held on to Trace, and the only hope she had. ''Mr. O'Hurley, we can't afford to joke about this.''

''Careful how you use *we*.'' Trace waited until her fingers uncurled. ''Let me ask you, Dr. Fitzpatrick, is your brother a smart man?''

''He's a genius.''

''No, no, I mean does he have two grains of common sense to rub together?''

Her shoulders straightened again because she was all too ready to lay her head on the table and weep. ''Flynn is a brilliant scientist, and a man who under normal circumstances can take care of himself quite nicely.''

''Fine, because only a fool would believe that if he came up with the formula for Hammer, he'd stay alive. They like to call themselves terrorists, liberators, rebels. What they are is a bunch of disorganized fanatics, headed by a rich madman. They kill more people by mistake than they do on purpose.'' Frowning, he rubbed a hand over his chest. ''They've got enough savvy to keep them going, and pots of money, but basically, they're idiots. And there's nothing more dangerous than a bunch of dedicated idiots. My advice to your brother would be to spit in their eye.''

Her already pale skin was ghost white. ''They have his child.'' Gillian placed a hand on the table for support as she rose. "They took his six-year-old daughter." With that, she fled the cantina.

Trace sat where he was. Not his business, he reminded himself as he reached for the bottle again. He was on vacation. He'd come back from the dead and intended to enjoy his life. Alone.

Swearing, he slammed the bottle down and went after her.

Her anger had her covering ground quickly. She heard him call her name but didn't stop. She'd been an idiot to believe that a man like him could help. She'd be better off attempting to negotiate with the terrorists. At least with them she wouldn't go in expecting any compassion.

When he grabbed her arm, she swung around. Temper gave her the energy that lack of sleep and food had depleted.

"I told you to wait a damn minute."

"You've already given me your considered opinion, Mr. O'Hurley. There doesn't seem to be any need for further discussion. I don't know what Mr. Forrester saw in you. I don't know why he sent me to look for a man who would rather sit in a seedy little dive swilling whiskey than help save lives. I came looking for a man of courage and compassion and found a tired, dirty drunk who cares about no one and nothing."

It stung, more than he'd expected. His fingers stayed firm on her arm as he waved away a small boy with a cardboard box filled with Chiclets. "Have you finished? You're making a scene."

"My brother and niece are being held by a group of terrorists. Do you think I care whether I embarrass you or not?"

"It takes more than an Irish redhead on a roll to embarrass me," he said easily. "But I have a policy against drawing attention to myself. Old habit. Let's take a walk."

She very nearly yanked her arm away. The part of her that was pride burned to do it. The part that was love triumphed, and she subsided. In silence she walked beside him, down the narrow planks that led to the water.

The sand was white here against a dark sea and a darker sky. A few boats were docked, waiting for tomorrow's fishing or tomorrow's tourists. The night was quiet enough that the music from the cantina carried to them. Trace noted that somebody was singing about love and a woman's infidelity. Somebody always was.

"Look, Dr. Fitzpatrick, you caught me at a bad time. I don't know why Charlie sent you to me."

"Neither do I."

He stopped long enough to cup his hands around a match and a cigarette. "What I mean is, this situation should be handled by the ISS."

She was calm again. Gillian didn't mind losing her temper. It felt good. But she also knew that more was accomplished with control. "The ISS wants the formula as badly as Hammer. Why should I trust my brother's and my niece's lives to them?"

"Because they're the good guys."

Gillian turned toward the sea, and the wind hit her dead on. Though it helped clear her head, she didn't notice the first stars blinking to life. "They are an organization run by many men—some good, some bad, all ambitious, all with their own concept of what is necessary for peace and order. At the moment, my only concern is my family. Do you have family, Mr. O'Hurley?"

He drew hard on the cigarette. "Yeah." Over the border, he thought. He hadn't seen them in seven years, or was it eight? He'd lost track. But he knew Chantel was in L.A. filming a movie, Maddy was in New York starring in a new play. Abby was raising horses and kids in Virginia. His parents were finishing up a week's gig in Buffalo.

He might have lost track of the time, but not of his family.

"Would you trust the lives of any of the members of your family to an organization? One that, if they considered it necessary for the common good, might sacrifice them?" She closed her eyes. The wind felt like heaven, warm, salty and strong. "Mr. Forrester understood and agreed that what was needed to save my brother and his child was a man who would care more about them than the formula. He thought you were that man."

"He was off base." Trace pitched his cigarette into the surf. "Charlie knew I was considering retiring. This was just his way of keeping me in the game."

"Are you as good as he told me?"

With a laugh. Trace rubbed a hand over his chin. "Probably better. Charlie was never much for back patting."

Gillian turned again, this time to face him. He didn't look like a hero to her, with the rough beard and the grimy clothes. But there had been strength in his hand when he'd taken her arm, and she'd sensed an undercurrent of violence. He'd be passionate when it was something he wanted, she thought, whether it was a goal, a dream or a woman. Under usual circumstances, she preferred men with cool, analytical minds, who attacked a problem with logic and patience. But it wasn't a scientist she needed now.

Trace dipped his hands into his pocket and fought the urge to squirm. She was looking at him as though he were a laboratory rat, and he didn't like it. Maybe it was the hint of Ireland in her voice or the shadows under her eyes, but he couldn't bring himself to walk away.

"Look, I'll contact the ISS. The closest field office is in San Diego. You can feed them whatever information you have. Inside of twenty-four hours, some of the best agents in the world will be looking for your brother."

"I can give you a hundred thousand dollars." Her mind was made up. She had discarded logic for instinct. Forrester had said this man could do it. Her father had agreed. Gillian was throwing her vote with theirs. "The price isn't negotiable, because it's all I have. Find my brother and my niece, and with a hundred thousand dollars you can retire in style."

He stared at her for a moment, and then, biting off an oath, he walked toward the sea. The woman was crazy. He was offering her the skill of the best intelligence organization in the world, and she was tossing money in his face. A tidy sum.

Trace watched the sea roll up and recede. He'd never been able to hang on to more than a few thousand at a time. It just wasn't his nature. But a hundred thousand could mean the difference between retiring or just talking about retiring.

The spray flew over his face as he shook his head. He didn't want to get involved, not with her, not with her family, and not with some nebulous formula that might or might not save the world from the big blast.

What he wanted was to go back to his hotel, order up a five-star meal and go to bed on a full stomach. God, he wanted some peace. Time to figure out what to do with his life.

"If you're determined to have a free-lancer, I can give you a couple of names."

"I don't want a couple of names. I want you."

Something about the way she said it made his stomach knot. The reaction made him all the more determined to get rid of her. "I just came off nine months of deep cover. I'm burned out, Doc. You need someone young, gung ho and greedy." For the second time he ran his hands over his face. "I'm tired."

"That's a cop-out," she said, and the sudden strength in her voice surprised him enough to have him turning around. She stood straight, loose tendrils of hair flying around her face, pale as marble in the light of the rising moon. It suddenly struck him that in fury and despair she was the most stunning woman he'd ever seen. Then he lost that thought as she advanced on him, her Irish leading the way.

"You don't want to get involved. You don't want to be responsible for the lives of an innocent man and a young child. You don't want to be touched by that. Mr. Forrester saw you as some kind of a knight, a man of principle and compassion, but he was wrong. You're a selfish shell of a man who couldn't have deserved a friend like him. He was a man who cared, who tried to help for nothing more than the asking, and who died because of his own standards."

Trace's head snapped up. "What the hell are you talking about?" His eyes caught the light and glittered dangerously. In one swift, silent move he had Gillian by both arms. "What the hell do you mean? Charlie had a stroke."

Her heart was beating hard in her throat. She'd never seen anyone look more capable of murder than Trace did at that moment. "He was trying to help. They'd followed me. Three men."

"What three men?"

"I don't know. Terrorists, agents, whatever you chose to call them. They broke into the house when I was with him." She tried to even her breathing by concentrating on the pain his fingers were inflicting on her arms. "Mr. Forrester pushed me through some kind of hidden panel in his library. I heard them on the other side. They were looking for me." She could remember even now how hot and airless it had been behind the panel. How dark. "He was putting them off, telling them I'd left. They threatened him, but he stuck by the story. It seemed that they believed him."

Her voice was shaking. Trace watched her dig her teeth into her lower lip to steady herself. "It got very quiet. I was more frightened by the quiet and tried to get out to help him. I couldn't find the mechanism."

"Two inches down from the ceiling."

"Yes. It took me almost an hour before I found it." She didn't add that she'd fought hysteria the entire time, or that at one point she'd beaten against the panel and shouted, prepared to give herself up rather than stay in the suffocating dark. "When I got out, he was dead. If I'd been quicker, I might have been able to help him.... I'll never be sure."

"The ISS said stroke."

"It was diagnosed as one. Such things can be brought on by a simple injection. In any case, they caused the stroke, and they caused it while looking for me. I have to live with that." Trace had dropped his grip, and she'd grabbed his shirtfront without realizing it, her fingers curled tight. "And so do you. If you won't help me for compassion or for money, maybe you'll do it for revenge."

He turned away from her again. He'd accepted Charlie's death once. A stroke, a little time bomb in the brain set to go off at a certain time. Fate had said: Charlie, you've got sixty-three years, five months, on earth. Make the best of it. That he'd accepted.

Now he was being told it wasn't fate, it was three men. Fate was something he was Irish enough to live with. But it was possible to hate men, to pay men back. It was something to think about. Trace decided to get a pot of black coffee and do just that.

"I'll take you back to your hotel."

"But—"

"We'll get some coffee and you can tell me everything Charlie said, everything you know. Then I'll tell you if I'll help you."

If it was all he'd give, she'd take it. "I checked into the same hotel as you. It seemed practical."

"Fine." Trace took her arm and began to walk with her. She wasn't steady, he noted. Whatever fire had pushed her this far was fading fast. She swayed once, and he tightened his grip. "When's the last time you ate?"

"Yesterday."

He gave a snort that might have been a laugh. "What kind of a doctor are you?"

"Physicist."

"Even a physicist should know something about nutrition. It goes like this. You eat, you stay alive. You don't eat, you fall down." He released her arm and slipped his around her waist. She would have protested if she'd had the energy.

"You smell like a horse."

"Thanks. I spent most of the day bumping around the jungle. Great entertainment. What part of Ireland?"

Fatigue was spreading from her legs to her brain. His arm felt so strong, so comforting. Without realizing it, she leaned against him. "What?"

"What part of Ireland are you from?"

"Cork."

"Small world." He steered her into the lobby. "So's my father. What room?"

"Two-twenty-one."

"Right next door to mine."

"I gave the desk clerk a thousand pesos."

Because the elevators were small and heated like ovens, he took the stairs. "You're an enterprising woman, Dr. Fitzpatrick."

"Most women are. It's still a man's world."

He had his doubts about that, but he didn't argue the point. "Key?"

She dug into her pocket, fighting off the weakness. She wouldn't faint. That she promised herself. Trace took the key from her palm and stuck it in the lock. When he opened the door, he shoved her against the wall in the hallway.

"What's wrong with you?" she asked. She swallowed the rest when she saw him draw a hunting knife out of his pocket.

It was all he had. He hadn't considered it necessary to strap on a gun while on vacation. His eyes were narrow as he stepped into the room and kicked aside some of the debris.

"Oh, God." Gillian braced herself in the doorway and looked. They'd done a thorough job. Even someone inexperienced in such matters could see that nothing had been overlooked.

Her suitcase had been cut apart, and the clothes she hadn't unpacked were strewn everywhere. The mattress and the cushions from the single chair had been slit, and hunks of white stuffing littered the floor. The drawers of the bureau had been pulled out and overturned.

Trace checked the bath and the access through the windows. They'd come in the front, he concluded, and a search of a room this size wouldn't have taken more than twenty minutes.

"You've still got your tail, Doc." He turned but didn't sheath the knife. "Pick up what you need. We'll talk next door."

She didn't want to touch the clothes, but she forced herself to be practical. She needed them, and it didn't matter that other hands had touched them. Moving quickly, she gathered up slacks and skirts and blouses. "I have cosmetics and toiletries in the bath."

"Not anymore you don't. They dumped the lot." Trace took her arm again. This time he checked the hall and moved quietly to the room next door. Again he braced Gillian against the wall and opened the door. His fingers relaxed on the handle of the knife, though only slightly. So they hadn't made him. That was good. He signaled to her to come in behind him, double-locked the door, then began a careful search.

It was an old habit to leave a few telltales, one he followed even off duty. The book on his nightstand was still a quarter inch over the edge. The single strand of hair he'd left on the bedspread hadn't been disturbed. He pulled the drapes, then sat on the bed and picked up the phone.

In perfect Spanish that had Gillian's brow lifting, he ordered dinner and two pots of coffee. "I got you a steak," he said when he hung up the phone. "But this is Mexico, so I wouldn't expect it for about an hour. Sit down."

With her clothes still rolled in her arms, she obeyed. Trace pushed himself back on the bed and crossed his legs.

"What are they after?"

"I beg your pardon?"

"They've got your brother. Why do they want you?"

"I occasionally work with Flynn. About six months ago I spent some time with him in Ireland on Horizon. We had a breakthrough." She let her head tilt back against the cushion. "We believed we'd found a way to immunize the individual cell. You see, in ionizing radiation injury the main structure affected is the single cell. Energy rays enter the tissue like bullets and cause localized injury in the cells.

We were working on a formula that prevented molecular changes within the affected cells. In that way we could—''

''That's just fascinating, Doc. But what I want to know is why they're after you.''

She realized she'd nearly been reciting the information in her sleep and tried to straighten in the chair. ''I took the notes on this part of the project with me, back to the institute, to work on them more intensely. Without them it could take Flynn another year, maybe more, to reconstruct the experiment.''

''So you're the missing piece of the puzzle, so to speak?''

''I have the information.'' The words began to slur as her eyes closed.

''You're telling me you carry that stuff with you?'' God save him from amateurs. ''Did they get it?''

''No, they didn't get it, and yes, I have it with me. Excuse me,'' she murmured, and went to sleep.

Trace sat where he was for a moment and studied her. Under other circumstances he would have been amused to have a woman he'd known for only a few hours fall asleep in the chair of his hotel room in the middle of a conversation. At the moment, his sense of humor wasn't what it might have been.

She was deathly pale from exhaustion. Her hair was a fiery halo that spoke of strength and passion. Clothes lay balled in her lap. Her bag was crushed between her hip and the side of the chair. Without hesitation, Trace got up and eased it out. Gillian didn't move a muscle as he dumped the contents on the bed.

He pushed aside a hairbrush and an antique hammered-silver compact. There was a small paperback phrase book—which told him she didn't speak the language—and the stub of a ticket for a flight from O'Hare. Her checkbook had been neatly balanced in a precise hand. Six hundred and twenty-eight dollars and eighty-three cents. Her passport picture was better than most, but it didn't capture the stubbornness he'd already been witness to. She'd worn her hair loose for it, he noted, frowning a bit at the thick riot of curls that fell beyond her shoulders.

He'd always had a weakness for long, luxuriant, feminine hair.

She'd been born in Cork twenty-seven years before, in May, and had kept her Irish citizenship, though her address was listed as New York.

Trace pushed the passport aside and reached for her wallet. She could use a new one, he decided as he opened it. The leather had been worn smooth at the creases. Her driver's license was nearly up for renewal, and the picture on it carried the same serious expression as the passport. She had three hundred and change in cash, and another two thousand in traveler's checks. He found a shopping list folded into the corner of the billfold along with a parking ticket. A long-overdue parking ticket.

A flip through the pictures she carried showed him a black-and-white snapshot of a man and a woman. From the clothes he judged that it had been taken in the late fifties. The woman's hair was as neat as the collar and cuffs on the blouse she wore, but she was smiling as though she meant it. The man, husky and full-faced, had his arm around the woman, but he looked a bit uncomfortable.

Trace flipped to the next and found a picture of Gillian in overalls and a T-shirt, her head thrown back, laughing, her arms around the same man. He was older by perhaps twenty years. She looked happy, delighted with herself, and nothing like a physicist. Trace flipped quickly to the next snapshot.

This was the brother. The resemblance to Gillian was stronger than with the people Trace assumed were her parents. His hair was a tamer red, almost a mahogany, but he had the same wide-set green eyes and full mouth. In his arms he held a pixie of a girl. She would have been around three, he concluded, with that telltale mane of wildly curling red hair. Her face was round and pleased, showing a dimple near the corner of her mouth.

Before he realized it, Trace was grinning and holding the photo closer to the light. If a picture told a story, he'd bet his last nickel the kid was a handful. He had a weakness for cute kids who had the devil's gleam in their eyes. Swearing under his breath, he closed the billfold.

The contents of her bag might have told him a few things about her, but there hadn't been any notes. A few phone calls would fill in the blanks as far as Dr. Gillian Fitzpatrick was concerned. He glanced at her again as she sat sleeping, then, sighing, dumped everything back in her purse. He might have to wait until morning to get anything else out of her.

When the knock came at the door, she didn't budge. Trace let the room-service waiter set up the table. After giving Gillian three hefty shakes and getting no more than a murmur in response, he gave up. Muttering to himself, he slipped off her sandals, then gathered her up in his arms. She sighed, cuddled and caused him an uncomfortable pressure just under the ribs. She smelled like a meadow with the wildflowers just opening. By the time he'd gotten her into bed, he'd given up on the idea of sleeping himself.

Trace poured his first cup of coffee and settled down to eat his dinner—and hers.

Chapter Two

Gillian woke after a solid twelve hours of sleep. The room was dim, and she lay still, waiting for her mind to clear. Quickly, and in order, the events of the previous day came back to her. The bumpy, nerve-racking flight from Mexico City to Mérida. The fear and fatigue. The frustrating search from hotel to hotel. The dingy little cantina where she'd found the man she had to believe would save her brother and her young niece.

This was his room. This was his bed. Cautiously she turned her head—and let out a small groan. He was sleeping beside her, and in all probability he was as naked as the day he was born. The sheet slanted across his bare back, from below the shoulder blade to the waist. His face, a little less harsh, a little less forbidding, in sleep, was inches from hers. She felt then, as she had felt when she'd first seen him the evening before, that it was the face of a man a woman would never be safe with.

Yet she'd spent the night with him and had been safe—safe from him and from whatever forces were after her. More significantly, the moment she had stepped into the room and had finished unburdening herself, she had felt a wave of relief and confidence. He would help, reluctantly, resentfully, but he would help.

Sighing, she shifted in bed, preparing to get up. His hand shot out. His eyes opened. Gillian froze. Perhaps she wasn't as safe as she'd thought.

His eyes were clear and alert. His grip was firm, and just shy of being painful. Under his fingers, he felt her pulse speed up. Her hair was barely mussed, which told him that exhaustion had held her still through the night. The hours of sleep had faded the shadows under her eyes, eyes that watched him warily.

"You sleep like a rock," he said mildly, then released her and rolled over.

"The traveling caught up with me." Her heart was bumping as though she'd run up three flights of stairs. He was dangerous to look at, and too close. Perhaps it was the morning disorientation that caused her to feel that dull sexual pull.

Before she managed to resist it, her gaze had flicked down—the strong column of neck, the broad chest—and froze. A long red scar marred the tanned skin just right of his heart. It looked as though he'd been ripped open, then put back together. And recently.

"That looks . . . serious."

"It looks like a scar." His voice held no inflection at all as she continued to stare at the wound with horrified eyes. "You got a problem with scars, Doc?"

"No." She made herself look away, back at his face. It was as hard and blank as his voice. Not my business, she reminded herself. He was a violent man who lived by violent means. And that was exactly what she needed. She got out of bed to stand awkwardly, smoothing her clothes. "I appreciate you letting me sleep here. I'm sure we could have arranged for a cot."

"I've never had a problem sharing a bed." She was still pale. It gave her a delicate bone-china look that made him edgy. "Feel better?"

"Yes, I—" She reached a hand to her hair as she felt the first wave of embarrassment. "Thank you."

"Good, because we've got a lot of ground to cover today." He tossed the sheet aside and noted her instinctive flinch. His own discomfort turned to amusement. He wore flesh-colored briefs that left little room for modesty or imagination. Rising without any sign of self-consciousness, he gave her a slow, cocky grin. He liked the fact that she didn't avert her eyes. Whatever her thoughts, she stood where she was and watched him coolly.

Her throat had gone dry as dust, but she made a passable stab at casualness. "You could use a shower."

"Why don't you order up some breakfast while I do?" He turned toward the bath.

"Mr. O'Hurley..."

"Why don't you make it Trace, sweetheart?" He looked over his shoulder and grinned again. "After all, we just slept together."

The water was running in the shower before she managed to free the breath that was trapped in her lungs.

He'd done it on purpose, of course, she told herself as she sat on the edge of the bed. It was typical of the male of the species to flaunt himself. The peacock had his plumage, the lion his mane. Males were always strutting and preening so that the female would be impressed. But who would have guessed the man would be built like that?

With a shake of her head, Gillian lifted the phone. She didn't care how he was built as long as he helped her.

He'd have preferred it if she hadn't looked so frail and vulnerable. Trace kept the water cold to make up for three hours' sleep. His problem. Lathering his face, he began to shave in the shower by feel. He'd never been able to resist the damsel-in-distress routine. It had nearly gotten him killed in Santo Domingo. And nearly gotten him married in Stockholm. He wasn't sure which would have been worse.

It didn't help a hell of a lot that this one was beautiful. Beautiful women had an edge, no matter what modern-day philosophy said about intellect. He could admire a mind, but—call him weak—he preferred it packaged well.

By God, she was some package, and she'd dumped him into an international mess when all he wanted to do was wander around some ruins and go snorkeling.

Hammer. Why in the hell did it have to be Hammer? He'd thought he was done with the half-baked, destructive group of renegades. It had taken him more than six months to infiltrate the organization at one of the base levels. He'd been working his way up, nicely, keeping a low profile with a Slavic accent, his hair dyed black and a lot of facial hair to complete the disguise.

Ten miles out of Cairo, he'd made the mistake of discovering that the man he'd been working with on a small-arms deal had been making a few deals of his own on the side. Nothing to him, Trace thought now, bitterly. God knew he'd tried to tell the man he didn't give a damn about his private ventures. But in a panic, the terrified entrepreneur had blown a hole in Trace's chest and left him for dead rather than risk being reported.

It was well-known that the man who wielded the power and money at Hammer had little patience with private enterprise.

For nothing, Trace thought in disgust. The months of work, the careful planning, all for nothing because one half-crazed Egyptian had had a sweaty trigger finger.

As a result, he'd brushed close enough to death to want to spend some time appreciating life. Get drunk, hold a willing woman, lie on white sand and look at blue skies. He'd even started thinking about seeing his family.

Then she'd come along.

Scientists. He rubbed a hand over his chin and, finding it smooth enough, let the water beat over his head. Scientists had been screwing up the order of things since Dr. Frankenstein's day. Why couldn't they just work on a cure for the common cold and leave the destruction of the world to the military?

He turned off the taps, then reached for two undersized towels. Two phone calls the night before had given him enough information on Gillian Fitzpatrick to satisfy him. She was the genuine article, though he'd been wrong about the Swiss school. It was Irish nuns who'd taught her posture. She'd completed her education in Dublin, then gone on to work for her father until she'd accepted a position with the highly respected Random-Frye Institute in New York.

She was single, though there was a link between her and a Dr. Arthur Steward, head of research and development at Random-Frye. Three months ago she'd spent six weeks in Ireland, on her brother's farm.

A busman's holiday, Trace decided, if she had indeed worked on Horizon while she'd been there.

There was no reason to disbelieve her, no reason to refuse to do as she asked. He'd find Flynn Fitzpatrick and the angel-faced little girl. And while he was at it he'd find the men who'd killed Charlie. He'd get a hundred thousand for the first and a great deal of satisfaction for the second.

The towel covered him with the same nonchalance as the briefs. He walked back into the bedroom to find Gillian shaking out what was left of her clothes.

"Shower's yours, Jill."

"Gillian," she told him. Fifteen minutes alone had done a great deal to help her regain her composure. Since she was going to have to deal with Trace O'Hurley for some time, she'd decided to think of him as a tool rather than as a man.

"Suit yourself."

"I usually do. I don't have a toothbrush."

"Use mine." He pulled open a drawer of the bureau. He caught her look in the mirror and grinned. "Sorry, Doc. I don't have a spare. Take it or leave it."

"It's unhygienic."

"Yeah, but then, so's kissing if you do it right."

Gillian took her clothes and retreated to the bath without commenting.

She felt almost human when she came out again. Her hair was damp, her clothes were wrinkled, but the scent of food and coffee brought a very healthy pang to her stomach. He was already eating, poring over the newspaper as he did. When she moved to join him, he didn't bother to look up.

"I wasn't sure what you liked."

"This is fine," he told her over a mouthful of eggs.

"I'm so glad," she murmured, but the sarcasm bounced off him without making a dent. Because her hunger was urgent, she applied herself to her own plate and returned the compliment by ignoring him.

"They make it sound like it's only going to take a couple of nice chats to ratify the new SALT Treaty."

"Diplomacy is essential in any negotiation."

"Yeah, and—" He looked up. He knew exactly what it felt like to take a hard fist in the solar plexis. He knew how the body contracted, how the air vanished and the head spun. Until now he hadn't known he could experience the same sensation by looking at a woman.

Her hair curled damply past her shoulders, the color of a flame. Her skin was ivory, touched with a rose brought back by rest and food. Over the rim of her cup her eyes, as deep and rich a green as the hills of Ireland, looked into his questioningly.

He thought of mermaids. Of sirens. Of temptation.

"Is something wrong?" She was nearly tempted to reach out and take his pulse. The man looked as though he'd been struck on the back of the neck. "Trace, are you all right?"

"What?"

"Are you ill?" Now she did reach out, but he jerked back as if she'd stung him.

"No, I'm fine." No, he was an idiot, he told himself as he lifted his own coffee. She wasn't a woman, he reminded himself, she was his ticket to an early retirement and sweet revenge. "We need to clear up a few points. When did they snatch your brother?"

Relief came in a tidal wave. "You're going to help me."

He smeared more butter on a piece of toast. "You said a hundred thousand."

The gratitude in her eyes dulled. The warmth in her voice cooled. He preferred it that way. "That's right. The money is in a trust fund that came to me when I turned twenty-five. I haven't needed it. I can contact my lawyer and have it transferred to you."

"Fine. Now when did they take your brother?"

"Six days ago."

"How do you know who took him and why?"

It didn't matter that he was a mercenary, she told herself, only that he would save her family. "Flynn left a tape. He'd been recording some notes when they came for him. He left the tape on, and I suppose no one noticed during the struggle." She pressed a hand to her mouth for a moment. The sounds of the fight had come clearly over the tape, the crashing, the screams of her niece. "He didn't go easily. Then one of the men held a knife to Caitlin's throat. His daughter. I think it was a knife because Flynn said not to cut her. He said he'd go quietly if they didn't cut her."

She had to swallow again. The breakfast she'd eaten with such pleasure rolled toward her throat. "The man said he'd kill her unless Flynn cooperated. When Flynn asked what they wanted, he was told he was working for Hammer now. They instructed him to bring all his notes on the Horizon Project. Flynn said...he told them he'd go with them, he'd do whatever they wanted, but to let the child go. One of the men said they weren't inhuman, it would be too cruel to separate a child from her father. And he laughed."

Trace could see what this was doing to her. For both their sakes, he offered her no comfort. "Where's the tape?"

"Flynn's housekeeper had been at the market. She found the mess in the laboratory when she got back, and she phoned the police. They contacted me. Flynn's recorder had an automatic shutoff when he reached the end of the tape. The police hadn't bothered with it. I did." She linked her hands together as Trace lit a cigarette. "Ultimately I took the tape to Mr. Forrester. It was gone when I found him dead."

"How do you figure they know about you?"

"They would only have to have read Flynn's notes. It would have been recorded that I worked with him and took part of the project back with me."

"The men on the tape, they spoke English?"

"Yes, accented…Mediterranean, I think, except for the one who laughed. He sounded Slavic."

"Anyone use a name?"

"No." On a deep breath, she ran both hands through her hair. "I listened to the tape dozens of times, hoping I might catch something. They said nothing about where they were taking him, only why."

"Okay." Trace tipped back in his chair and blew smoke toward the ceiling. "I think we can get them out in the open."

"How?"

"They want you, don't they? Or the notes." He was silent for a moment as he watched that sink in. "You said you had them with you. I didn't find them in your bag."

The consideration in her eyes turned to indignation. "You looked through my belongings?"

"Just part of the service. Where are they?"

Gillian pushed away from the table to pace to the window. It seemed nothing was hers alone any longer. No part of her life could be private. "Mr. Forrester destroyed them."

"You told me you had them with you."

"I do." She turned back and placed a fingertip to her temple. "Right here. With a true photographic memory, one sees words. If and when it becomes necessary, I can duplicate the notes."

"Then that's what you're going to do, Doc, with a few alterations." He narrowed his eyes as he thought the plan through. It could work, but it all hinged on Gillian. "How are you fixed for guts?"

She moistened her lips. "It's not something I've had to test to any extent. But if you mean to use me as bait to find out where Flynn and Caitlin are being held, I'm willing."

"I don't want any grand sacrifices." He crushed out his cigarette before he rose and walked to her. "Do you trust me?"

She studied him in the hard, brilliant light of the Mexican sun. He was scrubbed and shaven and, she realized, no less dangerous than the man she'd met in the cantina. "I don't know."

"Then you'd better think it through, real careful." He cupped a hand under her chin. "Because if you want to stay alive, you're going to have to."

It was a long, mostly silent drive to Uxmal. Trace had made certain everyone in the hotel knew they were going. He'd asked for brochures, gotten directions in both English and Spanish, then gone to the gift shop to buy another guidebook and some film. He'd asked the clerk about mileage, restaurants along the way, and insect repellent. In general, he'd played the enthusiastic tourist and made a spectacle of himself.

Anyone looking for Gillian would know she could be found at the ruins of Uxmal.

The vegetation on either side of the road was thick and monotonous. The Jeep was canopied, but it didn't have air-conditioning. Gillian drank bottled lemonade and wondered if she'd be alive for the drive back.

"I don't suppose we could have found someplace closer."

"Uxmal's a natural tourist spot." The road was straight and narrow. Trace kept an eye on the rearview mirror. "We'll have some company, but not enough, I think, to put our friends off. Besides, one of the reasons I'm here is to check out the ruins." If they were being followed, the tail was first-class. Trace shifted in his seat and adjusted his dark glasses. "It's not as big or as popular as Chichén Itzé, but it's the most impressive site on the Puuc Route."

"I didn't think a man like you would be interested in ancient civilizations and pyramids."

"I have my moments." In truth, he'd always been fascinated by such things. He'd spent two months in Egypt and Israel using a cover as an anthropology major early in his career. It had given him a taste for both history and danger. "We should be able to pull this off, and soak up the atmosphere, as long as you follow orders."

"I agreed, didn't I?" Even with the thin buff-colored blouse and slacks she wore, the heat was irksome. Gillian concentrated on it rather than the anxiety that was gnawing at her gut. "What if they're armed?"

Trace took his eyes off the road long enough to shoot her a grimly amused look. "Let me worry about that. You're paying me to handle the details."

Gillian lapsed into silence again. She must be mad, she thought, trusting her life and the lives of her family to a man who was more interested in money than humanity. Taking another swig of warming lemonade, she tried to comfort herself by remembering what Charles Forrester had said of him.

"A bit of a renegade, and certainly not a man who would be considered a good team player. If he was, he'd be running the ISS by now. That's how good he is. If you want a man who can find a needle in a haystack—and you don't care if the hay gets a bit mangled in the process—he's the one."

"This is my brother's life, Mr. Forrester. And the life of a little girl, not to mention the possibility of nuclear repercussions."

"If, out of all the agents I've worked with, I had to pick one to trust my life to, it would be Trace O'Hurley."

Now she was trusting her life to him, a man she'd known less than twenty-four hours. He was crude, and more than a little rough around the edges. Since she'd met him he hadn't offered one word of sympathy about her family, and he hadn't expressed more than a passing interest in a formula that could change forever the balance of power in the world.

And yet... there was the quietly supportive way he'd slipped an arm around her waist when she'd been staggering with fatigue.

Who was he? A quick bubble of panic started in her throat as the question finally broke through. Who was this man she was trusting everything to?

"How long have you been a spy?"

He looked at her again, then back at the road, before he burst out laughing. It was the first time she'd heard the sound from him. It was strong, careless, and more appealing than she'd counted on. "Honey, this ain't James Bond. I work in espionage—or, if you like a cleaner term, intelligence."

Unless she was mistaken, there was a trace of bitterness there. "You didn't answer my question."

"Ten years, more or less."

"Why?"

"Why what?"

"Why are you in this kind of work?"

Trace punched in the cigarette lighter and ignored the little voice in his head that reminded him he'd been smoking too much. "That's a question I've been asking myself lately. Why physics?"

She wasn't foolish enough to think he cared. It was simply a way to switch the conversation away from himself. "Family tradition, and I had a knack for it. I was all but born in a laboratory."

"You're not living in Ireland."

"No, I was offered a position at Random-Frye. It was an excellent opportunity." To finally slip out from under her father's shadow.

"Like the States?"

"Yes, very much. At first it seemed everything moved faster than it should, but you find yourself catching up. Where are you from?"

He pitched the cigarette out into the road. "Nowhere."

"Everyone's from somewhere."

His lips curved at some private joke. "No, they're not. We're nearly there. Want to go over anything?"

Gillian drew a long, steadying breath. The time for small talk was over. "No."

The parking lot was half full. When the winter season got under way, the ruins, less than a two-hour drive from Cancun, would do a brisk business. With his camera slung over his shoulder, Trace took Gillian's hand. Her initial resistance only caused him to tighten his grip.

"Try to look a little romantic. We're on a date."

"You'll understand if I find it a bit difficult to look starry-eyed."

"Shoot for interested." He pulled the guidebook out of his back pocket. "The place dates back to the sixth and seventh Centuries. That's comforting."

"Comforting?"

"Over a thousand years and we haven't managed to destroy it. Up for a climb?"

She looked at him but couldn't see his eyes behind the dark lenses. "I suppose."

Hands linked, they started up the rough steps of the Pyramid of the Magician. She wasn't immune to the atmosphere. Even with sweat trickling down her back and her heart thudding with dull fear, she was moved by it. Ancient stones lifted by ancient hands to honor ancient gods.

From the top she could look out over what had once been a community filled with people.

For a moment she indulged herself and held herself very still. The scientist in her would have cocked a brow, but her ancestors had believed in leprechauns. Life had been in this place. Spirits still were. With her eyes closed, Gillian felt the power of the atmosphere.

"Can you feel it?" she murmured.

It was captured memories, lingering passions, that drew him to places. The realist in him had never completely overshadowed the dreamer. "Feel what?" he asked, though he knew.

"The age, the old, old souls. Life and death. Blood and tears."

"You surprise me."

She opened her eyes, greener now with the emotion that was in her. "Don't spoil it. Places like this never lose their power. You could raze the stone, put a high rise on this spot, and it would still be holy."

"Is that your scientific opinion, Doctor?"

"You *are* going to spoil it."

He relented, though instinct told him they would both be better off it he kept the distance. "Have you ever been to Stonehenge?"

"Yes." She smiled, and her hand relaxed in his.

"If you close your eyes and stand in the shadow of a stone, you can hear the chanting." His fingers had linked with hers, intimately, though neither of them were aware of it. "In Egypt you can run your hand along the stone of a pyramid and all but smell the blood of slaves and the incense of kings. Off the coast of the Isle of Man there are mermaids with hair like yours."

He had a fistful of it, soft, silky. He imagined it heating his skin with the kind of fire magicians conjure without kindling or matches.

She could do nothing but stare at him. Though his eyes were still hidden, his voice had become soft and hypnotic. The hand on her hair seemed to touch every part of her, slowly, temptingly. The little twist of need she had felt that morning became an ache, that ache, a longing.

She leaned toward him. Their bodies brushed.

"The view better be worth it, Harry. I'm sweating like a pig."

Gillian jerked back as if she'd been caught with her hand in the till as a middle-aged couple dragged themselves up the last of the stairs.

"A pile of rocks," the woman said when she took off her straw hat to fan her flushed face. "God knows why we had to come all the way to Mexico to climb a pile of old rocks."

The magic of the place seemed to retreat. Gillian turned to look out over the ruins.

"Young man, would you mind taking a picture of my wife and me?"

Trace took the disc camera from the slightly overweight man, who had an Oklahoman accent. It was the least he could do after they'd prevented him from making a mistake. Letting his mind wander off the task at hand and into more personal matters wouldn't get him his revenge, and it wouldn't get Gillian her family.

"Little closer together," he instructed, then snapped the picture when the couple gave two wide, frozen grins.

"Kind of you." The man from Oklahoma took back his camera. "Want me to take one of you and the lady?"

"Why not?" It was a typical tourist device. After handing over his camera, he circled Gillian's waist. She went stiff as a board. "Smile, honey."

He wasn't sure, but he thought he heard her call him an unflattering name under her breath.

As they started back down, Trace maneuvered so that Gillian's bag was between them. Looking down from the pyramid, he'd seen three men come onto the site together, then separate.

"Stay close."

Gillian set her teeth and obeyed, though at the moment she would have liked nothing better than to put as much distance as possible between them. It must have been too much sun, she decided, that had made her go so soft and light-headed. It certainly hadn't had anything to do with genuine emotion. Sunstroke, she told herself. Add that to the fact that she had always been highly sensitive to atmosphere, and it made a plausible answer to why she had nearly kissed him, and wanted to kiss him, had felt as if she were meant to kiss him.

"This isn't the best time to be daydreaming." Swinging an arm around her shoulders, Trace drew her tight against his body and steered her under an arch into the Nun's Quadrangle.

The position pleased him. The grand plaza was flanked on all four sides by structures that were really a series of interior rooms and doors. It left them enough in the open, while providing cover if cover proved necessary. If he had a choice, he wanted to deal with their friends one at a time.

"You're supposed to be appreciating the detail work on the stones."

Gillian swallowed a little ball of fear. "The carved arches and facades are classic Mayan architecture. The Puuc construction is recognizable in the finely cut stone."

"Very good," Trace murmured. He saw one of the men slip into the quadrangle. Just one, he thought. So they had, as he'd hoped, spread out to find her. Turning, he pressed her against a column and ran his hands down her body.

"What are you—?"

"I'm making a lewd suggestion," he said softly as he leaned close to her ear. "Understand?"

"Yes." It was the signal for her to act, but she found herself frozen. His body was hard and hot and, for reasons she didn't want to dissect, made her feel safe.

"A very lewd suggestion, Gillian," Trace repeated. "It has something to do with you and me naked in a twenty-five-gallon tub of whipped cream."

"That's not lewd, that's pathetic." But she sucked in a deep breath. "You filthy-minded swine." Putting her heart into it, Gillian swung back and brought her palm hard—a bit harder than necessary—across his face. She shoved him away and made a production of smoothing her hair. "Just because I agreed to an afternoon's drive doesn't mean I intend to spend the night playing your revolting games."

Eyes narrowed, Trace ran a hand over his cheek. She packed a punch, but they'd discuss that later. "That's fine, sweetheart. Now why don't you find your own way back to Mérida? I've got better things to do than to waste my time on some skinny broad with no imagination." Swinging around, he left her alone. He passed the man who stood three yards away, ostensibly studying an arch.

Gillian had to bite her tongue to keep herself from calling Trace back. He'd asked her if she had guts, and now she was forced to admit she didn't have as many as she'd hoped. Her hands trembled as she cupped her elbows. It didn't take long.

"Are you all right, miss?"

This was it. She had no trouble recognizing the voice from her brother's tape. Gillian turned around, hoping her overbright eyes and unsteady voice would be taken as indignation. "Yes, thank you."

He was dark, and not much taller than herself, with olive skin and a surprisingly kind face. She forced herself to smile. "I'm afraid my companion wasn't as interested in Mayan architecture as he pretended."

"Perhaps I could offer you a ride back."

"No, that's kind of you, but—" She broke off when she felt the prick of a knife at her side, just above her waist.

"I believe it would be for the best, Dr. Fitzpatrick."

She didn't have to feign terror, but even as her mind threatened to freeze with it, Gillian remembered her instructions. Stall. Stall as long as possible so that Trace could even the odds.

"I don't understand."

"It will all be explained. Your brother sends his best."

"Flynn." Regardless of the knife, Gillian reached out and grabbed the man's shirt. "You have Flynn and Caitlin. Tell me if they're all right. Please."

"Your brother and niece are in good health and will remain so as long as we have cooperation." He put his left arm around her shoulders and began to walk.

"I'll give you whatever you want if you promise not to hurt them. I have some money. How much—?"

"We're not interested in money." The knife urged her forward. However kind his face had been, the hand on the knife was merciless. "There is a matter of the missing experiments and the notes."

"I'll give them to you. I have them right here." She gripped the strap of her bag. "Please don't hurt me, or my family."

"It's to your advantage that you are more easily persuaded than your brother."

"Where is Flynn? Please, tell me where you're holding him."

"You'll be with him soon enough."

Trace found the second man behind the Governor's Palace. He strolled by, clicking his camera, then pressed the man's face into one of the twenty thousand intricately carved stones.

"Fascinating stuff, isn't it?" He had his hand around the man's neck in what would look like a brotherly embrace. They both knew it would take only a jerk to break bone. "If you want to keep the use of your right arm, don't look around. Let's make this quick while we've got some privacy. Where are you holding Flynn Fitzpatrick?"

"I don't know a Flynn Fitzpatrick."

Trace hitched the man's arm up another quarter inch. He could hear bone grinding against bone. "You're wasting my time." After a quick look around, Trace pulled out his hunting knife and placed the blade where ear met skull. "Ever heard of van Gogh? It only takes a few seconds to remove an ear. It won't kill you—unless you bleed to death. Now, once more—Flynn Fitzpatrick."

"We weren't told where he was taken." The blade nipped into flesh. "I swear it! Our instructions were to take him and the girl to the airport and turn them over. We were sent back for the woman, his sister."

"And your instructions for her?"

"A private plane at the airport in Cancun. We were not told of the final destination."

"Who killed Forrester?"

"Abdul."

Because time was pressing, Trace had to forgo the pleasure of making the man suffer. "Go to sleep," he said simply, and rammed his head into the stone.

Where was Trace? Gillian thought as she approached a small white compact. If he didn't come soon, she and the altered notes would be on their way to... She didn't even know where.

"Please, tell me where you're taking me." She stumbled, and the knife slashed through the cotton of her blouse to flesh. "I feel faint. I need a moment." When she leaned heavily against the hood of the car, the man relaxed enough to draw the knife away from her side.

"You can rest in the car."

"I'm going to be sick."

He made a sound of disgust and pulled her upright by the hair. Trace's fist sent him reeling back three feet. "She may be a bit of a bitch," he said mildly, "but I can't stand to see a woman manhandled. Look, honey, I just wanted to get you naked. No rough stuff."

Gillian let the bag slip out of her hands and fled.

"That's a woman for you. No appreciation." Trace shot the man, whose mouth was spurting blood, a grin. "Better luck next time."

The man swore. Trace knew enough Arabic to catch the drift. When a knife was drawn, he was ready. He wanted badly to pull out his own, to go head-to-head with this man he knew had killed his closest friend. But it wasn't the time, and it wasn't the place. He wanted not only the instrument, but also the man who'd given the order. Keeping his gaze locked on the blade, Trace lifted both hands and backed off.

"Listen, you want her that bad, she's all yours. One woman's the same as another as far as I'm concerned." When the man spit at his feet, Trace bent down as if to wipe off his shoe. He came up with a nickel-plated .45 automatic. "Abdul, isn't it?" The half-amused light in his eyes had become deadly. "I've already taken care of your two friends. The only reason I'm not going to put a hole in your head is that I want you to take a message to your boss. Tell him Il Gatto's going to pay him a visit.'' Trace saw the quick widening of the dark eyes and grinned. ''You recognize the name. That's good. Because I want you to know who kills you. Deliver the message, Abdul, and put your affairs in order. You don't have very long.''

Abdul still had the knife in his hand, but he was aware that a bullet was faster than a blade. He was also aware that Il Gatto was quicker than most. ''Il Gatto's luck will run out, the same as his master's.''

Trace leveled the gun to a point just under Abdul's chin. ''Yeah, but yours is ticking away right this minute. My finger's starting to sweat, Abdul. You'd better move.''

He waited until the man had gotten behind the wheel and driven off before he lowered the gun. It had been close, Trace realized as he slipped the gun back into the holster strapped to his calf. He'd nearly taken his revenge there and then. Trace straightened again. When his blood was cool and his mind clear, revenge would be that much sweeter.

He spun quickly when he heard footsteps behind.

Gillian had seen that look before—when she'd told him that Forrester had been murdered. She thought she'd seen it again when her head had been jerked up by the hair. But even now, though she was seeing it for the third time, her skin prickled cold.

''I thought I told you to stay with a crowd.''

''I saw,'' she began, then walked over to pick up her bag. It would sound foolish to say she'd stayed close in case he'd needed her help. ''I didn't know you had a gun.''

''You figure I was going to get your brother out with fast talk and a charming smile?''

''No.'' She couldn't meet his eyes now. She'd disliked but at least understood the world-weary, slightly grungy man she'd first met. She'd nearly liked and again had understood the cocky, smart-mouthed man she'd breakfasted with. But this one, this hard-eyed stranger who carried death within easy reach, she didn't understand at all. "Did you . . . the other two men, did you . . ."

"Kill them?" He said the word simply as he took her arm and led her back to the Jeep. He'd seen both fear and revulsion in her eyes. "No, sometimes it's better to leave people alive, especially when you know what's left of that life is going to be hell. I didn't get a lot out of either of them. They dropped your brother and the kid at the airport and were sent out for you. They didn't know where he was being held."

"How do you know they were telling you the truth?"

"Because these guys are the bottom of the food chain. They haven't got the brains to lie, especially when they know you'll slice off little pieces of their bodies."

The adrenaline washed out of her. "God, then how are we going to find him?"

"I've got some leads. And the word is *I*, not *we*. As soon as I find a safe house for you, you're going under."

"You're mistaken." She stopped in front of the Jeep. Her face was beaded with sweat but no longer pale.

"Sure, we'll discuss it later. Right now, I want a drink."

"And as long as you're working for me you'll drink in moderation."

He swore, but more good-naturedly than she'd expected. "Name ten Irishmen you know who drink in moderation."

"You, for one." She turned to walk around to her side of the Jeep when he swore again and grabbed her. She was about to snap at him when he pulled her shirt loose from the waistband of her slacks. "What the hell do you think you're doing?"

"You're bleeding." Before she could protest, he'd yanked her slacks down enough to expose her hipbone. The cut wasn't very deep, but it was rather long. Blood had seeped through to stain her shirt. For an instant—and an instant was often too long—the dull red haze of fury clouded his vision. "Why didn't you tell me he'd hurt you?"

"I didn't realize." She bent to examine the wound clinically. "I was trying to slow him down and stumbled. He gave me a jab, I guess for incentive. It isn't serious. Nearly stopped bleeding."

"Shut up." It didn't seem to matter at the moment that the cut was shallow. It was her skin, her blood. Trace half lifted her into the Jeep, then popped open the glove compartment. "Just be still," he ordered as he broke open a first aid kit. "I told you not to take any chances, damn it."

"I only— For heaven's sake, that hurts worse than the cut. Will you stop fussing?"

"I'm cleaning it, damn it, and you're going to shut up." He worked quickly, and none to gently, until she was cleaned and bandaged.

"Congratulations, Doctor," she said dryly, and only smiled when he lifted angry eyes. "I never expected a man like you to get so flustered at the sight of a little blood. As a matter of fact, I would have taken bets that—"

She was cut off quickly and completely when his mouth covered hers. Stunned, she didn't move a muscle as his hands came to her throat and passed up into her hair. This was the promise, or the threat, she had glimpsed from the top of the pyramid.

His mouth, hard and hungry, didn't gently persuade, but firmly, unarguably possessed. The independence that was an innate part of her might have protested, but the need, the desire, the delight, overlapped and won.

He didn't know why in hell he'd started this. It seemed his mouth had been on hers before he'd even thought of it. It had just been. He'd been frightened when he'd seen her blood. And he wasn't used to being frightened—not for someone else. He'd wanted to stroke and soothe, and he'd fought that foolishness back with rough hands and orders.

But, damn it, why was he kissing her? Then her lips parted beneath his and he didn't ask any longer.

She tasted as she smelled, of meadows and wildflowers and early sunlight on cool morning dew. There was nothing exotic here, everything was soft and real. Home... Why was it she tasted of home and made him long for it as much as he did for her?

What he'd felt at the top of the pyramid came back a hundredfold. Fascination, sweetness, bewilderment. He coated them all with a hard-edged passion he understood.

She didn't cringe from it. She lifted a hand to his face. The echo of her heartbeat was so loud in her head that she could hear nothing else. His kiss was so demanding, she could feel nothing else. When he drew away as abruptly as he had come to her, she blinked until her blurred vision cleared.

He was going to have to get rid of her, and fast, Trace thought as he stuck unsteady hands in his pockets. "I told you to shut up," he said briefly, and strode around the Jeep.

Gillian opened her mouth, then shut it again. Perhaps, until she could think clearly, she'd take his advice.

Chapter Three

Trace nursed a beer. He figured that if Abdul was smart the message would be delivered to the right people before nightfall. He intended to be out of Mexico in an hour. He gave a brief thought to warm Caribbean waters and lazy snorkeling, then picked up the phone.

"Make yourself useful and pack, will you, sweetheart?"

She turned from the window. "The name is Gillian."

"Yeah, well, toss the stuff in the suitcase. We're going to check out as soon as—Rory? Well, so how the devil are you? It's Colin."

Gillian's brows went up. In mid-sentence his voice had changed from a lazy American drawl to a musical Irish brogue. Colin, was it? she thought, folding her arms.

"Aye. No, I'm fit. Right as rain. How's Bridget? Not again. My God, Rory, do the two of you plan to populate

Ireland by yourselves?'' As he listened, Trace glanced up long enough to give her a mild look and gestured toward the bureau. With more noise than grace, Gillian began yanking out his clothes.

"I'm glad to hear it. No, I don't know when I might be back. No, no trouble, nothing to speak of, in any case, but I wondered if you'd do me a favor.'' He watched Gillian heap his clothes into the suitcase and took a pull on the beer. "I'm grateful. There was a plane, probably private, that left the airport in Cork ten days ago. I don't want you to ask who was on board or why. Understand? That's a lad. Just nose around and see if you can find out the destination. Lacking that, find out how many miles she was fueled for and where she might have put down to be refueled. I'll take it from there…. Important enough,'' he went on after a pause, "but nothing you should take risks for…. No.'' And this time he laughed. "Nothing to do with the IRA. It's more of a personal matter. No, I'm traveling. I'll get back to you. Kiss Bridget for me, but try to keep it at that. I don't want to be responsible for another baby.''

He hung up and looked at the twisted, mangled clothes in his suitcase. "Nice job.''

"And what was that all about … Colin?''

"That was about finding out where your brother is. You'd better toss whatever you want to keep in there, too. We'll deal with getting you another suitcase later.'' He was up and stuffing his snorkeling gear into a tote.

"Why the accent and the false name? It sounded to me as though that man was your friend.''

"He is.'' Trace went to gather up the things in the bath.

"If he's your friend,'' Gillian insisted as she tailed behind him, "why doesn't he know who you are?''

Trace glanced up and caught his own reflection in the mirror. His own face, his own eyes. Why was it that too often he didn't recognise himself? He dumped toothpaste and a bottle of aspirin into a travel kit. "I don't use my name when I'm working."

"You checked in as Trace O'Hurley."

"I'm on vacation."

"If he's your friend, why do you lie to him?"

He picked up his razor and examined the blade very carefully before he dropped it in the case. "He was a kid mixed up in a bad situation a few years ago. Gunrunning."

"That's what you meant by the IRA?"

"You know, Doc, you ask too many questions."

"I'm trusting the most precious things in my life to you. I'll ask questions."

He zipped the travel kit in one impatient movement. "I was on assignment when I ran into him, and I was using the name Colin Sweeney."

"He must be a very good friend to agree to do you this kind of a favor without any questions."

Trace had saved his life, but he didn't want to think about that. He'd saved lives, and he'd taken them. He didn't want to think about either at the moment. "That's right. Now can we finish packing and get out of here before someone pays us a visit?"

"I have another question."

He let out a little laugh. "Am I surprised?"

"What was the name you gave that man this afternoon?"

"Just a nickname I picked up a few years back in Italy." He stepped forward, but she didn't move away from the door.

"Why did you give it to him?"

"Because I wanted whoever gives the orders to know who was coming for him." Brushing past her, he dumped the rest of his things into the suitcase and snapped it shut. "Let's go."

"What does it mean?"

He walked to the door and opened it before turning back to her. There was a look in his eyes that both frightened and fascinated. "Cat. Just cat."

He'd known some day he would go back to the States. There had been times in a jungle, or a desert or a grimy hotel room in a town even God had forgotten when he'd imagined it: the prodigal son returns, brass band included. But that was the theatrical blood in him.

Other times he'd imagined slipping quietly into the country, the way he'd slipped out a million years before.

There were his sisters. At the oddest times he would think of them, want to be with them so badly he'd book a flight. Then he'd cancel it at the last minute. They were grown women now, with lives of their own, and yet he remembered them as they'd been the first time he'd seen them. Three scrawny infants, born in one surprising rush, nestled in incubators behind a glass nursery wall.

There had been a bond between them, as he supposed was natural between triplets, and yet he'd never felt excluded. They'd traveled together from the time they'd been born until he'd stuck out his thumb on a highway outside Terre Haute.

He'd seen them only once since then, but he'd kept track. Just as he'd kept track of his parents.

The O'Hurleys had never been the huge commercial success his father had dreamed of, but they'd gotten by. They were booked an average of thirty weeks of the year. Financially they were solvent. That was his mother's doing. She'd always had a knack for making five dollars stretch into ten.

It was Molly, he was certain, who had tucked a hundred dollars in fives and tens into the pocket of his suitcase a dozen years before. She'd known he was going. She hadn't wept or lectured or pleaded, but she had done what she could to make it easier for him. That was her way.

But Pop... Trace closed his eyes as the plane shuddered a bit with turbulence. Pop had never, would never, forgive him—not for leaving without a word, but for leaving.

He'd never understood Trace's need to find something of his own, to look for something other than the next audience, the next arrangement. Perhaps in truth he'd never been able to understand his son at all, or in understanding, hadn't been able to accept.

The only time Trace had gone back, hoping perhaps to mend a small portion of his fences, Frank had greeted him with tight-lipped disapproval.

"So you've come back." Frank had stood icily rigid in the tiny dressing room he'd shared with Molly. Trace hadn't known that his presence had made Frank see it for what it was. A dim little room in a second-rate club. "Three years since you walked out, and only a letter now and again. I told you when you left, there'd be no fatted calf for you."

"I didn't expect one." But he'd hoped for some understanding. Trace had worn a beard then, part of an affectation he'd grown for an assignment. The assignment had taken him to Paris, where he'd successfully broken up an international art fraud. "Since it was Mom's birthday, I thought...I wanted to see her." *And you—but he couldn't say it.*

"Then run off again so she can shed more tears?"

"She understood why I left," Trace had said carefully.

"You broke her heart." *And mine.* "You're not going to hurt her again. You're either a son to her, or you're not."

"Either the son you want me to be, or nothing," Trace had corrected, pacing the cramped little room. "It still doesn't matter to you what I need or feel, or what I am."

"You don't know what matters to me. I think you never did." Frank had to swallow the obstruction in his throat that was part bitterness and part shame. "The last time I saw you, you told me what I'd done for you hadn't been good enough. That what I could give you never would be. A man doesn't forget hearing that from his son."

He was twenty-three. He'd slept with a whore in Bangkok and gotten roaring drunk on ouzo in Athens, and he had eight stitches in his right shoulder from a knife wielded by a man he'd killed while serving his country. Yet at that moment he felt like a child being scolded without justice or cause.

"I guess that's the only thing I ever said to you that you really heard. Nothing's changed here. It never will."

"You've chosen your way, Trace." His son had no way of knowing that Frank wanted nothing more than to open his arms and take back what he'd thought he'd lost forever. And was afraid Trace would only turn away. "Now you'll have to make the best of it. At least have the decency to say goodbye to your mother and sisters this time."

It had been Frank, his eyes blurred with tears, who had turned away. Trace had walked out of the dressing room and had never gone back.

He opened his eyes now to find Gillian watching him steadily. She looked different with the short, dark wig he'd made her wear. But she'd stopped complaining about it—and the horn-rimmed glasses and drab, dun-colored dress. It was padded to make her look frumpy, but he couldn't quite get his mind off what was hidden underneath. In any case, she'd blend into the scenery, which was just what he wanted.

No one would mistake the woman sitting beside him for the spectacular-looking Doctor Gillian Fitzpatrick.

He'd switched planes and airlines in San Diego, charging the tickets to a credit card under one of his cover names. After rerouting in Dallas, he'd picked up the fielder's cap and sideline jacket he was wearing. Now, as they headed into Chicago, they looked like a couple of dazed, weary tourists who wouldn't rate a second glance.

Except he could see her eyes, those deep, dark, intense green eyes through the clear lenses.

"Problem?" he asked.

"I was going to ask you the same thing. You know, you've been brooding ever since we boarded."

He pulled out a cigarette and played with it. "I don't know what you're talking about."

"I'm talking about the fact that you're ready to bite my head of if I so much as say pass the salt. I'm wearing this hideous wig, aren't I? And this a very fashionable dress."

"Looks great."

"Then if you're not upset about my disguise, what is it?"

"Nothing's wrong with me," he said between his teeth. "Now back off."

Holding on to her temper, Gillian sipped the white wine she'd been served—with a pitying look from the flight attendant, she thought with some disgust. "There certainly is something wrong with you. I'm the one who should be having an anxiety attack, but I'm not, because we're actually doing something. But if there's a problem...I should be concerned about, I'd appreciate you telling me."

His finger tapped on the armrest between them. "Do you always nag?"

"When it's important. Lives are at stake, lives that mean the world to me. If you're worried about something, then I need to know."

"It's personal." Hoping to dismiss it, he pushed back his seat and closed his eyes.

"Nothing's personal now. How you feel will affect your performance."

He opened one eye. "You'd be the first woman to complain, sister."

She flushed, but didn't let up. "I consider myself your employer, and as such, I refuse to have you keep secrets from me."

He swore at her, quietly but with considerable imagination. "I haven't been back in a while. Even I have memories, and they're my business."

"I'm sorry." She took a deep breath. "I haven't been able to think about anything but Flynn and Caitlin. It never occurred to me that this might be difficult for you." He didn't seem like a man of deep feelings or genuine emotions. But she remembered the pain in his eyes when she'd spoken of Forrester. "Chicago...is it a special place for you?"

"Played Chicago when I was twelve, and again when I was sixteen."

"Played?"

"Nothing." He shook his head and tried to relax. "I spent a few days there with Charlie a few years back. Last thing I saw of the States was O'Hare Airport."

"Now it'll be the first thing you see again." She had a magazine in her lap, but instead of opening it she just ran a thumb along its edge. "I've never seen much of America except New York. I've always meant to. Flynn brought Caitlin to visit a couple of years ago, just after her mother died." She let out a long breath. "They were both like lost souls. We went up the Empire State Building and to Rockefeller Center and had tea at the Plaza. Flynn bought her a little windup dog from a street merchant. She slept with it every night." The emotion came so quickly, she could do nothing to block it. "Oh, God." She pressed both hands to her face. "Oh, God, she's only six."

There hadn't been a woman in his life to comfort in too many years to count, but he hadn't forgotten how. "Take it easy." His voice was soft as he put an arm around her. "They're not going to hurt her. They need your brother's cooperation too much to risk it."

"But what are they doing to her inside? She must be so frightened. The dark— She still can't sleep in the dark. Would they give her a light? Do you think they'd give her a light?"

"Sure they would." His hand stroked her hair just as his voice stroked her fears. "She's going to be fine, Gillian."

Tears ran down her cheeks even as she struggled to calm herself. "I'm sorry. The last thing I want to do is make a fool of myself."

"Go ahead." His hand ran rhythmically over her shoulder. "I don't mind."

With a watery laugh, she fumbled for a tissue. "I try not to think of her too much. I try to concentrate on Flynn. He's very strong and capable."

"And he's with her. He's taking care of her."

"Aye, they're taking care of each other." God, she needed to believe that. She needed to believe that before long she'd see them, whole and healthy and safe. "We're going to get them out, aren't we?"

There were no promises in this kind of game. He knew that better than most. But she was looking at him now with brimming eyes and such desperate trust that he had no choice. "Sure we are. Didn't Charlie tell you I was the best?"

"He did." She let out a little breath. Control was back, but she didn't have as tight a grip on it as she would have liked. If she didn't think about something else, every minute that passed seemed like an hour. "Tell me about your family. Do you have brothers?"

"No." He drew his arm away, because it would have been entirely too easy to leave it around her. "Sisters."

"How many?"

"Three."

"That must have made life interesting."

"They were okay." His lips curved as he lit a cigarette. "Chantel was the brat."

"Every family has one," she began. Then it hit her, and she sat up straight. "Chantel O'Hurley? Chantel O'Hurley's your sister? I've seen her movies. She's wonderful."

The pride came, more intense than he'd expected. "She's okay. Always leaned toward the dramatic."

"She's the most beautiful woman I've ever seen."

"And knows it."

"Then Maddy O'Hurley's your sister, too." More than a little stunned, Gillian shook her head. "I saw her on Broadway a few months ago. She's very talented. The stage just lights up when she's on it."

It always did, Trace thought. "She's nominated for a Tony."

"She deserves it. Why, the audience nearly brought down the roof when she went into the number at the end of the first act. You should have seen..." Her words trailed off when she realized that he should indeed have seen, but, for reasons yet unknown to her, hadn't. "Your third sister?" she asked, wanting to give him both time and room.

"Abby raises horses in Virginia." He crushed out his cigarette and wondered how he'd ever gotten started on his family.

"Yes, I think I read something about her. She married Dylan Crosby, the writer, recently. There was a write-up in the *Times*. Oh, of course, triplets. Your sisters are triplets."

"I thought scientists would be too busy, causing and solving the ills of the world to read gossip columns."

She lifted a brow and decided against taking offense. At least until she'd learned everything she wanted to know. "I don't keep my head buried in a test tube. The article mentioned that they grew up in show business, traveling around the country. Your parents still do. I don't remember reading anything about you."

"I've been gone a long time, remember?"

"But didn't you travel with them?" Intrigued by the idea, she smiled and shifted in her chair. "Did you sing and dance and live out of a trunk?"

"You know, for a doctor, you tend to glamorize the mundane." He felt the slight dip that meant they were starting their descent. "It's like going to the circus and seeing only the spangles and the red lights. Backstage there are elephant paddies up to your ankles."

"So you did travel with them." Gillian continued to smile. "Did you have a speciality?"

"God save me from plane rides with nosy women. I've been out of it for twelve years." He jerked his seat belt on. "I prefer thinking about today."

Gillian clicked her own belt into place. "I wanted to be a singer when I was a little girl. I always pictured myself in the spotlight." With a little sigh, she slipped the magazine back into the pocket of the seat. "Before I knew it, I was my father's lab assistant. Strange, isn't it, how our parents seem to map out our routes even before we're born?"

Charlie's house was behind a five-foot stone wall and was equipped with an elaborate security system. He left behind, as far as Trace knew, only an older sister who lived in Palm Beach and a nephew who ran a brokerage from somewhere in the Midwest.

Gillian sat in the rented car while Trace pressed a series of buttons on the panel outside the gates. They opened soundlessly. He hadn't spoken since the airport, not once during all the cruising and backtracking, looking for signs of surveillance or a tail. She was holding back her questions now. It was grief that silenced him here, and she knew he'd have to deal with it in his own way.

The trees were fading as winter closed in, but they still held a stubborn touch of color. Wind tore at the leaves and moaned through the branches. The elms would shade the drive in the summer, she thought, giving the old brick house a stately, sturdy feel. It was something she'd barely noticed on her first trip here, and it was something that she tried to concentrate on now.

The house didn't look deserted, but as if it were simply waiting to be occupied again. She thought of the man who had listened to her, who had given her brandy and a sliver of hope.

"He was crazy about this place," Trace murmured. He shut off the engine but sat looking at the two stories of worn brick and white trim. "Whenever he was away, he'd always talk about coming back. I guess he'd have wanted to die here." He sat a moment longer, then pushed open his door. "Let's go."

He had keys. Charlie had given them to him once.

"Use them sometime," he'd said. "Everybody has to have a home."

But he hadn't used them, not until now. The key slipped into the lock and turned with a quiet click.

The hallway was dim, but he didn't switch on the lights. He remembered the way well enough, and in truth he didn't yet have the heart to look at anything of Charlie's too closely.

He took her into a library that smelled of lemon and leather. The heat had been turned down because there was no one left to need the warmth. "You can wait here."

"Where are you going?"

"I told you I was coming here to find out where they took your brother. I'm going to find out, and you're going to wait here."

"And I told you that I'm involved with anything that has to do with Flynn. Besides, I might be able to help."

"If I need a physicist, I'll let you know. Read a book."

"I'm not staying here."

She was two steps behind him when he reached the doorway. "Look, Doc, there's such a thing as national security. I'm already bending the rules because Charlie seemed to think it was worth it."

"Then bend them a little more." She took his arm. "I'm not interested in state secrets and international affairs. All I want is to know where my brother is. I've worked on sensitive projects, Trace. I have clearance."

"You keep interfering with me, it's going to take a lot longer."

"I don't think so."

"Have it your way. But keep your mouth shut for once." He went up the stairs, trying to convince himself he wasn't making a mistake.

The carpet was new since Trace had been there, but the wallpaper was the same. So was the room three doors from the top of the stairs that Charlie had used for an office. Without hesitating, Trace went to the desk and pushed a button under the second drawer. A four-foot span of paneling swung out.

"Another tunnel?" Gillian asked. Her courage was fading fast.

"Workroom," Trace said as he stepped through. He threw a switch and discovered that Charlie had updated his equipment.

Along the top of the far wall were clocks, still running, that gave the time in every zone around the globe. The computer system spread beneath them, then continued in an L along the next wall. With the radio equipment opposite it, he could have contacted anyone from the local deejay to the Kremlin. "Pull up a stool, Doc. This could take a while."

Gillian jolted only a bit when the panel slid shut behind them. "What are you trying to do?"

"You want to bypass some paperwork, so I'm going to patch into the ISS computer."

"Do you think they know where Flynn was taken?"

"Maybe, maybe not." He switched on the terminal and sat. "But they should have a pretty good idea where Hammer's new headquarters are. Charlie had to go and get state-of-the-art on me." He punched a series of buttons. When the machine requested his code, he gave Charlie's. "Okay, that's a start. Let's see what this baby can do."

He worked in silence, but for the tapping of his fingers and the beeping of the machine, as Gillian looked on. He inched past one security block to ram into the next.

Patience, Gillian noted, more than a little surprised to find he had the quality, as he broke one code and slowly drew out more data. She began to find a rhythm to the numbers and symbols that appeared on the screen, then blinked out again, at Trace's command. As he worked, she began arranging and rearranging the system in her head.

"So damn close," Trace muttered as he tried another series. "The problem is there are enough variables to keep me at it for a week."

"Maybe if you—"

"I work alone."

"I was only going to say that—"

"Why don't you go down to the kitchen and dig up some coffee, sweetheart?"

Her eyes narrowed at the tone, and temper trembled on the tip of her tongue. "Fine." She whirled and faced the closed panel. "I don't know how to open the door."

"Button's on the left. Just put your finger on it and push."

Her mouth opened again, but, all too aware of what might come flying out, she pushed the button.

Typical hardheaded, egocentric male, Gillian decided as she marched down the stairs. Hadn't she lived with one, tried to please one, nearly all of her life? Why had fate decreed that in this, the most important thing she'd ever had to do, she'd be chained to another man who had no use for her opinion.

Make coffee, she thought as she found the kitchen. And if he called her sweetheart one more time, she'd give him what men like him deserved. The back of a woman's hand.

She started the coffee, too incensed to feel uncomfortable with rooting through a dead man's cupboards.

He'd had no business dismissing her. Just as he'd had no business kissing her the way he had. It had felt as if she were being devoured. And yet when it had finished she'd been whole. It had felt as if she'd been drugged. And yet her mind had been clear, her senses sharp.

However she'd felt, however it had finished, she would never be quite the same. She could admit that here, alone, to herself. She was too practical a woman for self-deception. Her feelings were perhaps more easily touched, perhaps more readily given, than she would have preferred, but they were her feelings, and she would never have denied them. She'd enjoyed the feel and taste of Trace's lips on hers. She would remember it for a long time. But she was also an expert on self-discipline. Enjoyable or not, she wouldn't allow it to happen again.

Trace was still working when she came back into the room. Without ceremony, she slammed the coffee cup down next to him. He acknowledged her with a grunt. Gillian took a turn around the room, told herself to keep her mouth shut, then jammed her hands into her pockets.

"Access, number 38537/BAKER. Tabulate access code five. Series ARSS28." Gillian blurted the series out almost like an obscenity. "And if you're not too pigheaded to try it, it may work. If not, switch the first number sequence with the second."

Trace lifted his coffee, pleased she'd left it black, surprised she'd made it well. "And what makes you think you can figure out the access code to one of the most sophisticated computer systems in the free world?"

"Because I've been watching you for the past hour and I do a little hacking as a hobby."

"A little hacking." He drank again. "Broken into any good Swiss bank accounts?"

She crossed the room slowly, almost, Trace thought not without admiration, the way a gunslinger might approach a showdown. "We're talking about my family, remember? Add to that the fact that I'm paying you, and the least you could do is try my suggestion."

"Fine." Willing to humor her to a point, Trace tapped out the sequence she'd recited.

ACCESS DENIED

With only a slight smirk, he gestured toward the screen.

"All right, then, transpose the numbers." Impatient, she reached around him and began hitting the keys herself. The only thing Trace noticed for a moment was that his shampoo smelled entirely different on her.

REQUEST FILE

"There we are." Pleased with herself, Gillian leaned closer. "It's rather like working out a system for blackjack. A professor and I played around with that last semester."

"Remind me to take you with me the next time I go to Monte Carlo."

They were closer. One step closer. Smiling, she turned her face to his. "What now?"

There wasn't a hint of amber or gray in her eyes. They were pure green and brilliant now. Even as he watched them, they changed, filling with speculation, awareness, memory. "You talking about the computer?"

She needed to swallow badly. "Of course."

"Just checking." Trace turned away again. They both let out a quiet breath. He began typing, and within seconds data came up on the screen.

He moved from screen to screen. After all, he knew quite a bit about Hammer already. He'd been briefed intensely before he'd gone undercover, and had learned more during his stint as a low-level delivery boy. During his assignment, he'd managed to pass along names, places and dates to the ISS, and he'd been on the verge of being transferred to the newly implemented main base before he'd been shot.

Frowning at the screen, he rubbed a thumb over the scar.

But he'd been sedated for days, hanging between life and death. His recovery had taken two months of hospital care. He'd been debriefed, the assignment had been blown and he'd taken off for a long—supposedly peaceful—vacation.

Quite a bit could change in two or three months. Charlie, being Charlie, would have keyed into it.

He breezed by the basic data. Hammer had been founded in the Middle East in the early seventies. With a combination of luck and money, and a complete disregard for life, they had pulled off a number of bombings, taken hostages. The last hijacking the organization had attempted had ended with someone's itchy finger pushing a detonator and blowing eighty-five innocent people and six terrorists to oblivion.

That was their style, he thought. Win some, lose some.

"Husad," Gillian said, honing in one name as Trace flipped screens. "Isn't he the leader?"

"He's the one with the bucks. Jamar Husad, political outcast, self-proclaimed general and complete lunatic. Come on, Charlie," he muttered at the machine. "Give me something."

"You're hardly looking," she began.

"I already know all this."

"How?"

"I worked for them for six months," he said half to himself.

"You *what*?" She took a step back.

Annoyance flickered in his eyes as he glanced up. "Relax, sweetheart, all for the good of the cause. I infiltrated."

"But if you were inside, then you should know where they would have taken Flynn and Caitlin. Why are we fooling with this computer when—"

"Because they moved. They were just getting set up in the new location when I got taken out."

"Taken out?" Puzzlement veered into horror. "You were shot?"

"Part of the job description."

"You were nearly killed—a scar like that..." She trailed off and laid a hand on his shoulder. "You were nearly killed by those people, but you're doing this."

He shook her hand away. He couldn't afford to let her feelings soften toward him. Then it would be too easy to let his soften toward her. "I got a personal investment here. There's a matter of a hundred thousand—my ticket to paradise."

She curled her fingers into her palm. "Do you expect me to believe you're only doing this for the money?"

"Believe what you like, but keep it to yourself. I've never known anybody who asks so many questions. I'm trying to concentrate. Yeah, yeah," he muttered. "I know they were in Cairo, that's old—

"All *right*. I knew I could count on Charlie." Trace leaned back. "New base of operations: Morocco."

"Morocco? Could they have taken Flynn and Caitlin all that way?"

"They'd want the best security for them. In Morocco, Hammer would have allies close." He continued to flip from screen to screen until he came to the end of the file. "Nothing on your brother here yet." He instructed the computer to print out the pages that interested him, then turned to Gillian. "It would only take a phone call to bring the ISS in on this. I want you to think about it."

She had thought about it, worried about it. "Why didn't Mr. Forrester do that?"

"I've got some ideas."

"But you're not going to tell me what they are."

"Not yet. Like you said, it's your family, you make the choice."

She moved away from him. It was more logical to call the ISS. They were an organization with sophisticated equipment, with manpower, with political clout. And yet...

Every instinct told her to go with this one man, the man Charles Forrester had called a renegade. With her hands linked, Gillian turned to him. He still didn't look like a hero. And she was still going with her instincts.

"One hundred thousand, Mr. O'Hurley, and I go with you every step of the way."

"I told you I work alone."

"Perhaps you haven't seen me at my best, but I'm a very strong and capable woman. If I have to, I'll go to Morocco alone."

"You wouldn't last a day."

"Maybe not. Hammer's agents are looking for me. If they find me, they'll take me to my brother. At least that way I'd know he and my niece were all right. I'd rather do it another way."

He stood up to do some pacing himself. She'd slow him down, but not by much. And if she stayed with him, he'd be able to keep an eye on her. He couldn't deny she'd held up in Mexico. If he had to play that kind of game again, he could use her.

"We go together, it doesn't mean we're partners, it means you take orders."

Gillian inclined her head but didn't say anything.

"When the time comes for me to move, you stay out of the way. I won't be able to worry about you then."

"You won't have to worry about me." She took a deep breath. "What do we do now?"

"First I check with Rory." He moved to the phone. "But I have a feeling we're catching a plane."

Chapter Four

Casablanca. Bogart and Bergman. Pirates and intrigue.
Foggy airports and sun-washed beaches. The name con-
jured up images of danger and romance. Gillian was determined to accept the first and avoid the second.

Trace had booked adjoining rooms in one of the more
exclusive hotels near United Nations Square. Gillian remained silent while he spoke to the desk clerk in fluid
French and was addressed as Monsieur Cabot.

André Cabot was the name on the passport he was using
now. He wore a conservative three-piece suit and shoes that
had a mirror gleam. His brown-rinsed hair was a bit mussed
from the drive, but he'd shaved. He stood differently, too,
she noted. Ramrod-straight, as though he'd come through
some military academy. Even his personality had changed,
she thought as she stood to the side and let him deal with
the details of checking in. He'd slipped so effortlessly into

the role of the brusque, slightly impatient French businessman, she could almost believe she'd lost Trace O'Hurley along the way and picked up someone else.

For the second time she felt as if she were putting her life into the hands of a stranger.

But the eyes were the same. A little shock passed through her when he turned and looked at her with the dark intensity she recognized but had yet to become accustomed to.

She remained silent as Trace took her arm and led her to a bank of elevators. Gillian still wore the wig, but the glasses were gone and the drab dress was replaced by an elegant silk outfit more suited to the image of Cabot's current mistress. Twenty stories later they were entering their suite and he hadn't said a word. Trace passed bills to the bell man in a slow, methodical fashion that indicated that he was a man who counted his francs.

She expected Cabot to disappear the moment the door was closed, but instead he spoke to her in lightly accented English. "For rooms of this price, the sheets should be threaded with gold."

"What—"

"See if the bar is stocked, *chérie*." He was moving around the room, checking lamps, lifting pictures from the wall. He turned to her only briefly, with a warning glance. "I would prefer a small glass of vermouth before I have the pleasure of undressing your lovely body." He picked up the phone, unscrewed the mouthpiece, and then, after a quick search, fastened it again.

"Would you?" She understood he was staying in character until he was certain there was no surveillance equipment in the rooms. Though it was unnerving, she accepted it. It was only the fact that he'd portrayed his character and hers as lovers that grated. Deciding two could play, she moved to a small wet bar and opened a cabinet door.

"I'm more than happy to fix you a drink, sweetheart."
She saw his brow lift as he checked the headboard, then the
mattress. "But, as to the rest, I'm a bit tired after the
flight."

"Then we'll have to see what can be done to bring your
energy back." Satisfied the first room was clean, Trace
walked to her. There was a long moment of silence before
he accepted the glass she'd poured. "Let's move into the
next room," he murmured, then turned and left her to follow. "Perhaps you're not as tired as you think."

As he began the same procedure on the second room,
Gillian sat on the bed. "It was a long flight."

"Then you should rest. Let me help you." He lifted a
print of the Cathedral of the Sacré Coeur. His hands, long-
fingered and sure, ran over the frame and the back. "You'll
rest better unconfined."

Gillian slipped out of her shoes to massage her arches.
"You seem to have only one thing on your mind."

"A man would be foolish to have more than one thing on
his mind once alone with you."

Gillian considered a moment. Perhaps she could grow to
like this André Cabot. "Really?" She lifted the glass he'd
discarded and sipped from it. "Why?"

He'd come closer to check the headboard. Pausing a
moment, he looked at her. There was a grin on her face that
said, "I dare you." She should have known better. "Because you have skin like a white rose that grows only
warmer and softer when I touch you." His hand brushed
her thigh, making her jolt. Trace continued to check the
mattress, but his eyes stayed on hers. "Because your hair
is fire and silk, and when I kiss you... When I kiss you, *ma
belle,* your lips are the same."

Her breath caught as he circled his hand around her
neck. He leaned closer so that when it was released again it

mingled with his. "Because when I touch you like this I can feel how much you want me. Because when I look at you I can see you're afraid."

She couldn't look away. She couldn't move away. "I'm not afraid of you." But she was fascinated. Whoever he was, he fascinated.

"No? You should be."

She didn't notice that his voice had changed, had become his own again, just before his mouth closed over hers. It was the same heat, the same strength, as before. Had it only been once before? she thought as her body went fluid, sliding beneath his onto the bed. Without a thought to reason, without a thought to consequences, she wrapped her arms around him.

Why did it seem so easy? His mouth was hard and hot, his hands were anything but gentle. And yet it seemed so easy to be with him now, so natural. So familiar. Surely his taste was a taste she'd woken to before. If she ran her hands over his back, she knew what muscles she would find. If she drew in a breath so that the scent of him filled her, it would be no surprise.

Perhaps she had known his face for only a matter of days. But there was something here that she had known all her life.

He must be going mad. It was as though she'd always been there for him. Would always be there. The feel of her body beneath his wasn't like that of any other woman. It was like that of the only woman. He knew, somehow, how her sigh would sound before he heard it, how her fingers would feel on his face before she lifted them to touch him.

He knew, he expected, yet it still stunned.

He could feel his pulse speed up until it beat in hundreds of points throughout his body. He could hear his own crazed murmuring of her name as he tore his mouth from hers to let it roam desperately over her face and throat. Then there was the need, growing to a rage inside him that was nothing like the desire he'd felt for other women.

He wanted all of her, mind, body, soul. He wanted her now. He wanted her for a lifetime.

It was that shocking thought that stopped him. There were no guaranteed lifetimes, especially not in the game he'd chosen to play. He'd learned to live for the moment. Tomorrow was up for grabs.

Whatever she was doing to him had to stop—if he wanted to live to collect his hundred thousand.

He ached. He could have hated her for that, but he rolled off her with a carelessness that left her still and speechless. "The room's clean." He picked up the glass to drain the last of the vermouth. And wished it was whiskey.

Her breathing was uneven, and her limbs were unsteady. There was nothing she could do about that, or about the unsated need crawling inside her. But she could hate him. With her whole heart and soul she could hate him.

"You bastard."

"You asked for it, sweetheart." He pulled out a cigarette and focused his mind on what lay ahead, instead of what had lain beneath him only moments before. "I've got some things to do. Why don't you take a nap?"

She came off the bed slowly, with the look in her eye that he'd noted before. It occurred to him that it was fortunate for both of them that his weapons were out of sight and reach.

She'd been humiliated before. She'd been rejected before. But she didn't intend to be either at his hands ever again. "Don't you ever touch me. I'll put up with your crude manners because I have no choice, but don't you ever put your hands on me again."

He wasn't sure why he did it. Anger had a way of urging a man to make a wrong and reckless move. He yanked her against him, even enjoying her fast and furious struggles as he clamped his mouth down on hers again. She was wild-fire now, hot, volatile and dangerous. He had an image, steamy and strong, of pulling her to the bed and letting violence feed violence. Before he could top one mistake with another, he let her go.

"I don't take orders, Gillian. Remember that."

Her hands curled into fists. Only the knowledge that she'd lose kept her from landing a blow. "There'll come a time you'll pay for that."

"Probably. Right now, I'm going out. Stay inside."

When the door closed behind him, she had the small satisfaction of cursing him.

He was gone only an hour. Most of Casablanca was as he remembered it. The little shops along the Boulevard Hansali still catered to the tourist trade. The port was still busy with European ships. He had walked through the original Arab town, still surrounded by old rampart walls. But he hadn't gone sightseeing. His contact in the bidonville, the shantytown near the shopping district, had been pleased to see him again, and agreeable enough after an exchange of a few dirham to give birth to a certain rumor about a hijacked shipment of American arms.

Trace arrived back at the hotel, satisfied that the first step had been taken and ready to start the next. The rooms were empty. He didn't panic, not at first. His training was a natural extension of his mind, just as his arm was a natural extension of his body.

After unstrapping his revolver from his calf, he began to search both rooms and baths. The balcony doors were still locked from the inside, though the curtains had been drawn. She'd taken her things out of his suitcase. Trace found them neatly put away in closets and drawers. The cosmetics she'd bought to replace those she'd lost stood on the counter in the bath. There were bath salts the color of sea foam, and a short cotton robe shades darker hanging on the back of the door.

Her purse was gone, and so were the notes inside it. The drumming at the back of his neck, slow and steady, was growing louder.

There was no sign of a struggle. It was hard for him to believe that a woman like Gillian would have submitted to anyone without a fight. It was just as difficult for him to believe that anyone could have traced them so quickly.

So where the hell was she? Trace thought as he felt the first twinges of panic. He ran a hand through his hair and tried to think calmly. If they had her... If they had her, then he would...

He couldn't think calmly when he kept seeing how Abdul had dragged her up by the hair. He couldn't think calmly when he remembered how her blood had felt on his hands.

When he heard the key in the lock, he whirled. It took only an instant to pull back control. Before the knob turned, he was behind the door, gun pointed up, body tensed. As the door opened, he grabbed a wrist. And yanked Gillian inside. Both of them received a shock when he dragged her into his arms.

"Damn it, where were you? Are you all right?"

She'd drawn in her breath to scream. The collision with Trace had knocked the air out of her again. She managed to nod, and then, feeling the tension in his body, she soothed him automatically.

"I'm fine." She ran a hand over his back. "Did something happen? I was only gone a few minutes."

And in a few minutes his imagination had worked at top speed. Trace cursed himself, then her. "I told you to stay inside. What the hell's wrong with you?" Furious with himself, he shoved her away. "I don't have time to baby-sit, damn it. When I give an order, you're to follow it."

To think she'd felt a flow of concern, Gillian thought, berating herself. She'd even felt a warmth at what she'd thought was his concern for her. Both those emotions froze quickly enough. "I hired you to find my brother, not to spend every spare moment shouting at me."

"If you'd show some sense, I wouldn't have to shout at you. You've been cut once, sweetheart." He could only hope the memory of that would shake her as much as it did him. "Keep this up and I might not be around next time to make sure it's not any worse than that."

"You're not my bodyguard. In any case, you're the one who went off without telling me where you were going or how long you'd be."

He didn't care to be reminded why he'd left so abruptly. "Listen, sister, the only reason you're here with me is because I might be able to use you to get your brother out. You won't be of much use if they've already got you."

"No one has me," she tossed back as she hurled her purse on the bed. "I'm here, aren't I?"

He hated to argue with logic. "I told you to stay inside. If you can't do what you're told, you're going to find yourself on the first plane back to New York."

"I go where I want, when I want." She planted her feet and almost hoped he'd try to put his hands on her again. "But, for your information, I did stay inside."

"That's strange. I could have sworn I pulled you into the room a few minutes ago."

"That you did, and nearly dislocated my shoulder in the process." She yanked a small bottle out of the bag she carried. "Aspirin, O'Hurley. There's a gift shop off the lobby downstairs, and I had a headache. Now, if you'll excuse me, I think I'm about ready to take the whole bottle." She stormed across the room. The bathroom door shut with a resounding slam.

Women, Trace thought as he strode into the adjoining room. He rarely thought they were more trouble than they were worth, but he was making an exception in Gillian's case.

After nearly a dozen years of fieldwork, he was still alive. And that was why he was considering retiring more and more seriously. The law of averages was against him. He was a man who believed in fate and believed in luck just as passionately. Sooner or later luck ran out. As it had for Charlie.

Lighting a cigarette, he stood at the window and looked out at Casablanca. The last time he'd been here it had had to do with smuggling. He'd nearly gotten his throat cut, but luck had still been with him. He'd been Cabot then, as well, the French businessman who didn't mind a shady, if profitable—deal.

His cover would hold. The ISS had invented it with the meticulousness they were best at. His nerve would hold, as long as he remembered that the woman in the next room was a means to an end and nothing more.

He heard the water running in Gillian's bath and checked his watch. He'd give her an hour to stew. Then they had business to attend to.

Gillian's temper wasn't the kind that flashed quickly and vanished. She knew how to hold it off, and how to nurse it along when it suited her. At the moment, she was reaping enormous satisfaction from keeping herself on the edge of fury. It gave her energy and blocked her fear.

She told herself she wasn't the least bit concerned about what was going on in the room next door as she changed into a simple blouse and skirt.

He probably intended to make her stay locked up in her room, eating a solitary dinner from room service. She attached a wide leather belt almost as if it were a holster. She'd be damned if she'd hole up here like a mouse. She might not be sure what she could do to help with Flynn's and Caitlin's release, but there had to be something. Trace O'Hurley was going to have to accept the fact that she was part of this thing. Starting now.

She moved to the door that joined the rooms and nearly ran into him.

"I was just coming in to see if you'd stopped sulking."

Her chin angled. "I never sulk."

"Sure you do, but since you've apparently finished we can go."

She opened her mouth, then shut it again. He'd said *we*. "Where?"

"To see a friend of mine." Eyes narrowed, he backed up to look at her. "Is that what you're wearing?"

Her automatic response was to look down at the wide circle skirt and blouse. "What's wrong with it?"

"Nothing, if you're going to tea at the rectory." While she sputtered and slapped at his hand, Trace unfastened two more buttons. He stood back, frowned, then nodded. "Helps a little."

"I've no desire to display myself for your benefit."

"Personally, I don't give a damn if you wear a cardboard box, but you've got a role to play. Don't you have any gaudy earrings?"

"No."

"Then we'll get some. And darker lipstick," he muttered before he stepped back. "Can you do anything with your eyes?"

"My eyes? What's wrong with my eyes?" Natural feminine vanity began to war with bafflement as Trace strode into her bath.

"Cabot's woman hasn't come straight out of a convent, know what I mean?" As he began to root through her cosmetics, she shoved him aside.

"No. Just what do you mean?"

"I mean you need a little more paint, a little more cleavage and a little less breeding." He picked up a smoky green eye shadow, examined it, then held it out. "Here, try for tart, will you?"

"Tart?" The word came out of her mouth with beautiful Irish indignation. "Tart, is it? Do you really believe I'd paint myself up so you can display me like a . . . like a . . ."

"Bimbo is what I had in mind. A nice-looking, empty-headed bimbo." He picked up her scent and gave the atomizer a squeeze. It smelled warmer on her skin, he thought, and he quickly pulled himself back. "This is drawing room stuff. Is this the only perfume you have?"

She unclenched her teeth only because it hurt to keep them clamped together. "It is."

"It'll have to do, then," he decided and sprayed it at her. "The hair, Doc."

She touched a hand to her wig almost protectively. "What's wrong with it?"

"Mess it up. The guy I'm going to see would expect me to travel with a pretty, empty-headed and very sexy woman. That's Cabot's style."

This time her eyes narrowed. "Oh, it is, is it?"

"Right. And you have to look the part. Don't you have anything slinky?"

"No, I don't have anything slinky." Her lower lip moved into a pout as she turned to look at herself in the mirror. "I wasn't coming on this trip to socialize."

"I've never known a woman not to have something slinky."

If looks really could have killed, he would have dropped like a stone. "You've never known this one."

Taking it in stride, Trace reached for her blouse again. "Well, maybe one more button."

"No." She pulled her blouse together. "I'm not parading around half dressed so you can keep up your image." Teeth gritted, she snatched the eye shadow from him. "Go away. I don't want you hovering over me."

"Five minutes," he told her, and with his hands in his pockets he strolled out of the bath.

She took ten, but he decided not to quibble. Anger had brought on a flush that she'd added to with blusher. She'd used shadow and liner liberally so that her eyes were big as saucers and had that heavy bedroom look.

He'd wanted flamboyant, and she'd delivered. For the life of him, he couldn't figure out why it made him angry.

"Cheap enough for you, Monsieur Cabot?"

"It'll do," he said, already at the door. "Let's go."

She felt like a fool, and as far as she was concerned she looked the part. Still, she had to remind herself she wasn't being left behind to worry and fret while Trace went about the business of finding Flynn. Drawing a breath, Gillian told herself that if she was playing a part she should play it well.

As they stepped out of the hotel, Gillian tucked her arm through his and leaned against him. He gave her a quick, wary look that had her smiling. "Am I supposed to be crazy about you?"

"About my money, anyway."

"Oh, are you rich?"

"Loaded."

She looked over her shoulder as she stepped into a cab. "Then why don't I have any jewelry?"

A smart aleck, he thought, and wished he didn't like her better for it. He put his hand firmly on her bottom. "You haven't earned it yet, sweetheart."

The makeup couldn't disguise the fire and challenge that leaped into her eyes. Because he'd gotten the last word, he felt a great deal better as he settled into the cab beside her. He gave the driver an address, then turned to her. "Speak any French?"

"Only enough to know whether I'm ordering calf's brains or chicken in a restaurant."

"Just as well. Keep your mouth shut and let me do the talking. You're not supposed to be too bright, in any case."

He was telling her to keep her mouth shut too often for her taste. "I've already deduced that your taste in women runs to the type in men's magazines. Glossy and two-dimensional."

"As long as they don't talk back. If you have to say anything, ditch the Irish. You've lived in New York long enough to have picked up the tone."

They were driving out of the section of the city marked by hotels and large, modern shops. Inland from the port and harbor was the old medina, the original Arab town, enclosed by walls and mazed with narrow streets. At any other time, it would have fascinated her. She would have wanted to get out and look, smell, touch. Now it was only a place where a clue might be found.

Trace—or Cabot, as Gillian was training herself to think of him—paid off the cab. She stepped out to look at the hodgepodge of little shops and the mix of tourists they catered to.

The charm was there, the age, the Arab flavor. Exotic colors, open bazaars, men in robes. The avenue was shaded, the shop windows were crammed with souvenirs and silks and local crafts. The women she saw were for the most part European, unveiled and trousered. The wind was mild and carried the scents of the water, of spice, and of garbage left too long.

"It's so different." With her arm tucked through Trace's again, she began to walk. "You read about such places, but it's nothing like seeing them. It's so. . . exotic."

He thought of the bidonville he'd visited that afternoon, the squatters' shacks, the squalor hardly a stone's throw away from charming streets and neat shops. A slum was a slum, whatever the language or culture.

"We're going in here." Trace stopped in front of a jeweler's with gold and silver and brightly polished gems in the window. "Smile and look stupid."

Gillian lifted a brow. "I'm not sure I'm that talented, but I'll do my best."

The bells on the door of the shop jingled when it opened. Behind the counter was a man with a face like a burnt almond and hair growing white in patches. He glanced up, and recognition came quickly into his eyes before he went back to the customers bargaining over a bracelet. Trace simply linked his hands behind his back and studied the wares in a display case.

The shop was hardly more than ten feet by twelve, with a backroom closed off by a beaded curtain. There was music playing, something with pipes and flutes that made Gillian think of a tune shepherds might play to their flocks. The scent in here was all spice—cloves and ginger—and a paddle fan lazily twirled the air around and around.

The floor was wooden and scarred. Though the jewelry gleamed, most of the glass was dull and finger-marked.

Remembering her role, Gillian toyed with necklaces of blue and red beads. She sighed, thinking how delighted little Caitlin would be with a few strands.

"Bon soir." His transaction completed, the shopkeeper cupped one hand in the other. "It's been a long time, old friend," he continued in French. "I did not expect to see you in my shop again."

"I could hardly come back to Casablanca without dropping in on an old and valued friend, al-Aziz."

The shopkeeper inclined his head, already wondering if a profit could be made. "You have come on business?"

"A little business..." Then he indicated Gillian by turning his palm upward. "A little pleasure."

"Your taste is excellent, as always."

"She's pretty," Trace said carelessly. "And not smart enough to ask too many questions."

"You would purchase her a bauble?"

"Perhaps. I also have a commodity to sell."

Annoyed with being shut out of the conversation, Gillian moved to Trace. She twined an arm around his neck, hoping the pose was sexy enough. She tried for the clipped New York accent of her assistant at the institute. "I might as well have stayed back at the hotel if you're going to speak in French all night."

"A thousand pardons, *mademoiselle*," al-Aziz said in precise English.

"No need to apologize," Trace told him after giving Gillian's cheek a light, intimate pat. The trace of Ireland was still there, but he doubted anyone who wasn't listening for it would have noticed. "There now, *chérie*, pick yourself out something pretty."

She wanted, quite badly, to spit in his eye, but she fluttered hers instead. "Oh, André, anything?"

"But of course, whatever you like."

She'd make it good, Gillian decided as she bent over the display counter like a child in an ice cream parlor. Good and expensive.

"We can speak freely, *mon ami*," Trace went on. He too rested against the counter, but he moved his hands quickly, competently, then folded them together on the glass top. "My companion understands no French. I assume you're still . . . well connected."

"I am a fortunate man."

"You'll remember a few years ago we made a deal that was mutually profitable. I'm here to propose another."

"I am always happy to discuss business."

"I have a similar shipment. Something that was liberated from our capitalist friends. I find the shipment, shall we say, too volatile to store for any length of time. My sources indicate that a certain organization has relocated in Morocco. This organization might be interested in the supplies I can offer—at the going market rate, of course."

"Of course. You are aware that the organization you speak of is as volatile as the supplies you wish to sell?"

"It matters little to me, if the profit margin is agreeable. Are you interested in setting up the negotiations?"

"For the standard ten-percent commission?"

"Naturally."

"It's possible I can help you. Two days. Where can I reach you?"

"I'll reach you, al-Aziz." He smiled and ran a fingertip along the side of his jaw. It was a trait peculiar to Cabot. "There is a rumor I find interesting. A certain scientist is, let us say, employed, by this organization. If I had more information about him, the profit could very well increase, by perhaps twenty percent."

Al-Aziz's face was as bland as his voice. "Rumors are unreliable."

"But simple enough to substantiate." Trace drew out a money clip and extracted some bills. They disappeared like magic into the folds of al-Aziz's cloak.

"Such things are rarely impossible."

"Oh, darling, can I have these?" Gillian grabbed Trace's arm and drew him over to a pair of long gold earrings crusted with red stones. "Rubies," she said with a long, liquid sigh, knowing perfectly well they were colored glass. "Everyone at home will simply die of envy. Please, darling, can I have them?"

"Eighteen hundred dirham," the shopkeeper said with a complacent smile. "For you and the lady, sixteen hundred."

"Please, sweetheart. I just adore them."

Trapped in his own game, Trace nodded to al-Aziz. But he also managed to pinch Gillian hard as the shopkeeper drew the earrings out of their case.

"Oh, I'll wear them now." Gillian began to fasten them on as Trace took more bills from his clip.

"Two days," Trace added in French. "I'll be back."

"Bring your lady." The shopkeeper's face creased with a smile. "I can use the business."

Trace steered her out to the street. "You could have picked out some glass beads."

Gillian touched a fingertip to one earring and sent it spinning. "A woman like me would never be satisfied with glass beads, but would probably be foolish enough to believe paste was rubies. I wanted to do a good job."

"Yeah." The earrings glittered with a lot more style on her than they had in the case. "You did okay."

With a hand on his arm, Gillian pulled up short. "Wait a minute. I'm nearly breathless after that compliment."

"Keep it up."

"There, that's better. Now are you going to tell me what that was all about?"

"Let's take a walk."

Chapter Five

At least she wasn't cooped up in a hotel room. Gillian tried to comfort herself with that as she sat in a noisy club that was fogged with smoke and vibrating with recorded music. Nursing a glass of wine, she sat observing the life around her. The clientele was young, and again mostly European. Though her traveling had been limited by her work, Gillian thought you could have found an almost identical place in London or Paris.

It occurred to her that she'd seen more of the world in the past two weeks than she had in all her life. Under other circumstances she might have enjoyed the noise and confusion, the edgy party atmosphere. Instead, she leaned closer to Trace.

"You have to tell me what was said, what's being done."

He'd chosen the club because it was loud and the clientele were self-absorbed. Whatever they said wouldn't carry beyond the table at which they sat. He'd chosen it for those reasons, and because he was postponing going back to the hotel, where he would be alone with her.

"Al-Aziz is a businessman. So is Cabot." Trace nibbled on a stale bread stick. "I made him a business proposition."

"What does that have to do with Flynn?"

"I get al-Aziz interested. With any luck he gets Hammer interested. We set up a meeting and I find out a hell of a lot more than we know now."

"You're going to meet with those people?" For some reason, her blood froze at the thought. For him, she realized. She was afraid for him. "But they know who you are."

Trace took a sip of his whiskey and wondered how long it would be before he was back in a country that served a proper drink. "Abdul knows who I am. Goons like him aren't generally in on arms transactions."

"Yes, but— Arms?" Her voice dropped to a passionate whisper. "You're going to sell them guns?"

"They damn well better think so."

"That's crazy. Setting up business transactions, pretending you'll be selling arms to terrorists. Certainly there has to be a better way."

"Sure. I could have walked into al-Aziz's and told him you were Dr. Gillian Fitzpatrick, whose brother had been kidnapped by Hammer. I could have appealed to his humanitarian instincts. Before the sun came up in the morning you'd be in the same position your brother's in now. And I'd be dead."

Gillian frowned into her wine. "It certainly seems a roundabout way of accomplishing something."

"You stick to your equations, Doc, I'll stick to mine. In a few days I should be talking with the general himself. I have a feeling that wherever he is, your brother's close by."

"You really think Flynn's near here?" As she leaned closer, her fingers gripped his. "I wish I could be sure. I wish I could feel something."

"The computer said Morocco. Rory confirmed that the plane was logged for Casablanca. Wherever he is now, he was here. So we start here."

He seemed so confident, so sure of the plan of attack. There was nothing she wanted, needed, more than to believe in him. "You'd met al-Aziz before, hadn't you? He seemed to know you."

Trace felt an itch between his shoulder blades. He'd have preferred sitting with his back to the wall. "We've dealt before."

"You've used him to sell guns before."

"The ISS used him," Trace said. He broke another bread stick in half. "A few years back there were plans for a coup the ISS wanted to endorse. Anonymously. Cabot made a nice profit, al-Aziz made his commission, and democracy took a giant step forward."

She knew such things happened. She'd grown up in a country divided by war. She lived in a country whose faith had been strained by secret deals and political machinations. But that didn't make it right.

"It's wrong."

"This is the real world," he countered. "And most of it's wrong."

"Is that why you do it?" She'd drawn away from him, but she couldn't ignore the impulse to move closer. "To make things right?"

There'd been a time—it seemed a lifetime ago—when he had been idealistic enough to believe that things could be made right. When he'd lost that, where he'd lost that, he couldn't have said. And he'd stopped looking.

"I just do my job, Gillian. Don't try to make a hero out of me."

"It didn't occur to me." She said it dryly enough to make his lips curve. "I just think it would make it easier if I understood you."

"Just understand that I'm going to get your brother and his kid out."

"And then?" She made a conscious effort to relax. There was nothing she could do now but wait. Wait, and try to probe beneath the surface of the man who held her life in his hands. "Will you retire?"

"That's the idea, sweetheart." The smoke around him was expensive—French, Turkish. The music was loud, the liquor just tolerable. He wondered when it had hit him that he'd spent too much time in places like this. He nearly laughed out loud. For all intents and purposes, he'd been born in a place like this. Sometime over the past year he'd realized he wanted out as badly as he'd wanted out a dozen years before. Only he was long past the point where he could just stick out his thumb.

"Trace?"

"What?"

She wasn't sure where he'd gone, but she knew it wasn't the time to ask. "What will you do... when you retire?"

"There's a place in the Canary Islands where a man can pick fruit right off the tree and sleep in a hammock with a warm woman. The water's clear as glass, and the fish jump right in your lap." He took another long sip. "A hundred thousand dollars in a place like that, I could be king."

"If you didn't die of boredom first."

"I've had enough excitement to last me the next thirty or forty years. Honey-skinned women and a salt-free diet."

He clicked his glass against hers. "I'm going to enjoy myself."

"André!"

Trace twisted in his chair and found his mouth captured in a long, steamy kiss. About halfway through, recognition dawned. He could remember only one woman who smelled like a hothouse flower and kissed like a vampire.

"Désirée." Trace ran a hand down her bare arm as she snuggled into his lap. "Still in Casablanca."

"Of course." She gave a throaty laugh and tossed back a mane of spiky midnight hair. "I'm partners now in the club."

"Come up in the world."

"But yes." She had skin like a magnolia and a heart that pumped happily with poison. Despite it, Trace had maintained a distant affection for her. "I married Amir. He's in the back, or he'd slit your throat for putting your hands on me."

"Nothing's changed, I see."

"You haven't." Blithely ignoring Gillian, Désirée ran her fingertips over Trace's face. "Oh, André, I waited weeks for you to come back."

"Hours, anyway."

"Are you staying long?"

"Few days. I'm showing my friend the charms of North Africa."

Désirée glanced around, took a sweeping up-and-down look, then cast Gillian into oblivion. "There was a time when my charms were enough for you."

"Your charms were enough for any army." Trace lifted his drink and kept his eye on the door of the back room. He knew Désirée wasn't exaggerating about Amir. "I've got a little business, *ma belle*. Do you still listen well at keyholes?"

"For you—and a price."

"Flynn Fitzpatrick. Scientist. Irish, with a small daughter. How much will it cost me to find out if they're in Casablanca?"

"For such an old, dear friend . . . five thousand francs."

Trace shifted her off his lap before taking out his money clip. "Here's half now. As an incentive."

She bent down and slipped the money into her shoe. "It's always a pleasure to see you, André."

"And you, *chérie*." He rose and brushed his lips over her knuckles. "Don't give Amir my best."

With another laugh, Désirée weaved her way through the crowd.

"You have fascinating friends," Gillian commented.

"Yeah. I'm thinking of having a reunion. Let's go."

Gillian made her way out of the smoke and into the clear night. "What were you saying?"

"Just reminiscing about old times."

She lifted a brow. "I'm sure they were fascinating."

Despite himself, he had to smile. Désirée had a heart of coal, but what an imagination! "They had their moments."

She fell silent for a moment, struggling. At last she gave up. "That woman was your type? Slinky?"

Trace knew enough about women to know when laughter was dangerous. He coughed instead. "Let's just say she's *a* type."

"I'm aware of that, and I doubt she's terribly attractive once you've scraped off the three layers of makeup."

"No need to be jealous, sweetheart. We're old news."

"Jealous?" She made the word sound like a joke and despised herself because it wasn't. "I would hardly be jealous of any woman you'd . . . you'd . . ."

"Come on, you can spit it out."

She shrugged off the arm he'd draped companionably around her shoulders. "Never mind. What did you pay her for?"

"To dig up some information."

"How would a woman like that be able to get any information?"

Trace looked down at her, saw that she was serious, and could only shake his head. "Diplomacy," he said.

She couldn't sleep. The energy that had been so sorely depleted only days before was back in full force. She was in Africa, a continent she had only read about in books. The Sahara was to the south. She was only steps away from the Atlantic, but from this side of the world it seemed a different ocean. Even the stars seemed different.

She didn't mind the strangeness. During her childhood she'd often dreamed of going to faraway places, but she'd contented herself with books. Her decision to emigrate to America had been the result of a craving to see something new, to be her own woman in a way she could never have been if she'd remained in Ireland with her father. So she'd gone to America to pursue her own goals, to live her own life. Now her father was ill and her brother was missing.

Gillian pulled on her robe, then threw open the terrace doors. How many times had she asked herself if things would somehow have been different if she'd stayed. It seemed foolish, even egotistical, to believe it. And yet the nagging doubt remained.

Now she was in Africa with a man who changed his identity in the blink of an eye. It would be through him and her own determination that things were put right again.

Put right. With a sigh, Gillian leaned on the railing and looked out at the lights and shadows of Casablanca. He said he didn't believe in putting things right, only in doing his job. Why didn't she believe that? It seemed to fit the style of the man. What it didn't fit were her feelings about him.

Almost from the first moment, she'd felt both drawn and repelled. There was something in his eyes, though only rarely, that told her he could be both kind and compassionate. There was the way he'd looked at her, looked to her, at the top of the Pyramid of the Magician. Part of him was a dreamer, part of him an icy realist. It seemed impossible to combine the two.

What he was, what he did, made her uneasy. All her life she'd believed in right and wrong, good and evil. Until she'd met him, she hadn't considered there could be so many shades in between. Nor had she realized until she'd met him that she could be attracted to a man who lived his life in those shades.

But it was a fact—not a theory, not a hypothesis, but a fact—that she was attracted, that she did trust, that she did believe. She couldn't take her emotions into a laboratory and dissect them, analyze them. For perhaps the first time in her life, she was stuck with a problem that no amount of logic or experimentation could solve. And the name of the problem was Trace O'Hurley.

She'd been jealous, quite fiercely jealous, when that woman had draped herself all over Trace in the club. When she'd murmured to him in intimate French and put her hands all over him, Gillian had wanted, badly, to grab her by the hair and yank out a few lacquered hunks. That simply wasn't in her nature. Or rather she'd never known it was.

She'd been jealous of Flynn from time to time, but only in the way a sister might be of a favored brother. And her love for him had always been much deeper than her envy. At university she'd had a few jealous pangs over girls with straight blond hair and blue eyes. But that had been very much a surface thing, without passion or depth.

The jealousy she'd felt tonight had been hot and violent and very difficult to control. It had also been unfamiliar. She hadn't been jealous of the woman's exotic looks or of her sinuous body, but of the fact that she'd twined that body around Trace's and kissed him as though she could have eaten him alive.

And he'd seemed to enjoy it.

Gillian crossed her arms over her chest and looked out at the smattering of lights that were still glowing in the city. She didn't care for jealousy any more than she cared for confusion. Trace O'Hurley apparently equaled both.

She jolted at a quick scraping sound, then whirled to see the flare of a match on the terrace beside hers.

He was in the shadows. They seemed to suit him best. She wondered how long he'd been there, silently watching.

"I didn't know you were there." And she wouldn't have, she realized, unless he'd allowed her to. "I couldn't sleep." When he didn't respond, she fiddled with the tie of her robe and cleared her throat. "I thought you'd gone to bed."

"Time change throws your system off."

"Yes, I suppose that's it." She curled her fingers around the railing again, wishing it was that simple. "We've been in so many time zones in the past few days. I'd have thought you'd be used to it."

"I like the night." That was true enough, but he'd come onto the terrace because he'd been restless, and because he'd been thinking of her.

"Sometimes I'll go up on the roof of my building. It's the only way you can see the stars in New York." She looked up at them now. "Back in Ireland, all you had to do was walk outside." With a shake of her head, she looked out at the city again. "Do you ever miss it?"

"Miss what?"

"Your home."

He drew on the cigarette, and his face was washed in red light for an instant. "I told you, I don't have one."

She moved to the side of the terrace that ran along the side of his. "Just the Canary Islands? How long can a man live on fruit and fish?"

"Long enough."

Though the night had cooled, he wore only baggy drawstring pants. Gillian remembered, quite clearly, the wild thrill of being held against that body. And the confusing emptiness of being pushed away from it. No, emotions couldn't be analyzed, but she could try to analyze their source.

"I wonder what it is you're running from."

"Running to." Trace pitched his cigarette over the balcony and onto the street below. "A life of luxury, sweetheart. Coconut milk and half-naked women."

"I don't think you can do it. You've already given a chunk of your life to your country."

"That's right." Unconsciously he rubbed at the scar on his chest. "What's left is mine." Her scent was soft again. The breeze carried it from her skin to his.

"You know, one of the things Mr. Forrester told me about you was that if you played by the rules more regularly you'd be running the ISS."

"Charlie had delusions of grandeur."

"He was tremendously proud of you."

"He recruited me. He trained me." Trace moved restlessly to the railing. "He'd want to think he'd done a good job of it."

"I think it was more than that. Affection and pride don't always go together." She thought of her father. "You should have the satisfaction of knowing he liked who you were, as well as what he'd made you. I know you cared for him, and that you're doing this as much for him as for the money. The reasons shouldn't matter to me, but they do. Trace?''

He didn't want to look at her now, with the moonlight slanting down and her scent hanging in the air. He kept his eyes on the street below. ''Yeah?''

''I know that Flynn and Caitlin will be all right. That they'll be safe soon because you're here.'' She wished he was close that she could reach out and touch him. She was grateful he wasn't. ''And when I have them back I'll never be able to repay you. So I want you to know now that whatever happens in the meantime, whatever has to be done, I'm grateful.''

''It's a job,'' he said, his teeth clenched, because the low, warm voice tended to make him forget that. ''Don't make me out to be some knight on a white charger, Gillian.''

''No, you're not that, but I think I'm beginning to understand what you are, Trace.'' She walked to the terrace doors. ''Good night.'' Because she hadn't expected him to answer, she closed the door on his silence.

''But how can you expect me to browse through shops and snap pictures as if I were nothing more than a tourist?''

Trace steered Gillian toward another display window. ''Because today you *are* nothing but a tourist. Show a little enthusiasm, will you?''

''My brother and my niece are prisoners. I'm afraid it's a little difficult for me to work up any enthusiasm over a bunch of crockery.''

''Authentic North African Art,'' Trace said.

''We're wasting time poking around when we should be doing something.''

"Any suggestions?" His voice was low as he continued to stroll, her arm caught firmly in his. Brightly striped awnings shaded the wares spread on outside tables. There was leather, and there was the flash of metal and the smell of horse. "You want me to break into where you brother's being held, guns blazing, maybe a knife between my teeth?"

He did a good job of making her feel like a fool. Gillian shrugged it off. "It makes better sense than buying trinkets and taking snapshots."

"In the first place I don't know where they're holding him. Hard to break into something until you've got the address. In the second place, if I tried that kind of TV tactics I'd be dead and your brother would be no better off. Let's sit." Satisfied with the position, he chose a shaded table on the terrace of a small café. "Why don't you tell me what's eating you?"

Gillian pushed her sunglasses more firmly on her nose. "Oh, I don't know. It might have something to do with the fact that Flynn and Caitlin have been kidnapped. Or perhaps I just got up on the wrong side of the bed."

"Sarcasm doesn't suit you." He ordered two coffees, then stretched out his legs. "You played the game well enough yesterday."

Gillian looked down at her hands. The sun glinted off the gold band of her watch. She studied the play of light until their coffee was served. "I couldn't sleep. Most of the night I just lay there waiting for morning. There was this feeling I couldn't shake. Something was wrong, dreadfully wrong, and I was going to be too late to put it right again." She looked up at him then, certain she would despise him if he laughed at her.

"You've been through a lot in the past few days." He said it easily, without the sympathy she would have bristled at or the edge she would have resented. "It wouldn't be normal for you to sleep like a baby."

"I suppose not, but if I just felt we were doing something..."

"We are." He put his hand on hers, then immediately drew it away again. "Drink your coffee."

The touch had been quick, and he was already resenting it. The fact that she thought she understood made her smile. "Being kind makes you uncomfortable."

"I'm not kind." He lit a cigarette, knowing he'd do better if he kept his hands occupied.

"Yes, you are." A little more relaxed, Gillian picked up her cup. "You'd prefer not to be, but it's difficult to change your nature. You can become other people." The coffee was hot and strong, and exactly what she'd needed. "But you can't change your nature. Whatever name you use, underneath it you're a kind man."

"You don't know me." He let smoke fill his lungs. "Or anything about me."

"As a scientist, I'm trained to observe, to analyze, categorize, hypothesize. Would you like to hear my hypothesis about you?"

"No."

The tension that had been locked in her muscles throughout the night eased. "You're a man who looked for adventure and excitement and undoubtedly found more than he'd bargained for. I'd say you believed in freedom and human rights strongly enough to spend a great deal of your life fighting for them. And you've been disillusioned and you nearly lost your life. I'm not certain which disturbs you more. I don't think you lied when you told me you were tired, Trace. But you lie every time you pretend not to care."

She was close, much too close, to the heart of things, much closer than anyone else had ever stepped. He'd found that life was more comfortable with distance. When he spoke, it was with the single goal of reestablishing it. "What I am is a trained liar, thief, cheat and killer. There's nothing pretty or glamorous or idealistic about what I do. I follow orders."

"I think the question isn't so much what you do as why you do it." For now, she stopped asking herself why it was so important for her to believe that, and just believed. "The whys became less clear, so you have a fantasy about retiring to some little island where you won't have to think about it."

Trace crushed out his cigarette. "You said physicist, not psychiatrist, right?"

"It's simply a matter of logic. I'm a very logical person." She set her cup back neatly in its saucer. "Then there's the matter of your behavior toward me. Apparently you're attracted."

"Is that so?"

She smiled then, always more secure when things were spelled out clearly. "I think it would be foolish to deny that a physical attraction exists. That can be listed as fact rather than theory. Yet, even on that basis, your behavior is contradictory. On each occasion when you've acted on that attraction, you've chosen to back off in favor of annoyance and frustration."

He didn't care to have his attractions, physical or otherwise, dissected like some embalmed frog. Trace waited until the waiter had freshened both cups before he leaned toward Gillian. "You can be grateful I backed off."

Their faces were very close over the little round table. Her heart began to drum, but she found the sensation more unique than unpleasant. "Because you're a dangerous man?"

"I'm the most dangerous man you'll ever meet."

She wasn't about to argue with that. "I explained to you before, I can take care of myself."

She reached for her coffee, and Trace closed his hand over her wrist. The grip was firm enough to make her eyes narrow. "You wouldn't know where to begin with me, Doc. And you sure as hell wouldn't know where to end. Count your blessings."

"My family's been kidnapped, I've seen a man die and had a knife to my back. There's little you could do to frighten me." She jerked her hand away and, with every outward appearance of calm, lifted her cup. Her heart beat fast and hard in her throat.

"You're wrong." This time he smiled. "If I decide to have you, you'll find out how wrong."

Her cup hit the saucer with a snap. "I'm ready to go."

"Sit." It was the sudden change in his voice that made her obey. "Drink your coffee," he said mildly as he picked up his camera.

"What is it?"

"Al-Aziz has a visitor." The camera was one of the few pieces of ISS equipment Trace was fond of. He pushed a button, and a man stepping out of a black car twenty yards away filled the viewfinder. He recognized the face from briefings, and he smiled again. Kendesa was the general's right hand, a man of taste and intelligence who just managed to balance the general's fanaticism.

"You know who it is?"

Trace took two shots out of habit. "Yeah." He lowered the camera.

"What does it mean?"

"It means they took the bait."

Gillian moistened her lips and struggled to stay calm. "What do we do now?"

Trace lit another cigarette. "We wait."

Al-Aziz's visitor stayed twenty minutes. When he came back out, Trace was up and moving. By the time Kendesa stepped into his car, Trace and Gillian were in a cab. "I want you to stay with that car," he told the driver, pulling out bills. "But keep a nice distance."

The driver pocketed the money before he started the engine. Gillian groped for Trace's hand and held on.

"He knows where Flynn is, doesn't he?"

"He knows."

She pressed her free hand to her lips as they drove. "What are you going to do?"

"Nothing."

"But if he—"

"Let's just see where he's going." Because her hand was icy, he kept it in his. The black car stopped at one of the more exclusive hotels in the business district. Trace waited until Kendesa was inside. "Stay here."

"But I want to—"

"Just stay here," he repeated, and then he was gone. As the minutes passed, fear became annoyance. Gillian slid to the door and had her fingers around the handle when Trace pulled it open.

"Going somewhere?" He let the door slam behind him. Settling back, he gave the driver the name of their hotel.

"Well?"

"He just checked in this morning. He hasn't given them a day of departure. I'd say that means he intends to stay until business is completed."

"Aren't you going to go in and make him tell you where Flynn is?"

`Trace spared her a look. "Sure, I'll go on up to his room, rough him and his three guards up a bit and drag the truth out of them. Then I'll march up to wherever they're holding your brother and blast him out single-handed."

"Isn't that what I'm paying you for?"

"You're paying me to get him out—in one piece." As the cab pulled up at the curb, Trace handed the driver more bills. "Let's play this my way."

Knowing her temper couldn't be trusted, Gillian remained silent until they were in their rooms. "If you have a plan, I think it's time you filled me in."

Ignoring her, Trace walked over to the bed and began to fiddle with what Gillian had taken for a compact portable stereo.

"This is hardly the time to listen to music." When he continued to say nothing, she stormed over to him. "Trace, I want to know what you have in mind. I refuse to be kept in the dark while you sit here and listen to the radio. I want to know—"

"Shut up, will you?" When he played back the tape, the voices came out barely audible, and speaking Arabic. "Damn." He adjusted the volume and strained.

"What is that?"

"Our friends talking, almost out of reach of the bug I planted yesterday."

"You . . . I never saw you plant anything."

"That boosts my confidence." He rewound the tape to the beginning.

"I can't think of any place you could have hidden it."

"I left it out in plain view. People find things a lot quicker if you hide them. Didn't you ever read Poe? Now be quiet."

The voices were barely distinguishable, but he recognized al-Aziz's. He could decipher the formal greetings, but from there on could translate only a few snatches. He heard Cabot's name, and some basic monetary negotiations.

"What does it say?" Gillian asked when he shut the tape off again."

"I don't know enough Arabic to make much sense of it."

"Oh." She tried to block off the disappointment. Running her hands over her face, she sat on the bed beside him. "I guess you'd hoped they speak in French or English."

"It would have been helpful." Trace removed the tape and slipped it into his pocket. "Now we need an interpreter."

Her hands dropped in her lap. "You know someone who'll help us?"

"Almost anyone's willing to help for a price." He checked his watch. "The club ought to be pretty quiet now. I think I'll go to see Désirée."

"I'm going with you."

He started to refuse, then thought better of it. "Just as well. I can use you as a cover in case Amir's around. With you hanging all over me, he won't think I'm trying to tickle his wife's fancy. Or anything else."

"I'm so glad I can be useful."

They found Désirée in the apartment above the club. Though it was nearly noon, she answered the door heavy-eyed and in a sexily rumpled robe that slipped provocatively off one shoulder. Her eyes brightened considerably at the sight of Trace.

"André. What a nice surprise." She spotted Gillian, pouted a moment, then stepped back to let them in. "You used to come visiting alone," she said in French.

"You used to be single." Trace glanced around the wide, dim room, with its fussy pillows and its china knicknacks. The room was crammed with furniture, and the furniture covered with things. Possessions had always been important to Désirée. Apparently she'd finally acquired them. "You've come up in the world, *chérie*."

"We make our own way in life." She walked to a table and chose a cigarette from a glass holder. "If you've come for your information, you haven't given me much time." She held the cigarette, waiting until Trace crossed the room to light it.

"Actually, I've come on other business." She smelled of perfume that clung from the night before, no longer strong, but still overpowering. "Is your husband in?"

Her brow lifted as she glanced in Gillian's direction. "You were never one for group games."

"No games at all." He took the cigarette from her and drew on it himself. "Amir. Is he here?"

"He had business. He's a busy man."

"Your Arabic was always excellent, Désirée." Trace drew the tape from his pocket. "Two thousand francs for a translation of this tape, and a memory lapse immediately afterward."

Désirée took the tape and turned it over in her palm. "Two thousand for the translation, and three more for the loss of memory." She smiled at him. "A woman must make a living where she can."

There had been a time when he would have enjoyed negotiating with her. He wondered why that time seemed to have passed. "Done."

"Cash, darling." She held out an empty hand. "Now."

When Trace handed her the money, she went over to a stereo. "Amir enjoys his toys," she said as she slipped the tape into the player. After switching it on, she adjusted the volume. Almost at once, her expression changed. With the touch of a finger, the player fell silent again. "Kendesa. You said nothing of Kendesa."

"You didn't ask." Trace sat and gestured for Gillian to join him. "The deal's struck, Désirée. Play it my way and your name will never be mentioned."

"You mix in very bad company, André. Very bad." But the money was still in her hand. After a moment's consideration, she slipped it into her pocket, then switched the machine back on. "Kendesa greets the swine al-Aziz. He asks if business is good." She listened for another moment, then turned the machine off again. "They speak of you, the Frenchman Cabot, who has an interesting business proposition for Kendesa's organization. Al-Azia has humbly agreed to act as liaison."

She turned the machine on again, then repeated the process of listening before turning it off to translate. "Kendesa is very interested in your product. His sources have confirmed that you are in possession of a shipment of American arms intended for their Middle Eastern allies. A shipment of this size and—" she groped for the word a moment "—quality is of interest to Kendesa's superior. And so are you."

She switched the tape on again and lit a cigarette as the two voices murmured through the speakers. "Your reputation is satisfactory, but Kendesa is cautious. His organization is most concerned with another project at this time, and yet your product is tempting. Kendesa has agreed to have al-Aziz arrange a meeting. They discuss commission. Then it becomes interesting. Al-Aziz asks of this Fitzpatrick. He tells Kendesa he has heard rumors. Kendesa tells him to mind his shop and his tongue."

Désirée turned the tape off. It ejected smoothly. "Tell me, André, are you interested in guns or in this Irishman?"

"I'm interested in the largest profit." He rose to take the tape from her. "And your memory, Désirée?"

She fondled the bills in her pocket. "Quite blank." She smiled, then ran a hand up his chest. "Come back for a drink tonight. Alone."

Trace cupped her chin in his hand and kissed her. "Amir is a large, jealous man who has a talent with knives. Let's just treasure the past."

"It was an interesting one." She sighed and watched him walk to the door. "André, the Irishman was in Casablanca."

He stopped, clamping his hand around Gillian's arm before she could speak. "And now?"

"He was taken east, into the mountains. That's all I know."

"There was a child."

"A girl. She's with him. It would have to be a great deal more profitable to ask questions now that I know who is involved."

"You've asked enough." He drew out bills and set them on the table by the door. "Forget this, too, Désirée, and enjoy your large husband."

When he closed the door, Désirée considered for a long moment, then walked to the phone.

"He was here," Gillian said, torn between relief and fresh terror. "They were both here. There has to be a way of finding out where they were taken. Oh, God, they were so close."

"Don't get ahead of yourself. The mountains to the east isn't a street address."

"But it's another step. What do we do now?"

"We get some lunch. And we wait for Kendesa to move."

Chapter Six

I want to go with you."

Trace straightened the knot of the hated tie. "It's out of the question."

"You haven't given me a reason." Gillian stood planted behind him, scowling at his reflection. He looked so smooth, she thought, a world away from the man she'd found in the cantina. She wondered what dramatic turn her life had taken to make her prefer the rough, unshaven and slightly dirty man she'd first met to the urbane and cologned one who stood in front of her.

"I don't have to give you reasons, just results."

At least that much hadn't changed, she thought wryly, standing her ground. "I explained to you right from the beginning that I'd be going through this step-by-step with you."

"You're going to miss this step, sweetheart." Trace checked the plain brushed-gold links at his cuffs. "You just stay here and keep a light burning in the window." Turning, he gave her a friendly pat on the cheek.

"You look like a stockbroker," she muttered.

"No need for insults." Trace picked up a briefcase filled with papers and inventories he'd spent the better part of the night putting together.

"You're meeting with Kendesa, and I think I should be there."

"It's a business meeting—bad business. I take a woman along to a meeting where I'm talking about dealing arms to terrorists, Kendesa's going to wonder why. He wonders hard enough and he could check you out. He checks deep enough, he could find out that my woman is the sister of Hammer's most prized possession." He stopped long enough to wipe away a smudge on his shoe. "It's not a good bet."

It was because it was too logical to argue with that Gillian was angry. "I'm not your woman."

"They better think you are."

"I'd rather be buried up to my neck in hot sand."

He glanced at her. She stood by the window, spitting mad and stunning. "I'll keep that in mind. Why don't you spend a couple hours making up a list of alternatives? It might put you in a better mood."

When he opened the door, she prepared to hurl abuse. "Be careful," she said instead, hating herself for it.

He paused again. "Concern. I'm touched."

"It's nothing personal." But her palms were sweaty at the idea of him going alone. "If anything happened to you I'd have to start from scratch."

With a little laugh, he stepped into the hall. "Stay inside, Doc."

The moment the door closed at his back, he left Trace O'Hurley behind. He had a certain affection for each of his covers. Without that, it would have been difficult for him to play any of them convincingly for what were often long stretches of time. André Cabot was fussy, and often pompous, but he had excellent taste and extraordinary luck with women. Trace felt that redeemed him.

Still, Cabot's charm hadn't made a dent in Gillian's defenses. So she doesn't like Frenchmen, Trace decided as he settled into a cab. Apparently she preferred stodgy American scientists like that Arthur Steward she spent so much time with in New York. The man was fifteen years older than she, and more interested in white mice than romance. Trace had told himself it was simply standard procedure to check him out. Nothing personal.

Trace shifted his briefcase and reminded himself that Cabot was concerned only with making a profit. He wouldn't have given a woman like Gillian a second thought once she was out of sight. The trouble was, Trace O'Hurley was thinking about her entirely too much.

She was still a puzzle to him, and he was used to figuring any angle, any woman. They shared the same set of rooms, yet she gave the arrangement a sense of innocence and propriety. She was vulnerable and passionate, frightened and determined. She was logical, yet enough of a dreamer to feel the power of a Mayan ruin. She spoke easily, even clinically, of his attraction to her. But there had been a fire, hot and vital, when he'd kissed her.

She was right about one thing—he wanted her, and bad. What she didn't know, what he couldn't explain even to himself, was that he was terrified of what might happen if he acted on that need.

When the cab drew up to the curb, Trace pulled himself back. He was right about something, too. He was thinking about her too much.

He counted out bills as Cabot would, carefully. With obvious reluctance, he added the minimum tip. After straightening the line of his jacket, he walked into the lobby of Kendesa's hotel.

He spotted one of the bodyguards but walked to the bank of elevators without pausing. He was on time to the minute. That was another of Cabot's traits. The elevator took him to the top floor, to the executive suite, often reserved for dignitaries and visiting heads of state.

The door was opened at the first knock by a burly guard who looked uncomfortable in his dark Western suit. "Your weapon, monsieur," he said in stilted French.

Trace reached inside his jacket and removed a .25 automatic. Cabot carried a small pistol rather than chance ruining the line of his jacket.

The guard pocketed it before gesturing him into the parlor of the suite. A bottle of wine was open on the table. Fresh roses stood in a vase beside it. The room was cushioned from the noise and heat of the day. Noting that the terrace doors were not only shut but locked, Trace took his seat. Kendesa didn't keep him waiting.

He wasn't an imposing man. Whatever passions stirred him were kept firmly strapped down and controlled. He was small in stature and impeccably and conservatively dressed. Unlike the man he represented, he wore no ostentatious jewelry, no vivid colors. He was dark and blandly handsome, rather like a news anchorman, and moved with the steady grace of a career soldier.

He was a man who exuded trust and moderation, and in the past eighteen months he had been responsible for the execution of three political hostages. He was holding the wildly fanatical Hammer together by the skin of his teeth.

"Monsieur Cabot." Kendesa offered his hand. "It's a pleasure to meet you."

"*Monsieur.* Business is always my pleasure."

With a politely interested smile, Kendesa took his seat. "Our mutual friend indicated you have some supplies that may be of interest to me. Some wine? I think you'll find it agreeable." Kendesa poured two glasses. Trace let him drink first.

"I've recently acquired certain military supplies that I believe your organization would find useful." Trace sipped and found the wine dry and light. Cabot's preference. He smiled. Kendesa had done his homework.

"My sources tell me that these supplies were intended for the Zionists."

Trace lifted a shoulder, pleased that the money he'd spent in the bidonville had been invested wisely. "I'm a businessman, *monsieur*. I have no politics, only a profit margin. The supplies could still be shipped where the Americans originally intended, if the price was right."

"You're frank." Kendesa tapped a finger on the side of his glass. "The United States had not admitted openly that these supplies were...confiscated. In fact, it's difficult to prove that they ever existed."

"Such things are embarrassing. For myself, I prefer that the entire business be kept quiet until the final transactions are complete." Setting his wine aside, Trace lifted his suitcase. "This is a list of the arms my associates are holding. I can assure you they are top-quality. I've checked samples myself."

Kendesa took the papers but continued to watch Trace. "Your reputation in such matters is unimpeachable."

"*Merci.*"

Kendesa's brows lifted slightly as he scanned the list. Trace had made it irresistible. "This particular weapon, the TS-35. My sources tell me it was not to be completed for several months."

"It was completed and tested five weeks ago," Trace told him, knowing the news would be out in a matter of weeks in any case. "It is a beautiful piece of work. Very light-weight, and compact. The Americans are very clever in some areas." He drew out another sheet of paper. "My associates and I have settled on a price. Shipping can, of course, be arranged."

"The total seems high."

"Overhead. Inflation." He spread his hands in a purely Gallic gesture. "You understand."

"And I am a cautious man, you understand. Before negotiations can be initiated, it would be necessary to inspect a portion of your product."

"Naturally, I can deal with that myself, if you like." He moved his fingertip over his jawline consideringly. "It will take me a few days to make the arrangements. I prefer to do so in a place you have secured. In today's atmosphere, transactions of this nature have become only more delicate."

"The general is residing in the east. Such a transaction cannot be completed without his approval."

"Understood. Though I'm aware much of the buying and selling are your province, I would prefer discussing the matter with the general."

"You will bring your samples to us, in one week." In a week he would have a complete report on Cabot and the enterprise. "The general has established his headquarters in an area east of Sefrou that he has christened el Hasad. It will be arranged for you to be met in Sefrou. From there, your transportation will be seen to."

"I will contact my associates, but I see no problem with those arrangements. One week, then." Trace rose.

Kendesa rose, as well. "A question on another matter, *monsieur*. You inquired about a scientist who has recently joined our organization. I would ask what your interest is."

"Profit. There are several parties interested in Dr. Fitzpatrick and his particular skills. The Horizon project, once completed, could generate an incredible amount of income."

"We are not only interested in money."

"I am," Trace said with a cool smile. "You might think of what the scientist is worth, if you can persuade him to complete the project. The arms we are currently negotiating over would be little more than toys." He folded his hands, and the gold at his wrists winked dully. "If your organization finds the proper partner, you could not only be rich, but as powerful politically as any developed country."

It was something he had considered already, though he would have preferred making the first move. "Your outlook is intriguing."

"Only speculation, *monsieur*, unless you can indeed convince the man to produce for you."

Kendesa brushed that aside easily. He was a man who was accustomed to cooperation—or submission. "That is only a matter of time. I will speak with the general on this, as well. Perhaps it can be discussed." Kendesa led him to the door. "I would tell you, Monsieur Cabot, that you might be more cautious in choosing your associates."

"I beg your pardon?"

"I speak of the French woman, Désirée. She thought a greater profit could be made through blackmail. She was mistaken."

Trace merely lifted a brow, but he felt a cold gnawing at his stomach. "She is as greedy as she is beautiful."

"And now she is dead. Good afternoon, *monsieur*."

Trace gave a slight bow. He held on to Cabot until he was back in his room. There he gave way to fury by slamming a fist into the wall.

"Damn the woman!" Couldn't she have been satisfied with the easy money he'd passed her? She'd killed herself. He could tell himself she'd killed herself, and yet he felt the weight of another life on his hands.

For a moment he closed his eyes and forced the image of his island into his mind. Soft breezes, warm fruit, warmer women. The minute he had the cash in his hand he was getting out.

Trace went to the bottle of whiskey on his dresser, poured a double and washed the taste of Kendesa's wine from his mouth. It didn't help. Slamming the glass down again, he went into the next room to tell Gillian they were a step closer.

She was sitting on the bed, her back very straight, her hands folded in her lap. She didn't glance over as he came in, but continued to stare out the window at a slice of sky.

"Still sulking?" The whiskey hadn't helped, but maybe dumping a little excess temper on her would. "I don't know which is more tiresome, listening to you bitch or putting up with your moods." Yanking off his tie, he tossed it in the general direction of a chair. "Snap out of it, Doc, unless you don't want to hear what I found out about your brother."

She looked at him then, but he didn't see recrimination or temper in her eyes. There wasn't the anticipation he'd expected, but grief, raw and dry-eyed. He'd started to peel out of his jacket, and now he drew it off slowly.

"What is it?"

"I called my father." Her voice was quiet, hardly more than a whisper, but steady. It was the tone that stopped him from nagging at her for using an unsecured line. "I thought he should know we were close to finding Flynn. I wanted to give him some hope, some comfort. I know he felt helpless having to send me instead of doing it himself." She closed her eyes and waited for her strength to rebuild. "I got his nurse. She's staying at the house, looking after it. He died three days ago." She unlinked her fingers, then curled them together again. "Three days. I didn't know. I wasn't there. They buried him this morning."

He came to her in silence to sit beside her, to slip an arm around her. She resisted only a moment, then allowed herself to lean against him. The tears didn't come. She wondered why she felt so cold and numb, when hot, raging grief would have been a relief.

"He was all alone when he died. No one should die alone, Trace."

"You said he'd been ill."

"He was dying. He knew it, and he really didn't want to live the way he'd become. Weak and feeble. All his research, all his brilliance, couldn't help him. He only wanted one thing—for me to bring Flynn home before he died. Now it's too late."

"You're still going to bring Flynn home."

"He loved Flynn so. I was a disappointment to him, but Flynn was everything he wanted. The worry of the past days only made him worse. I wanted him to die easy, Trace. Even after everything, I wanted him to die easy."

"You did everything you could. You're doing what he wanted."

"I never did what he wanted." Her cheeks were hot and wet now, but she didn't notice. "He never forgave me for going to America, for leaving him. He never understood that I needed to breathe, needed to look for my own life. He only understood that I was going away, rejecting him and his plans for me. I loved him." Her voice caught on the first sob. "But I could never explain myself to him. And I never will. Oh, God, I didn't get to say goodbye. Not even that."

She didn't object when he drew her closer, to rock, to stroke, to soothe. He didn't speak, only held, as the tears came, fast and violent. He understood grief, the fury and the ache of it, and knew it wasn't words that dulled both, it was time. Gathering her close, he lay down with her while she wept out the first pains.

He understood the guilt. He and Gillian were as different as black and white, but he, too, had had a father who had made plans, who hadn't understood and hadn't forgiven. And he knew that guilt made grief more painful even than love.

He brushed his lips across her temple and held on.

When she was quiet, he continued to stroke her hair. The light was still strong through the windows. Wanting to draw the curtains closed, he started to rise. Gillian tightened her hold.

"Don't go," she murmured. "I don't want to be alone."

"I'll close the drapes. Maybe you can sleep."

"Just stay with me a little while longer." She brushed a hand over her face to wipe away the tears. Emotional outbursts were something she'd always been prone to, and one more thing her father hadn't understood. "He was a hard man, my father, especially after my mother died. She knew how to reach him. I'll always regret that I couldn't." Taking a long breath, she shut her eyes again. "Flynn and Caitlin are the only family I have left. I have to find them, Trace. I have to see that they're safe."

"I have a pretty good idea where they are."

She nodded. All her faith, all her hopes, were tied up in him now. "Tell me."

He gave her a brief sketch of his meeting with Kendesa, but stopped short of mentioning Désirée. That was still on his conscience. She listened but didn't move away. Her head stayed on his shoulder, her hand on his chest. As he spoke, something he'd closed off long before began to crack open. He couldn't explain why he felt stronger because his arms were around her. He couldn't explain why, even knowing what had to be done in the next few days, he felt almost at peace lying in the bright room with her hair against his cheek.

"You think Flynn and Caitlin are with this General Husad?"

"I'd give odds on it."

"And in a week you'll meet with him."

"That's the plan."

"But he'll expect you to have some of these guns. What will happen when you don't?"

"Who says I won't?"

She did move then, slowly drawing her head back so that she could see his face. His eyes were half closed, but the grimness around his mouth hadn't faded. "Trace, I don't understand. You told them you had a shipment of American arms. You don't. How can you take them samples of what you don't have?"

"I have to go shopping for a few M-16s, 40-millimeter grenade launchers and odds and ends."

"I don't think the local department stores carry them."

"The black market does, and I've got connections." He let the silence hang for a moment. "Gillian, it's time to let the ISS in on this."

"Why? Why now?"

"Because I've established cover, I've made contact. They'll be annoyed, but they aren't stupid enough to blow the operation at this stage. If something goes wrong, they'll need to have the information so they can move on it."

She was silent for a long time. "You mean if you're killed."

"If I'm taken out, a lot of time will be wasted in getting to your brother. With ISS backing from this point, we cover more bases."

"Why should they hurt you? You're selling them the guns they want."

He thought of Désirée. "The guns are one thing, Horizon is another. These people aren't businessmen, and they don't have the honor of a Manhattan street gang. If they think I know too much, or might infringe on their territory, eliminating me would be the best way of protecting their interest. It's a toss of the dice which way they'll play it. You don't want to risk your brother's life on a toss of the dice."

Nor did she want to risk his. It came to her now as they lay close, without passion, without anger, that she'd become as concerned for him as for her family. He wasn't simply an instrument to free Flynn and Caitlin with any longer, but he was a man who drew her, infuriated her, aroused her.

She looked down and saw that her hand had curled against his chest. Holding on, she thought, to something that wasn't hers. "Maybe we should let the ISS take over from here."

"Let's not go overboard."

"No, I mean it." She shifted away and sat up. She wanted more now. She wanted him to hold her, not in comfort, not in reassurance, but in desire. "The more I think about it, the crazier it seems for you to go in alone. Anything could happen to Flynn and Caitlin . . . to you."

"I've worked alone and come out in one piece before."

"And the last time you worked against them you nearly died."

Because this sudden attack of nerves intrigued him, Trace sat up and took her by the shoulders. "Don't you believe in destiny, Gillian? We do things to move it along, to protect ourselves from it, but in the end, what's meant is meant."

"You were just talking about luck."

"Yeah, I don't figure there's a contradiction there. If my luck's in, and I'm meant to come out, I will."

"You're not a fatalist."

"Depends on the mood. But I'm always a realist. This job is mine, for a lot of reasons." And she wasn't the least of them. "But I'm practical enough to know when it's time for backup."

"I don't want anything to happen to you." She said it quickly, knowing it was as foolish as it was useless.

His look sharpened. Before she could turn away, he cupped her chin in his hand. "Why?"

"Because . . . I'd feel responsible."

It wasn't wise to push, but he wasn't always wise. "Why else?"

"Because I'd be alone, and I've nearly gotten used to you, and . . ." Her voice trailed off as she lifted a hand to his cheek. "And there's this," she murmured, bringing her lips to his.

The light was still bright, but it seemed to her that the room went dim, the colors softened and the world tipped out of focus. The emotional roller coaster she'd already experienced went speeding around an unexpected curve, leaving her giddy and exhilarated. She pressed against him, already anticipating the next plunge.

She was as warm and sweet as any fantasy. She was real and vital. More than he'd ever wanted freedom or wealth or peace of mind, he wanted her. He felt reason slipping against the pull of need, and he held himself back. To need anything too much was to risk losing.

But her hands were so soft, so soothing. His own were in her hair, dragging her closer, even as he told himself it was wrong for both of them. Her scent was like a quiet promise, lulling him into believing he could have and keep. He ached from needing to touch her, to feel how her body might move against his hands.

He had to remind himself that there was no promise, neither from her nor to her. There couldn't be.

When he drew her away, she reached out again. Trace tightened his grip and held her back. "You listen to me. This is all wrong. You know it and I know it."

"No, I don't."

"Then you're an idiot."

She knew how to handle rejection. She braced herself for it. "You don't want me?"

He swore, once, then twice. "Of course I want you. Why shouldn't I? You're beautiful. You've got brains and guts. You're everything I've ever wanted."

"Then why—?"

He dragged her out of the bed. Before she could draw in the breath to protest, he was holding her in front of the mirror. "Look at yourself, you're a nice, well-bred woman. A physicist, for God's sake. You came from a nice upper-class family, went to good schools and did what you were told." When temper had her pulling away, he yanked her back again. "Look at me, Gillian." He gave her one hard shake until her head snapped up and her eyes met his in the mirror. "I spent most of my life dancing from second-rate club to second-rate club. I never spent more than a handful of days a year in a real school. I never learned to play by the rules. I've never owned a car or a piece of property, and I've never stayed with a woman for long. Do you want to know how many people I've killed in twelve years? Do you want to know how many ways there are to do it?"

"Stop it." She pulled away from him, only to whirl back. "You're trying to scare me, and it won't work."

"Then you *are* an idiot."

"Maybe I am, but at least I'm an honest one. Why don't you just admit that you don't want to be involved? You don't want to feel anything for me."

He drew out a cigarette. "That's right."

"But you do." She tossed her head back, daring him to deny it. "You do feel, and you're the one who's scared."

Her point, he thought as he blew out smoke. But he'd be damned if he'd let her know it. "Let's get something straight, sweetheart. I don't have time to give you the hearts and flowers you'd like. We've got a priority, and it's in the mountains east of here. Let's concentrate on that."

"You can't run forever."

"When I stop, you'll wish to God I'd kept going. I've got some things to do." He walked out.

Gillian did something she hadn't done in years. She picked up the nearest breakable and heaved it at the door.

Chapter Seven

After the number of years you've had in service, Agent O'Hurley, I'm sure you're aware that there's such a thing as procedure."

Captain Addison—British, balding and straight-line ISS—sat in Trace's room, drinking coffee and looking annoyed. It was his job to oversee and coordinate operations in this part of the world. After nearly fifteen years of field duty, he was quite content to do so from behind a desk. Under these particular circumstances, he'd been ordered to handle the business face-to-face. The break in routine did nothing to please him.

He'd been set to go back to London on holiday when the call had reached him at his Madrid base. Now he was in godforsaken Morocco, in the middle of an incident that would very likely keep him from his steak-and-kidney pie for some time to come.

"You have, I presume, some sort of valid explanation?"

"I was on vacation, Captain." Trace drew easily on his cigarette. Types like Addison amused him more than they annoyed him. It was the possibility that he could become similarly straitlaced that had kept him away from desks and paperwork. "My own time. I thought the ISS might be interested in what I stumbled into."

"Stumbled into," Addison repeated. He pushed his rimless glasses up on his nose and gave Trace a very cool and very clear stare. "We both know you didn't stumble into anything, Agent O'Hurley. You acted on your own, without ISS sanction."

"The woman came to me." Trace didn't bother to put any emphasis into the explanation. He knew very well that men of Addison's type preferred agents to sweat. "I followed up an interesting story and came by some even more interesting information. If you don't want what I've got, it doesn't matter to me. I've still got a week before I punch in."

"The correct procedure would have been to inform the ISS the moment Dr. Fitzpatrick contacted you."

"I consider that a judgment call, Captain. My judgment."

Addison folded his hands. Though he'd been divorced for five years, he still wore a gold wedding band. He'd gotten used to the weight on his finger. "Your record shows a high percentage of infractions."

"Am I fired?"

A creature of habit and order, Addison bristled at Trace's careless arrogance. But he, too, had his orders. "Fortunately—or unfortunately, depending on one's viewpoint— your record also show a high percentage of successful assignments. To be frank, O'Hurley, I don't care for showboating of this kind, but the Horizon project and Dr. Fitzpatrick and his daughter take precedence over personal feelings."

Trace hadn't missed the order of importance. Nor had he expected anything else. "Then I take it I'm not fired."

"You will maintain your cover as André Cabot, but from this point on we go by the book. You will keep in constant contact with the ISS base in Madrid on your progress. You will report directly to me." This, too, gave him no pleasure. One didn't easily keep a rogue agent under one's thumb. "We have arranged for one crate of American-made weapons to be delivered to you in Sefrou in four days. Your contact there will be Agent Breintz. Once you have confirmed Dr. Fitzpatrick's location and assessed the situation, you'll be given further orders. Headquarters feels you should keep the arms negotiations straightforward. If you do find yourself in Husad's lair, it's code blue."

Again, it was nothing he hadn't expected. Code blue meant simply that if his cover didn't hold the ISS would destroy his files, his identity. It would be as if Trace O'Hurley had never existed.

"I need a TS-35 in the crate."

"A—" Addison laid his hands carefully on the arms of his chair. "You told them about the TS-35?"

"The Soviets will know about it in a week—if they don't already. Everyone else will know before the month is out. If I dangle one in front of their noses, Husad might decide I'm a useful ally. He might loosen up enough about Fitzpatrick to let me have a tour, especially if I tell him that my associates are willing to help finance Horizon."

"They may be maniacs, but they're not fools. If they had a prototype, it wouldn't take them long to duplicate the weapon."

"If we don't get Fitzpatrick out and secure the Horizon project, the TS-35 isn't much more than a peashooter."

Addison rose and paced to the window. He didn't like it. He didn't like O'Hurley. He didn't like having his plans interfered with. But he hadn't reached his position by not knowing when and how to play his cards. "I'll arrange it. But the weapon is to be brought back out or destroyed."

"Understood."

With a nod, Addison turned back. "Now, about the woman." He glanced toward the door that led to Gillian's room. "Since Agent Forrester saw fit to tell her about you and she's now aware of the operation, she'll have to be debriefed."

Trace lifted the pot of coffee and poured himself a cup. "Good luck."

"Your humor eludes me, O'Hurley. I'd like to speak with her now."

With a shrug, Trace rose to walk to the door. He pushed it open and stuck his head inside. Gillian stopped pacing and looked at him. "Your turn."

Gillian swallowed, wiped her hands on her slacks, then walked through the doorway.

"Dr. Fitzpatrick." With the first congenial smile Trace had ever seen on his face, Addison crossed to offer her his hand. "I'm Captain Addison."

"How do you do?"

"Please, sit down. Can I offer you a cup of coffee?"

"Yes, thank you." Gillian sat, back straight, chin up, while Trace lounged in the chair beside her.

"Cream, Doctor?"

"No, black, please."

Addison handed her a cup, then sat down cozily with his own. Gillian was almost afraid he was going to talk about the weather. "Dr. Fitzpatrick, I must tell you how concerned the ISS is about your family's welfare. Our organization is dedicated to ensuring the freedom and basic human rights of people everywhere. A man like your brother is of great importance to us."

"My brother is of even greater importance to me."

"To be sure." He smiled again, almost avuncularly. "Though we believe you and Agent O'Hurley acted impulsively, we think we can turn these impulses to our advantage."

Gillian looked at Trace, saw by the lazy way he moved his shoulders that he would be no help and looked back at Addison. "I acted in what I believed, and still believe, is my brother's best interests, Captain. He and Caitlin are my only concern."

"Of course, of course. I can assure you that even now the ISS is putting all its skill and experience into freeing your brother. We hope that will be accomplished quickly. In the meantime, I'd like you to come back to Madrid with me and remain under ISS protection."

"No."

"I beg your pardon?"

"I appreciate the offer, Captain, but I'm staying with Agent O'Hurley."

Addison put his arms on either side of his cup and linked his hands. "Dr. Fitzpatrick, for your own safety, and for the security of this operation, I must insist you come under ISS protection."

"My brother and my niece are in the mountains east of here. I won't sit in Madrid and wait. I'm quite confident that Agent O'Hurley can protect me, if you feel protection is warranted. As to the operation's security, I was involved long before you or the ISS, Captain. I'm sure my clearance can be upgraded if necessary."

"My orders are to take you to Madrid."

"Your orders are of no concern to me, Captain." It was that tone of voice, used rarely but effectively, that had helped secure her a top position at the institute. "I have no ties to the ISS, or to anyone but my family. General Husad wants me, as well. As long as there's a chance that that can be used to get Flynn out, I'm willing to take the risk."

"Dr. Fitzpatrick, I understand and appreciate your emotional involvement, but it's simply not possible—"

"It is possible, unless the ISS also indulges in kidnapping private citizens."

Addison sat back to collect his thoughts, then tried another tactic. "Agent O'Hurley is highly trained, certainly one of our best." Trace merely lifted a brow, knowing that had stuck in Addison's throat. "However, his energies will be centered on the operation."

"And so will mine, as long as I can be useful."

"Agent O'Hurley will tell you himself that it's against policy to use a civilian."

"Go to Madrid, Gillian." Trace said it quietly, and broke a promise to himself by putting a hand over hers. It wasn't a matter of policy. He'd already said to hell with policy. But it was a matter of what would be best, and safest, for her.

"I'm going with you." She turned her hand over so that their palms met. "That was the deal."

"Don't be stupid. It could get ugly from here."

"That doesn't matter."

Because he thought he understood, he drew his hand away again. Rising, he walked to the window and lit a cigarette. What the hell had he done to earn that kind of trust? He didn't know the answer to that any more than he knew how to make her see reason. "I told you before, I don't have time to baby-sit."

"And I told you, I can take care of myself." She put the hand, still warm from his, in her lap as she turned back to

Addison. "I've established myself as Cabot's woman. There wouldn't be any reason to question my traveling with him as far as Sefrou. If I have to wait there, I'll wait. Unless you intend to forcibly detain me, which I assure you would cause some nasty publicity, I'm going."

Addison hadn't expected resistance. His files on Gillian had indicated that she was a dedicated scientist, a woman who lived quietly and followed the rules. "I have no intention of forcibly detaining you, Dr. Fitzpatrick, but let me ask you this—what would happen if you were discovered and taken to Husad?"

"Then I'd try to find a way to kill him." She said it passionlessly. It was a decision she'd come to at dawn, after spending the night searching her soul. And it was because of the lack of passion, because of the simplicity, that Trace turned from the window to stare at her. "I would never allow him to use my knowledge or the skill I've worked all my life to attain against me. The Horizon project was never intended for a man like him. One of us would die before he got it."

Addison pulled off his glasses and began polishing them with a white handkerchief. "I admire your dedication, Doctor, and I appreciate your feelings. However, Agent O'Hurley will have his hands full over the next few days."

"She holds her own," Trace said from the window.

Addison pushed his glasses back on. "She's a civilian, and a target."

"She holds her own," Trace repeated as he and Gillian looked at each other. "I can use her. Cabot's been traveling with a woman. He always does."

"Then we'll assign another agent."

"Gillian's already established. She'll go with or without ISS sanction, so we might as well make the best of it."

It wasn't the fact that he was outnumbered. Addison had been outnumbered before. There was, however, the fact that any change of routine at this point could endanger the operation. Gillian Fitzpatrick wasn't one of his people, but if she insisted on risking her life, the ISS would use her.

"Very well. I can't stop you, but I can't approve. I hope you won't live to regret this decision, Doctor."

"I won't regret it."

"The notes. Since you refuse to come to Madrid with me, I must insist you give me your notes on Horizon so that I can secure them."

"Of course. I wrote them—"

"She wrote them in technical terms," Trace said, interrupting her. He aimed a long, cool glance at her that had her subsiding. "You probably won't be able to make much out of them."

"I'm sure our scientists will be able to interpret them. If you'll get them for me?"

"Of course."

"She's your responsibility," Addison said in an undertone when Gillian left the room. "I don't want any civilian casualties."

"I'll take care of her."

"See that you do." Addison rose and brushed back what was left of his hair. "At least without the notes she won't be able to make things worse than they are."

Gillian came back with her neatly folded papers. "This is all I have on the area I worked on."

"Thank you." Addison took them and slipped them into his briefcase. He turned the combination lock before straightening again. "If you change your mind, you have only to ask O'Hurley to contact us."

"I won't change my mind."

"Then goodbye, Doctor." He shook his head. "I hope that when this is over you and your brother can work on Horizon in peace." He gave a brief nod to Trace. "Report at six-hour intervals."

Gillian waited until the door had closed before she sat on the edge of the bed. "What an unfortunate man to work for. Do you deal with him often?"

"No, thank God." He went back to the coffee, but it was only lukewarm. "Not all ISS brass are like him."

"That's good news for the free world." She waited until he'd paced the room twice before speaking again. "I have some questions."

"Am I supposed to be surprised?"

"Could you sit?" In a gesture that might have been of annoyance or amusement, she waved toward a chair. "Over there. There's no danger of you touching me accidentally from that distance."

He paused long enough to give her a level look. "I don't touch accidentally."

"Well, that clears that up." She waited. Restless and edgy, he took the chair. "Why did you change your mind?"

"About what?"

"About taking me with you."

"Agreeing with Addison went against the grain."

Gillian folded her hand and spoke with the patience of a Sunday-school teacher. "I think I'm entitled to a genuine answer."

"That's genuine enough." He lit a cigarette. "And I meant what I said. I think you'll do okay."

"Your flattery leaves me speechless."

"Look, I figure you've got the biggest stake in this. Maybe you've got a right to stick around." He watched her through a haze of smoke. "That's all there is."

Or all she'd get, Gillian thought. She opted to accept it. For now. "All right. Now tell me why you didn't want me to tell Addison the notes had been doctored."

"Because the real ones are in your head. I figure that's where they belong."

"He's your superior. Don't you have an obligation to be straight with him?"

"First I go with the gut, then I go with regulations."

Gillian said nothing for a moment. She respected what he'd said, admired him because she knew he meant it. Hadn't that been the reason she'd chosen to trust him? "Once before you told me you thought you understood why Mr. Forrester didn't go directly to the ISS. I think it's time you tell me."

Trace tapped the ashes of his cigarette. The sun was dropping lower in the sky. Twilight was nearly on them. He remembered he'd been watching another sunset just before he'd seen her the first time. Perhaps he was doomed to think of her whenever night approached.

"Why don't you want Hammer to have the formula?"

"That's a ridiculous question. They're a group of terrorists headed by a madman. If they had the serum, nuclear war would be almost inevitable." She fell silent as he simply sat and looked at her. "Surely you're not comparing the ISS with one of the most radical organizations on the globe? The ISS is dedicated to ensuring international law and order, to saving lives, to protecting democracy." This time it was she who rose to pace. "I don't have to tell you what they represent. You're one of them."

"Yeah, I'm one of them. Weren't you the one who said it was an organization run by men, some good, some bad?"

"Yes." She couldn't have said why her nerves were beginning to fray. The room was dimmer, the light soft and pleasant. "And I still believe that if I had gone to them in the beginning, the project would have come first, my brother and my niece second. Meeting Captain Addison did nothing to change my mind. Still, the project was done under their auspices, and it was always intended to be handed over when completed. My father believed in the system."

Trace took one last long drag. "And you?"

"My family comes first. When they're safe, we'll go from there."

"Complete the project and hand it over to the ISS?"

"Yes, of course." A little paler, she turned back to him. "That was what my father was working toward. What are you saying, Trace?"

"Just that I figure the intent of the ISS is one thing and possible results another. Think about it, Gillian, a serum that protects you from the effects of nuclear fallout. A miracle, a shield, a scientific breakthrough, whatever you want to call it. Once it's proven, how much easier is it going to be for someone to decide to push the button?"

"No." She hugged her chest and turned away again. "Horizon is a defense, only a defense, one that could save millions of lives. My father— None of us who have worked on it ever intended for it to be used destructively."

"Do you figure the scientists involved in the Manhattan Project ever expected Hiroshima? Or maybe they did. They had to know they were busy creating a bomb in the name of a scientific breakthrough."

"We're creating a defense, not a weapon."

"Yeah, a defense. And some German physicists were just fooling around with experiments fifty years ago. I wonder if they'd have gone on with it if they'd known they were forming the basis of a weapon that has the power to wipe life off the planet."

"But the weapon's there, Trace. We can't go back and prevent its creation." She'd turned back to him now. The light coming through the window behind her had gone a pure rose. "Horizon's meant to balance that, to ensure that life will go on if that final button is pushed. Horizon is a promise of life, not a threat."

"Who decides who gets the serum, Gillian?"

She moistened dry lips. "I don't know what you mean."

"Do you plan to inoculate everyone? That's not practical, probably not even feasible. Maybe we should only shoot for the countries in the United Nations. Better yet, just the countries whose political beliefs mesh with ours. Do we use it on the very old or the terminally ill? It's bound to be expensive. Who pays for it, anyway? The taxpayers? Well, do the taxpayers want to foot the bill for the inoculation of criminals? Do we go in and give the mass murderers a shot in the arm, or do we get selective?"

"It doesn't have to be that way."

"Doesn't have to, but it usually is, isn't it? The world's not perfect, Doc. It ain't ever going to be."

She wanted to believe it could be, but she'd been fighting off those very same questions and doubts for a long time. "My father devoted most of his life to Horizon. My brother might lose his because of it. What is it you're asking me to do?"

"I'm not asking you to do anything—I'm just theorizing."

She came to him then, knowing he would distance himself, however hard she struggled to close the gap. "What disillusioned you, Trace? What made you stop believing that what you do can make a difference?"

"Because it doesn't. Oh, maybe for a while, maybe here and there, but in the long view, none of it really means a damn." He started to reach for another cigarette but pushed the pack aside instead. "I'm not ashamed of anything I've done, but that doesn't mean I'm proud, either. I'm just tired of it."

She sat across from him, no longer sure of her own thoughts, her own goals. "I'm a scientist, Trace, not a politician. As far as Horizon goes, my input has been minimal. My father didn't share a great many of his hopes with me. I do know that it was his belief, his dream, that his work would bring some lasting good. Perhaps the kind of peace we all claim to want but do so little to secure."

"You don't get peace from a serum, Doc."

"No, perhaps not. Some of the questions you've asked I've asked myself, but I haven't gone very far with them. Maybe I haven't done enough with my life to be disillusioned." She closed her eyes a moment, because nothing seemed clear, and especially not her life. "I don't know enough of what you do—or have done—to understand. I have to take it on faith. I believe, in the long view, you have made a difference. If you're tired, if you're dissatisfied, it may be because you're more of a dreamer than you'll admit. You can't change the world—none of us can—only little pieces of it."

She wanted to offer him a hand, but she held back, knowing that rejection now would prevent her from finishing. "These last few days with you have made a difference with me."

He wanted to believe. And wanting, he discovered, could hurt. "You're romanticizing again, Doc."

"No, I'm being as honest as I know how. As logical as the situation permits. You've made a difference in the way I think, the way I feel, the way I act." She pressed her lips together. Did he have any idea how difficult it was for her to strip herself bare this way? She cleared her throat, telling herself it didn't matter. She was going for broke. "I've never thrown myself at a man before."

"Is that what you're doing?" He picked up a cigarette but only ran it through his fingers. He wanted to be casual, even amused, but the ache was spreading.

"It would be obvious to anyone but you." She had to get up, to move. Why did it always seem she had to beg and bargain for affection? "I haven't asked you for a commitment." Though she wanted one. "I haven't asked for a pledge of love or fidelity." But she would give one to him if he asked. "I've only asked you to be honest enough to...to..."

"Sleep with you?" When the cigarette snapped in his fingers, Trace dropped the pieces in the ashtray. "I've already given you the reasons why that's not in the cards."

"You gave me a bunch of foolishness about our differences. I don't want you to be my twin." She had to take a quick, steadying breath. "I want you to be my lover."

Need and longing twined so tightly inside him that he had to make a conscious effort to stand and walk toward her. He would make it quick, he promised himself, he would make it cruel and save both of them. "A fast tussle in the sheets, no strings attached? Some nice uncomplicated sex without the pretty words?"

Color flooded her face, but she kept her eyes steady. "I expect no pretty words from you."

"That's good, because I don't have any." He curled his fingers into the V of her blouse and dragged her closer. She was trembling. Good. Her fear would make it that much easier. "You're out of your league, Doc. A one-night stroll through paradise isn't your style."

She started to back away but made herself stand firm. "What difference does it make? You said you wanted me."

"Sure, and maybe I'd get a kick out of showing you what life's all about. But you're the permanent kind, sweetheart. If I ever start thinking about a house in a nice neighborhood, I'll give you a call. Meanwhile, you're just not my type."

It was, as he'd intended, a solid slap in the face. She backed away, turned and started toward her room. She heard the sound of liquid hitting glass as she grasped the doorknob.

All her life, Gillian thought on a sudden wave of fury. All her life she'd taken that kind of casual criticism without a murmur. She'd grown up with it, come to expect it. But she was a grown woman. Her shoulders straightened. Her own woman, she added with a touch of malice as she turned back. It was time to stop freezing up or walking away and take the next risk.

Trace sipped warm whiskey and braced himself for what he thought would be a rousing argument. He'd have preferred it if she'd just gone into her room and slammed the door, but she was entitled to take a few shots. If she needed to, he'd let her aim and fire. He lifted the whiskey a second time. And choked on it.

"What the hell are you doing?"

Gillian calmly finished unbuttoning her blouse. "Proving you're wrong."

"Stop it." She let the blouse slide to the floor, then reached for the hook of her slacks. "Damn it, Gillian. Put your shirt on and get out of here."

She stepped out of her slacks. "Nervous?"

The teddy was virgin white, without lace, without frills. Her legs were creamier, with long thighs. Despite the whiskey, his mouth went dry as dust. "I'm not in the mood for one of your experiments." With damp hands he fumbled for a cigarette.

"Nervous, definitely." She tossed her hair back. One strap fell down her shoulder as she started toward him.

"You're making a mistake."

"That's more than a possibility." She stood in front of him so that the last light of day streamed over her hair and face. "But it'll be mine, won't it?"

If he'd ever seen anything more beautiful, he couldn't remember it. If he'd ever wanted anything more intensely, he'd long since forgotten it. But he was sure he'd never feared anything more than this small, lovely, half-naked woman with eyes like jade and hair like fire.

"I'm not going to touch you." He lifted his glass and drained the last drop. His hand trembled. It was all she needed to complete her confidence.

"All right. I'll touch you."

She had no guide to work with, no standard formula she had tested. Her experience with men wasn't nonexistent, but it had been limited by a strict upbringing and a demanding career. Somehow she understood that even if she'd known hundreds of men this time would have been different. Relying on instinct and need, she stepped closer.

Her hands were steadier than his as she ran them up over his chest. With her eyes on his, she enjoyed the firm, hard feel of muscle as she moved them over his shoulders. She had to rise on her toes to reach his mouth. Then her lips were soft and coaxing as they played across his. With her body pressed against his, she felt his heart thudding.

He held his body tense, as if he were expecting a blow. Once he caught himself reaching for her, but he dropped his hands again and curled them against the dresser at his back. He thought he knew her well enough to be sure a lack of response would humiliate her to the point where she would leave. To keep her safe from him. What he hadn't counted on was that she'd come to understand him, as well.

While her lips toyed with his, she unbuttoned his shirt so that her hands could move freely over the flesh beneath. Her own heart was drumming, her vision clouding, as she murmured her approval. If she had been an accomplished seductress, she could have done no better.

"I want you, Trace." Her lips trailed over his jaw to his throat. "I have since the beginning. I tried not to." On a shuddering breath, she wrapped her arms around his waist, then ran them up his back. "Make love with me."

He put his hands to her shoulders before she could kiss him again. He knew that if his mouth was on hers a second time there would be no reason, no chance. "This isn't a game you can win." His voice had thickened. The words seemed to burn his throat. "Back off, Gillian, before it's too late."

The room was dark. The moon had yet to rise. He could see only the glimmer of her eyes as she looked at him. "You said you believe in destiny. Don't you recognize me, Trace? I'm yours."

Perhaps it was that and that alone he feared most. She was as inescapable as fate, as elusive as dreams. And now, just now, she was wrapped around him like a promise.

"Then I'm yours. God help you."

He lowered his mouth to hers with all the fire, all the force, all the fury, that he'd held back. He'd wanted to save her, and himself. Now it was up to fate, and luck. Whatever promises he'd made he'd break. He would touch her, would have his fill of her. The night would take care of itself.

He let his hands roam over her. The thin material slid under his palms. More enticement. It rose high on the thigh, so he could move from texture to texture, arousing them both. Her skin was like cream, cool, white, rich. Fascinated, he slipped his fingers under the material and found the heat. At once she dug her fingers into his back. Bracing her against him, he drove her up until her knees buckled. When she was limp, he swept her into his arms.

"This is just the beginning," he told her as he laid her on the bed. "Tonight I'm going to do all the things to you I imagined the first time I saw you." Her hair spread out like a fan of flame on the plain white cover. The first sprinkling of moonlight filtered in, along with a breeze that smelled faintly of the sea. "I can take you places you've never been. Places you may wish tomorrow you hadn't gone."

She believed him. Excited, afraid, she reached up to him. "Show me."

She hadn't known anyone could kiss that way. Before he'd shown her passion, temper, restraint. Now the restraint had been lifted, to be replaced by a devastating skill. His tongue teased and tormented, his teeth aroused and provoked. She found herself responding with a totality she'd never experienced. Already more involved than she'd ever been before, she dragged him back again and again.

Then he began to touch.

He had the hands of a musician, and he knew how to play a woman. Fingertips stroked, pressed, lingered, until she was breathless beneath him. Her murmurs were soft, then urgent, then delirious. She reached for him, held him, demanded with a strength that seemed to have been born of the moment. She fumbled for the snap of his pants, ready to take him to her, ready to give back this pleasure that she thought could reach no higher. Then his fingers found a new secret. Her body tensed, shuddered, then went lax.

No, she'd never been to this place before. It was dark, and the air was thick and sweet. Her arms felt so heavy, her head so light. She felt the trace of his lips down her throat to where the material lay on her breast. He dipped his tongue beneath to run over the peak. She could only moan.

He caught the strap in his teeth and lowered it slowly while his hands continued to work their magic. This was how he'd wanted her, weak from pleasure, drugged with desire. He could taste where he chose. Such sweetness. Even as her skin grew hot and damp, there was such sweetness. He could have fed on it for days.

The moonlight grew brighter, the passion darker.

He drew the material down and down, following the path with his mouth. He could make her shudder. And did. He could make her moan. And did. He let her sigh with quiet delight, murmur with easy pleasure, then shot her back to desperation.

Catapulted up, Gillian reached for him. They rolled together, caught in a need that was so close to being fulfilled. Again she struggled to undress him, and this time he made no protest. She moved quickly. When they were naked, he moved more quickly.

When he plunged into her, she let out a strangled cry. Half mad, she grabbed his hair and dragged his mouth to hers. He took her hard and fast, but she found herself more than able to match her rhythm to his. More than that, it seemed to her that their hearts beat in the same rhythm. She felt him form her name against her mouth, heard the sudden shudder of his breath as emotion merged with passion. She saw as her eyes fluttered open the dark intensity of his.

Then he buried his face in her hair and they took each other.

Chapter Eight

It had been a mistake to stay with her. To sleep with her through the night. To wake beside her in the morning. Trace had known when they'd wrapped themselves around each other in the night that he'd pay. A man always paid for his mistakes.

The problem was, it felt so damn good.

In sleep she was as warm, as soft, as pliable, as she had been in passion. Her head was nestled on his shoulder as if it belonged there. Her hand, curled loosely in a fist, lay over his heart as if a claim had been staked. He wished, in those early-morning moments, that such things were true. Knowing better wasn't easy, it just was.

The odd and uneasy thing was that the desire hadn't dissipated. He still needed, still craved, just as sharply as he had the night before, when she'd put her hands on him for the first time.

He wanted to gather her close, to wake her slowly, erotically, and send them both spinning back to where they'd gone before sleep had claimed them. He wanted, somehow more intensely, to gather her close, to stroke her hair and absorb the quiet excitement of dozing with her through the morning.

He couldn't do either. Though Trace would never have considered himself noble, he was thinking of her. He was a man who did his job and did as he chose. He lived as hard as he worked and had no ties to anyone. In Gillian he recognized a woman to whom home and hearth and family came first. He had no doubt she was good at what she did, that she was devoted to her work, but there were white picket fences and flower gardens buried inside her. A man who'd never had a home, who'd chosen never to have one, could only complicate the life of a woman who made one wherever she went.

But she felt so good curled around him.

He drew away more abruptly than he'd intended. When she stirred and murmured something, he rose to pull on his loose drawstring pants. He didn't have to turn around to know she was awake and watching him.

"You can sleep a while longer," he told her. "I've got some things to do."

Gillian drew the sheet with her as she sat up. She'd been half awake, or thought she had been. Perhaps she'd dreamed that he'd been stroking her hair. "I'll go with you."

"Well-bred ladies don't belong where I'm going."

Strange how quickly a chill could come. She'd lain half dreaming, warm and secure. Now she was cold and alone again. Her fingers tensed on the sheet, but her voice came out calmly. "I thought we were going to work together."

"When it suits, sweetheart."

Her fingers began to work on the sheet. "When it suits whom?"

"Me." He reached for a cigarette before he turned back to her. It was just as he'd thought. She looked more beautiful now than she had any right to, with her skin pale, her hair vivid, her eyes dark and heavy. "You'd get in the way."

"Apparently I already am." She fought back humiliation as she tossed the sheets aside to gather up what she could find of her clothes. Holding them in front of her, she paused long enough to look at him. She would say what she had to say, she told herself. Too often in the past she'd taken an emotional slap with a bowed head. No more.

"I don't know what you're afraid of, O'Hurley, except yourself and your own feelings, but there's no need to behave this way."

"I'm just doing what comes naturally." He drew on the cigarette. It tasted as bitter as his thoughts. "Look, if you're going to order breakfast, get me some coffee. I'm going to take a shower before I go out."

"It's fine to regret what happened. That's your privilege." She wouldn't cry. That she promised herself. "But it isn't fine to be cruel about it. Were you thinking I'd expect a pledge of undying love? Did you have it in your mind that I'd be waiting for you to fall on your knees and tell me I'd changed your life? I'm not the fool you think I am."

"I've never thought you were a fool."

"That's good, because I'm not." It was satisfying, she'd discovered, very satisfying, to bite back. "I didn't expect those things from you. But I didn't expect that you'd treat me as if I were something you'd bought and paid for and had the right to discard in the morning. I didn't expect that, either, Trace. Maybe I should have."

She walked quickly into her room and, tossing the crumpled clothes aside, headed straight for her shower. She wouldn't weep for him. No, by the saints, there wouldn't be one tear wasted on him. Turning the spray up to near scalding, she stepped into the shower. All she needed was to be warm again, to wash the scent of him from her skin, to rinse the taste of him from her mouth. Then she would be fine again.

She wasn't a fool, she told herself. She was simply a woman who'd made an error in judgment and now had to deal with it. She was an adult, one who made her own decisions and accepted fully and freely the consequences of her own actions.

But she was a fool. As big and as stupid as they came. Gillian pressed the heels of her hands against her eyes as the water streamed over her. Damn him, and her. Who else but a fool fell in love with a man who would never give anything back?

When the curtain whipped back, her head snapped up. She turned and gave Trace a cool, disinterested stare. The hurt wasn't his problem, she told herself. And she'd see him in hell before she'd let it show. "I'm busy at the moment."

"Let's get something straight. Just because I didn't babble over you like an idiot this morning doesn't mean I think of you as someone I could have picked up off the street."

Gillian picked up the soap to rub it in slow circles over her shoulder. So he was angry. It was there, darkening his eyes and his voice. That, too, was satisfying. "It occurs to me that I'm better off not giving a damn what you think. Your pitiful excuses don't interest me, O'Hurley, and you're getting water all over the floor." She snatched the curtain back into place. It didn't even have time to settle before he tore it open again.

His eyes were furious, and his voice entirely too soft and steady. "Don't ever close a door in my face."

She wondered why she should feel like laughing at this point in her life. "It's not a door I'm closing, it's a curtain. A door would be more effective, but this will have to do." She pulled it closed again. Trace ripped it from the rod in one angry tug. As the little metal hooks jingled against the rod, Gillian tossed wet hair out of her eyes. "Well, now, that was a brilliant move. If you've finished taking out your foulness on an inanimate object, you can go."

He kicked the torn curtain aside. "What the hell do you want?"

"At the moment, to wash my hair in peace." Deliberately she stuck her head under the spray. Despite her determination, she let out a quick yelp when she was dragged back. He stood in the tub with her now, his cotton pants plastered to his legs. Water bounced off them both and onto the tile.

"I don't have time for this guilt trip. I've got a job to do, and we're going to clear the air so I can concentrate on doing it."

"Fine. The air's clear." She smacked the soap back in its holder. "You want absolution? You've got it."

"I've got nothing to feel guilty about." He stepped closer, and the spray hit his chest. "You threw yourself at me."

With one hand, Gillian dragged her hair back from her face. The steam rose, clouding the room. "Aye, that I did. You fought like a tiger, but I overpowered you." She shoved a hand into his chest. "Better clear out, O'Hurley, before I force myself on you again."

"You smart-mouthed little—" He'd started forward, then had the breath knocked out of him as her fist connected with his stomach. As the water beat down on both of them, they stared at each other in equal surprise. All at once Gillian let out a gurgle of laughter and covered her mouth with her hand.

"What the hell's so funny?"

"Nothing." She choked back another laugh. "Nothing at all, except you look like a bloody fool, and I feel like one." Still laughing, she turned her face into the spray. "Be on your way, O'Hurley, before I really get tough."

He touched a hand to his stomach for a moment, amazed that she'd gotten one in under his guard. He was slipping. Then, because the anger had disappeared, he laid a hand on her shoulder to turn her around again. "You pack a hell of a punch, Doc."

It might have been her imagination, or wishful thinking, but she thought he was speaking of more than her fist. "Thank you."

"You know you run the water too hot."

"I was in the mood for hot."

"Uh-huh." He touched her cheek, running his thumb over the light sprinkling of freckles. She wondered if he knew he was apologizing. "Why don't I wash your back?"

"No."

He slipped his arms around her. "Then you can wash mine."

"Trace." She brought her hands up in a small defensive gesture. "This isn't the answer."

"It's the only one I've got." He lowered his head to rub his lips over hers. "I want you. Isn't that what you wanted to hear?"

If only it were so simple. If only she cared less. She let the sigh come as she pressed her cheek to his. "Last night was special. I can accept that it didn't mean anything to you, but I can't afford to get in any deeper, because it did mean something to me."

He was silent for a moment, knowing they would both be better off without the words even as he understood that they had to be said. "It meant something to me, Gillian." He framed her face in his hands so that he could look at her as he took the risk. "It meant too damn much."

Her heart broke a little. "And that makes things hard for you."

"Hard for me, maybe impossible for you." He would have let his hands drop, but she caught them in hers. "I'm no good for you."

"No, you're not." She smiled as she pulled his arms around her. "Neither's chocolate cake, but I can never resist that, either."

He wasn't sure it was wise to take Gillian to the bidonville, but he'd nearly convinced himself it was necessary. She might be better off seeing how low he had to sink in his job, and what kind of people he often did business with. What had happened between them that morning hadn't changed his mind about the senselessness of their relationship, but it had made him realize that a bond had formed, like it or not. It was up to him to be certain she had a clear-eyed view of what she was getting into.

So he took her on a roundabout route until he'd lost both Kendesa's tail and the shadow Addison had assigned to him. The first he not only expected but accepted as part of the game. The second proved to him that the ISS, or perhaps Addison alone, had decided against giving him a free hand. That only meant he had to take it.

Once he was certain he'd ditched both teams, Trace took one last circle before heading toward the shacks and squalor of the bidonville.

Because he wanted to go on foot, he carried a pistol under his jacket, another strapped to his calf, and a silent and very effective switchblade. Though his visit this trip had been brief, he knew his way here, just as he knew his way through so many other slums and ghettos.

There were plenty of unemployed men loitering in the narrow streets and cramped alleyways. But the two of them were never approached. Trace didn't walk like a tourist who'd lost his way or a curiosity seeker who'd come to take snapshots of the other side of Casablanca.

It stank. Gillian said nothing as she walked beside Trace. She wondered if he sensed it as she did. The smell was more than sweat, animal and rot. Over that there was the scent of anger and hatred. She'd seen poverty in Ireland, she'd witnessed the homeless and destitute in New York, but she'd never seen such misery and squalor as this.

There was blood here, newly spilled. There was disease waiting patiently to take hold. And there was death, more easily understood than life. She saw men watching her with hard black eyes. Veiled women never lifted theirs.

Trace approached a shack. It couldn't be called anything else, though it had glass in the windows and an excuse for a yard. A scrawny dog bared its teeth but backed away when Trace continued forward. There was a vegetable garden scratched into the ground. Someone had weeded it, and the rows were straight.

Trace knocked on the door of the shack before taking a long, sweeping view of the street. They were still watched, that was expected, but what went on in the bidonville stayed in the bidonville. Kendesa wouldn't find out about his visit unless Trace arranged it himself.

The door was opened by a small woman in a dark dress and veil. Her eyes showed the quick light of fear as she looked at Trace.

"Good morning. I've come to speak to your husband." His Arabic was rusty but competent enough. Gillian watched the woman's eyes dart here and there before she bowed the door the rest of the way open.

"If you would be pleased to sit."

Whatever filth and dirt were outside, the inside of the shack was neat as a pin. The floors and walls were scrubbed and still smelled lightly of the harsh soap used. The furniture was sparse, but without a speck of dust. In the center of the room sat a small boy in a cloth diaper. He grinned up at Trace and Gillian and pounded on the floor with a wooden spoon.

"I will bring my husband." The woman scooped up the child and disappeared through the back door.

Gillian bent to pick up the wooden spoon. "Why is she afraid of you?"

"Because she's smarter than you are. Sit down, Doc, and look a little bored. This shouldn't take too long."

With the spoon still in her hand, Gillian sat on a spindly chair. "Why are we here? Why did we come to this place?"

"Because Bakir has something for me. I've come to collect it." Trace slipped a hand inside his jacket as the door opened. He let it relax again when he saw that the man was alone.

Bakir was a little weasel of a man with a thin build and a narrow face. His eyes were small and dark. When he smiled, his teeth gleamed white and sharp. He was dressed in a gray robe that might have started off as spotless as the room. Now it was grimy at the hem. Two fresh grease stains spoiled the sleeve. Gillian felt an instant and uncontrollable revulsion.

"Ah, old friend. You were not expected until tomorrow."

"Sometimes the unexpected is preferable."

Though they spoke in English—Trace wasn't feigning an accent—Gillian said nothing. She wished quite fiercely that she had remained behind. The shack didn't seem clean and harmless now that Bakir had come inside.

"You are in a hurry to complete our business?"

"Do you have the merchandise, Bakir? I have other matters to attend to today."

"Of course, of course, you're a busy man." He glanced at Gillian and, with a grin, said something in Arabic. Trace's eyes went hard as stone. His reply was only a murmur, but whatever he said was enough to make Bakir blanch and bow. Pushing a table aside, he lifted a portion of the floor to reveal a wide trench beneath.

"Your assistance, please."

Trace bent to the task. Between the two of them, they hauled up a long wooden crate. Moving in silence now, Bakir pulled a crowbar from the trench and pried off the lid. Gillian's fingers tensed when Trace pulled out the first rifle.

It was black and oiled. She knew by the ease with which he lifted and sighted that he'd used one before. He broke it open and, in the practical manner of a man who understood guns, examined it.

"Almost like new," Bakir offered.

Instead of acknowledging him, Trace put the rifle back and drew out another. He performed the same careful examination on it, then on the next and the next, as he pulled them out of the crate. Each time he lifted a new one, Gillian's heart jolted.

He looked so natural with a gun in his hands. The same hands that had held and stroked and aroused her only a short time before. He was the same man. And yet as she looked at him now she wondered how he could seem so different in this place, with a crate of weapons at his feet and one in his hand.

Satisfied that the guns and ammunition were in order, Trace nodded. "You'll have the merchandise shipped to Sefrou. This address." He passed Bakir a sheet of paper. "Shipment tomorrow."

He reached into his jacket for an envelope fat with ISS money. He wondered what Addison's reaction would be when he learned Trace had requisitioned it.

The envelope disappeared into the folds of Bakir's cloak, but his hand remained on it. "As you wish. It may interest you that certain powers have offered great rewards for information on Il Gatto."

"Make the shipment, Bakir, and remember what would be done to anyone found to have done business with Il Gatto."

Bakir only grinned. "My memory is excellent."

"I don't understand." Gillian stayed close to Trace's side as they started down the narrow street. "Where did you get that money?"

"From taxpayers." As he walked he let his gaze swing right and left. "This is an ISS-backed operation now."

"But you gave him money for those guns. I thought Captain Addison was arranging for the weapons."

"He is." He took her arm to steer her around a corner.

"Well, if Addison's arranging for the weapons you're to show Husad, why did you pay that man for more?"

"Backup. If things don't go Addison's way, I don't figure on trying to get your brother out with a pistol and a charming smile."

Gillian felt the knot of tension in her stomach tighten. "I see. Then they're for you."

"That's right, sweetheart. Keep walking," he said when she hesitated. "This isn't the neighborhood for window-shopping."

"Trace, what good are those weapons going to do you, one man, alone?"

"Isn't that what you hired me for?"

"Yes." She pressed her lips together as she kept pace with him. "Yes, but—"

"Having second thoughts?"

She was having more than second thoughts. But how could she explain to him that the past few days had changed everything? How could she tell him that he was now every bit as important to her as the man and the child she wanted so desperately to see safe? He would laugh at her concern—or, worse, be annoyed by it.

"I don't know what I think anymore," she murmured. "The longer this goes on, the less real it seems. When it first started, I thought I knew exactly what had to be done. Now I'm not sure of anything."

"Just let me do the thinking."

A man in a grimy white robe stumbled in front of them. He only had time to gesture toward Gillian and mutter something in a drunken slur before Trace had the switchblade out. Gillian saw the sun glint off steel as Trace issued a quiet warning. Still grinning, the man lifted both hands palms up and teetered out of the way again.

"Don't look back," Trace ordered as he pulled Gillian along with him.

"Did he want money?"

He'd stopped believing anyone could be that naive. She was good for him, he thought. Too damn good. "For starters," he said simply.

"This is an awful place."

"There are worse."

She looked at him then as the beat of her heart began to calm again. "You know how to walk here, how to talk here, but that doesn't make you like that man back in that shack.''

"We both make a living."

They skirted around the walls and went into the shopping district. "You know, I think you'd like me to believe you were like him. That would be more comfortable for you."

"Maybe. We'll get some coffee, hang around here long enough for the tails to pick us up again."

"Trace." Though it shamed her, she felt safe again away from the sights and smells of the slums. "Is it just me, or do you fight off anyone who gets too close?"

He didn't know how to answer her. Worse, he wasn't sure he could afford to dig too deeply for the real answer. "Seems to me we were pretty close last night."

She met his look levelly, her eyes clear and serene. "Yes, we were, and you still haven't dealt with it."

"I've got a lot on my mind, Doc." He pulled out a chair at a small café and sat down. After a moment's hesitation, Gillian joined him.

"So have I. More than I bargained for." She let him order coffee and hoped that before long she would be back in her room, where she could pull down the shades, close her eyes and block out the morning, if only for a little while. "I have another question."

"Sweetheart, I've never known you not to."

She put a hand on his before he could light a cigarette. "That man, Bakir, he didn't know you as Cabot."

"No, I used him in an operation a few years back."

"He's an agent?"

Trace laughed but waited until their coffee was served before speaking again. "No, Doc, he's a snake. But reptiles have their uses."

"He knows who you are. Why would he deliver the shipment instead of simply keeping the money you've given him and telling Husad who and where you are?"

"Because he knows that if Husad didn't manage to kill me I'd come back and slit his throat." Trace lifted his coffee. Out of the corner of his eye he noted that the first tail had picked them up again. "Bad business risk."

Gillian stared at her coffee. It was black and thick. She knew that if she drank it it would take the chill from her skin, but she didn't pick up the cup. "I was raised to respect life," she said quietly. "All life. So much of the work I've done has been to try to make life better, easier. I can't deny that science has had too much to do with destruction, but the goal has always been to preserve and advance. I've never in my life hurt anyone intentionally. It's not that I'm such a saint, but more, I think, that I've never had to make that choice."

She wrapped both hands around her cup but still didn't pick it up as she lifted her gaze to Trace's. "When Captain Addison asked me what I would do if Husad took me, I was telling the truth. I know in my heart that I could take a life. And it frightens me."

"You're not going to find yourself in the position where you have to put that to the test." He put a hand over hers briefly, because no matter how hard he tried he couldn't keep himself from offering comfort.

"I hope not, because I know not only what I would do, but that I could live with it afterward. I suppose what I'm trying to say is that we're not so different, you and I."

He looked away from her, because the need to believe she was right was too sharp. "Don't bet on it."

"I already have," she murmured, and drank her coffee.

Chapter Nine

Gillian told herself that the move to Sefrou was bringing her another step closer to Flynn. He was close now. She could look out at the unfamiliar streets and mountains and almost feel how close.

It was a rare thing now for her to allow herself more than a few moments alone. Alone she would think too clearly of what had happened, what could be happening, to her brother and niece. The fear that she was too late, or would ultimately be too late, was a dark secret she kept buried inside her heart.

She didn't spend her nights weeping. The emotional release of tears wouldn't help Flynn. There were the nightmares, the sometimes hideous, often violent dreams she pulled herself out of on almost a nightly basis. Thus far she had been able to bring herself out of the nightmares without causing a disturbance that woke Trace. At least she could be grateful for that. She didn't want him to know she was weak enough to be frightened into cold chills by dreams. He had to think of her as strong and capable. Otherwise he might change his mind about letting her play any part in freeing Flynn.

Strange how well she had come to know him. Gillian watched a small compact car wind through the streets below while the silence of her hotel room hung around her. It was at times like this, when she was alone, that she worked hardest to concentrate on the practical aspects of Flynn's release. When that didn't work, she concentrated instead on Trace. Who he was, what made him tick, what secrets he kept locked in his heart.

She had come to understand him, though he told her little with words. More than once she had imagined them meeting socially in New York, under normal, even pedestrian, circumstances. A dinner date, a show, a cocktail party. She knew they would have become lovers wherever they'd met, but she also knew that under other circumstances it would have happened slowly and with more caution.

Destiny. She had never really thought about her own before Trace. Now she believed, as he did, that some things were meant. *They* were meant. She wondered how long he would continue to fight his feelings, the feelings she sensed in him whenever he held her. Words of affection wouldn't come easily from a man who'd deliberately shut those doors in his life. She was certain the reason for that had to do with his family.

If there was one thing Gillian was accustomed to, it was reticent males. She could be patient until he opened up to her. And she was optimistic enough not to doubt that he would.

She was so in love. She leaned on the windowsill with a sigh. All her life she'd waited for this feeling, the one that made the heart pound and the brain giddy, the one that made everything seem more vivid. True, she'd never expected to experience love for the first time in the midst of the biggest crisis of her life. But, crisis or not, the feeling was there, big and bold and beautiful.

Gillian knew she would have to wait to share it. There'd come a time when she could speak of it freely, laugh and steep herself in the feelings between them. She hadn't waited all her life to fall in love only to be denied the pleasure of expressing it. But she could wait.

One day, when Flynn and Caitlin were safe, when the violence, the fear, the intrigue, were nothing more than a vague memory, she would have her time with Trace. A lifetime. She couldn't afford to doubt that. What had happened in the past few weeks had taught her that happiness had to be grabbed with both hands and treasured with a full heart.

Yes, she would bide her time, and accept her destiny.

But how she wished he'd come back. How she hated being left alone.

Gillian understood he had a role to play and a job to do. Neither Cabot's mistress nor Dr. Gillian Fitzpatrick had a place in the morning meeting between Flynn and his ISS contact in eastern Morocco. The ISS agent would see that André Cabot received his supply of arms, just as Bakir would see that Il Gatto received his.

She could only wait while the man she loved armed himself and stepped into the hornet's nest.

Because her nerves were building quickly, Gillian searched for something to do. She had already unpacked and rearranged her belongings three times. Trace's case was open, but his clothes were jumbled inside. He'd taken out only what he needed that morning. For lack of something better to do, Gillian began to shake out, refold and put away his clothes.

She found she could enjoy the small task, smoothing out a shirt, wondering where he'd bought it, how he looked wearing it. She could draw in his scent from his rumpled garments. His taste in clothes was certainly eclectic. There was everything from denim to silk, from bargain basement to Saville Row.

How many men did he carry around in this case? she wondered as she folded a T-shirt that was thin to the point of transparency at the shoulders. She wondered if he ever had to stop and think, to bring back to the front of his mind who he really was.

Then she found the flute, wrapped carefully in felt beneath a tailored shirt of satin piqué. It was polished but had the look of something old and well used. Experimentally Gillian lifted it to her lips and blew. The note came clear and sweet and had her smiling.

He came from a family that made its living making music. He hadn't left that behind, not completely, no matter how hard he pretended he had. She imagined he played when he was alone and lonely in some foreign place. Perhaps it reminded him of the home he claimed not to have, of the family he'd chosen not to see for years.

She placed her fingers over the holes, then lifted two at random, enjoying the sound that came when she blew into the mouthpiece. She'd always had an affection for music, though her father had considered the study of chemicals more important than the piano lessons she'd once hoped for. She wondered if someday Trace would teach her to play a real melody, something sentimental, from the country she'd left behind.

She set the flute on the bed, but didn't rewrap it. There were books in the case, as well, Yeats and Shaw and Wilde. Gillian picked one and leafed through familiar passages. A man who described himself in such harsh terms carried Yeats along with a weapon. She'd sensed that contradictory combination long before she'd seen evidence it existed; indeed, she'd fallen in love with the many sides of the enigma that was Trace O'Hurley.

Nerves forgotten, fears banked, she set the books on the table beside the bed. She was humming to herself as she put the last of the shirts away. When she started to close the case, she noticed a notebook tucked in one of the side pockets. Without thinking, she drew it out and set it on the edge of the dresser. She put the case in the closet beside hers, fussed to be sure the trousers were hung by the crease, then wandered back toward the window. As she passed the dresser, she knocked the notebook to the floor. The words and musical notes caught her eye as she bent to pick it up.

The sun rises, the sun sets, but I wait for the dream.
The nights are too long to be alone.
Days pass without sweetness in sunlight that streams.
The nights are too dark to be far from home.

Enchanted, she sat on the bed to read. Her hand went to the flute and rested there.

It had been a few years since Trace had worked with Breintz. They'd put together a tidy little job in Sri Lanka five or six years before, and then, in the way of people in their business, they'd lost touch. Outwardly Breintz had changed. His hair had thinned, his face had widened. There were folds of wrinkles under his eyes that gave him a lazy basset-hound look. He sported a sapphire stud in his ear and wore the robe of the desert people.

After an hour's discussion, Trace was reassured. However much Breintz's appearance had changed, inside he was still the same sharp-witted agent he'd worked with in the past.

"It was decided against using the usual routes for the shipment." Breintz's clipped English had a controlled musicality Trace had always found agreeable. "It would be too possible for another terrorist group to trace it, or even for an overenthusiastic customs official to cause problems. In this I have used my contacts. The shipment comes by private plane to an airstrip a few miles east of here. Those who need to be paid off have been."

Trace nodded. In the dim rear booth of the nearly empty restaurant he indulged in one of Breintz's Turkish cigarettes. Over the scent of rich smoke he could smell meat—some sort of sausage—grilling. "And once the shipment arrives, I move accordingly. The whole thing should be over in a week."

"If the gods permit."

"Still superstitious?"

Breintz's lips curved, more in patience than in humor. "We all hold on to what works." Breintz let out smoke in three puffs, watching the rings form and vanish. "I don't believe in advice, but in information. Understand?"

"Yes."

"Then I will pass on this information, though you are likely aware already. I am in my fourth year of association with terrorists in this small, beleaguered part of the world. Some are fanatically religious, some politically ambitious, some simply blinded by anger. Such things, when accompanied by a disregard for human life, are dangerous, and, as we have too often found, not easily controllable. There is a reason, old friend, why none of the more established revolutionary organizations recognize Hammer. Religion, politics and anger become unpalatable even to the radical when they are driven by madness. Husad is a madman—a clever and magnetic one, but a madman. If he discovers your deception, he will kill you in any of several unpleasant ways. If he does not discover your deception, he will still kill you."

Trace drew again on the Turkish cigarette. "You're right, I'm already aware. I'm going to get the scientist and the kid out. Then I'm going to kill Husad."

"Assassination attempts have failed before, to the disappointment of many."

"This one won't."

Breintz spread his hands. "I am at your service."

With a last nod, Trace rose. "I'll be in touch."

Trace knew he would be moving toward a conclusion in a matter of days. He was grateful for it. Since his first assignment with the ISS, he'd accepted the fact that any job he agreed to take could kill him. It hadn't been a matter of his not caring whether he lived or died. Trace had always had a definite preference for living. It had simply been a matter of his acknowledging the risks and making damn sure he was around to collect his pay. Over the past few days, staying alive had become even more important.

He hadn't changed his mind concerning himself and Gillian, but he'd had to accept the fact that he wanted more time with her. He wanted time to hear her laugh, as she'd done so rarely since they'd met. He wanted time to watch her relax, as she did only when she'd convinced herself she could let go for short snatches of time. He wanted, more than he cared to admit, to have her care for him with the same depth and devotion that she cared for her family.

It was stupid. It was certainly wrong for her. But that was what he wanted.

He would give her back her brother, and the child she sometimes murmured for in her sleep. He would do what he had come to Morocco to do, and then he would have one clear night with her. One night, all night, without the tensions, the fears, the doubts, that hovered around her now. She thought he didn't sense them, but he did. He wanted to give her peace.

She hadn't wanted his sympathy, so he didn't offer it. The passion he did give should have been easy, yet it was tinted with the sweetest, sharpest ache he'd ever known. The ache was longing, a longing to give more than was asked, to take more than was given. To make promises, and to accept them.

He couldn't do that, but he could have that one night with her when her family was safe and the threat was past. Then he could give her the gift of backing out of her life.

To have that one night, to walk away with more than he'd ever had before, all he had to do was stay alive.

Kendesa's tail dropped him in the lobby. Trace felt secure knowing Kendesa was taking precautions. He felt even better knowing that his meeting with Breintz would be reported. The other agent's cover was as tight as they came. Trace strolled down the corridor to his room, thinking how glad he would be to get out of the suffocating suit and tie.

When he opened the door he was stunned, then furious.

Gillian looked up at him, her eyes damp and her smile brilliant. "Trace, I'm so glad you're back. These songs are so lovely. I've read them all twice and still haven't decided if I have a favorite. You have to play them for me so I can—"

"What the hell are you doing digging around in my things?"

The tone caught her so off guard that she simply stared at him, the notebook open in her lap. When he crossed to her to snatch the notebook, she felt the full brunt of his fury. She didn't cringe away. She just sat very still.

"I don't suppose it occurred to you that even though I'm working for you, even though I'm sleeping with you, I'm still entitled to my privacy."

She went very pale, as she did whenever stress took over. "I'm sorry," she managed in a very careful voice. "You were gone so long, and I needed something to do, so I thought I'd put your things away for you. I came across the flute and the notebook as I was finishing up."

"And didn't stop to think that what was written in the notebook might be private?" He stood, holding the book in his hand, as thoroughly embarrassed as he'd ever been in his life. What he'd written had come straight from the heart and was nothing he'd ever intended to share with anyone.

"I beg your pardon." Her voice was stiff with formality now. She didn't bother to tell him how the notebook had fallen open, since he was so obviously interested only in the end result. "You're right, of course. I had no business messing about with your things."

He'd hoped for an argument. A good shouting match would have helped him turn the embarrassment into something more easily dealt with. Instead, her quiet apology only made him feel more embarrassed and a great deal like a moron. Opening a drawer, he tossed the book in, then slammed it shut again.

"Next time you're bored, read a book."

She rose as her own temper bristled. She'd gotten such pleasure, such innocent pleasure, out of the words the man was capable of writing. Now she was being punished for discovering this secret part of him. But it was his secret, she reminded herself before she could open her mouth in anger. It was his, and she'd intruded on it.

"I can only repeat that I'm sorry, I was completely in the wrong, and you have my word that the mistake won't be repeated."

No, she wasn't going to argue with him, Trace realized as he walked over to wrap the flute in felt. There was too much hurt in her eyes, hurt he'd put there by being so unreasonably hard about an innocent act. "Forget it." He set the flute in the drawer beside the book and shut them both away. "The meet with Breintz went according to plan. The guns are here. I figure Kendesa will make contact tomorrow, the next day at the latest."

"I see." She looked around for something to do, something to occupy her hands. She settled on clasping them together. "Then it should all be over soon."

"Soon enough." For reasons that escaped him, he wanted to apologize, to hold her and tell her he was sorry for being an idiotic ass. He stuck his hands in his pockets. "We can go down for lunch. There's not much to see in this place, but you could get out of the room awhile."

"Actually, I thought I'd lie down, now that you're back and I know everything's all right. I've really been more wound up than hungry." And though she'd thought never to feel that way again, she wanted desperately to be alone.

"All right. I'll bring you something back."

"Some fruit, maybe." They kept their distance, because neither had the nerve to take the first step. "I never seem to have much of an appetite when I'm traveling."

He remembered the first night, when she'd fallen asleep without dinner, how pale and drained she'd been when he'd carried her to bed. She was pale now, too. He wanted, very badly, to stroke the color back into her cheeks. "I won't be long."

"Take your time."

She waited until he was gone before she lay down on the bed. Curling into a ball always seemed to help somehow. It concentrated the hurt into one tight place where it was more easily dealt with. She wouldn't weep. She let her eyes close and tried hard to concentrate on nothing. She wouldn't let her emotions swing wild, the way they had when she'd been young and had thought to surprise her father.

She'd tidied up his office, polishing wood and shining glass. He'd been furious, too. She sighed and struggled to clear the memory from her mind. Furious that she'd infringed on his private space, touched his personal things. She might have broken something, misplaced something. It hadn't mattered that she'd done neither.

Sean Brady Fitzpatrick had been a hard man, and loving him had been one long exercise in frustration. Gillian sighed again. Apparently she was a very slow learner.

He hadn't eaten anything. Nor had he finished the whiskey he'd ordered. Trace had never known a woman who could make a man feel more of a fool when she was clearly in the wrong. Those songs had never been intended for anyone but himself. He wasn't ashamed of them, it was just that he'd indulged himself, or parts of himself, in the writing of them. They were his innermost thoughts, innermost feelings, dreams he admitted to having only on the rarest of occasions. He wasn't sure he could handle her knowing what was inside him, what he sometimes longed for on the longest of lonely nights. The songs could erase the differences and the distance between them, whether he wanted them to or not.

He shouldn't have hurt her. Only the stupid or the heartless hurt the defenseless. Discovering he could be both left an unpleasant taste in his mouth. He'd have liked to blame that on her, too, but he thought too clearly once anger had passed.

He laid the rose on the little basket of fruit and opened the door.

She was sleeping. He'd hoped she would be awake so that he could make his gesture of apology quick and painless. Growing up with women had taught him that they forgave easily, often smugly, as though men's cloddish behavior was to be expected. It wasn't a sweet pill to swallow, but at least it was a small one.

Trace set the basket on the dresser before moving toward her. She was curled up tight, as if to ward off another blow. That was one more brick on his back. Muttering a curse, he pulled the spread up over her. She'd left the shade up. He walked over to draw it down and dim the room. It made a quiet sound that had her stirring in sleep.

"Caitlin."

Though the little girl's name came in a murmur, Trace heard the fear in it. Not sure what to do, he sat on the edge of the bed and began to stroke her hair. "She'll be all right, Gillian. Just a few more days."

But his touch and his reassurance seemed to set off a new reaction. He felt her begin to tremble. Even as he stroked the hair from her temple, sweat pearled cold on her skin. Though he let no more than a second pass, he could see she was fighting to pull herself out of the dream. Her face went a deathly white as he took her by the shoulders and drew her up.

"Gillian, wake up." He gave her a squeeze that had her muffling a scream. "Come on, Doc, knock it off." Her eyes were wide and terrified when they flew open. Trace kept his grip firm until he saw comprehension come into them. "You okay?"

"Yes, yes, I'm fine." But she couldn't stop shaking. All the other times she'd been able to control the shaking. "I'm sorry."

"You don't have to apologize for having a nightmare."

"For making a fool out of myself, then." She drew away, just a little, but enough to make him realize what a twist rejection gave the heart.

"Want some water?"

"Yes. I'll get it."

"Sit down, damn it. I'll get it." He felt like a ham-handed jerk. Giving the tap a violent twist, he filled a glass to the rim with tepid water. Gillian sat on the bed, fighting back tears she was certain would put a cap on her humiliation and struggling to ignore a roiling stomach that came from holding back too long. "Take a couple of sips and relax."

But her hands were shaking, and she only managed to spill water on both of them. "I'm—"

"If you apologize again, I swear I'll belt you." He took the glass and set it aside and then, feeling an awkwardness he'd never experienced with women, slipped an arm around her. "Just relax. Why don't you tell me about it? It usually helps."

She wanted to lean her head against his shoulder. She wanted him to hold her, really hold her, murmuring something sweet and foolish, until the terror passed. She wanted a miracle, she told herself. As a scientist, she knew that the world was fresh out.

"It was just a dream, unpleasant, that's all. Like the rest of them."

"What rest of them?" He cupped her face in his hand so that he could turn it up to his. "Have you been having nightmares all along?"

"It's not surprising. The unconscious mind—"

He swore and tightened his grip. He remembered how she had trembled, how the sweat had beaded cold and clammy on her skin, how glazed with fear her eyes had been. "Why didn't you tell me?"

"I didn't see the point."

He let her go then, slowly, and rose to his feet. If she had aimed a blow directly at his solar plexus, she wouldn't have been any more accurate. He gave a brief, humorless laugh. "Well, I guess I had that one coming, didn't I?"

A new fear was growing, one that warned her that she might be suddenly, violently, physically sick. She was too afraid to try to stand, too restless to stay where she was. "You'd just have been annoyed, as you are now. And I'd just have been embarrassed, as I am now." She shifted so that she could press a hand against the churning of her stomach.

"Seems you've got me pegged," he murmured. He opened his mouth to say more but was surprised to see that she'd gone even paler. Moving instinctively, he turned her toward the edge of the bed and pushed her head between her knees. "Just breathe deep. It'll pass in a minute. Come on, love, nice deep breaths."

Even as the faintness faded, the tears burned in her eyes. "Just leave me alone, will you? Just go away and leave me alone."

There'd been a time, not so long before, when he would've been only too happy to oblige her. Now he simply ran a hand up and down her spine, murmuring to her, until he felt her breathing even out. "I think we've both taken the easy way for too long." Gathering her up, he lay down beside her and held her close. He recognized more surprise than resistance and decided he deserved that, as well. "I think you should know I don't expect Superwoman. I know what you're going through, and I know that even someone as strong as you needs an outlet. Let me help."

She tightened her arms around him. Though the tears fell quietly, the release was complete. "I need you." Her body absorbed the warmth of his as tension fled. "I've tried so hard not to be afraid, and to believe everything really is going to be all right. Then the dreams... They kill all of you. And I can't stop them."

"The next time you have a dream, remember, I'm right here. I'm not going to let it happen."

She could almost believe in miracles when he moved his fingers gently through her hair, his lips gentle at her temple. "I don't want to lose you, either." She tilted her face up to his, hoping she would at least see acceptance.

"I've come through tighter spots than this." He touched his mouth to her forehead, realizing how comforting it could be to give comfort. "Besides, my retirement fund's riding on this one."

Her lips curved a little. "The Canary Islands."

"Yeah." Oddly, he couldn't picture the palm trees and calm waters. "I'm not going to let you down, Gillian."

She touched a hand to his face. "When this is over, I wonder if it would be an intrusion if I visited you there for a few days."

"I might be up to some company. The right company." He nestled her head in the curve of his shoulder again. The glass on the table beside them vibrated against the wood. Water sloshed over the edge again. Beneath them, the bed shook.

"What—"

"Earth tremor." He tightened his grip. "Just a little one. Morocco's prone to earthquakes."

"Is that all?" When the vibration ceased, Gillian let out the breath she'd been holding. "I could give you some scientific data on earthquakes, crustal plates, faults." She let out a calmer breath when the world stayed steady. "But I can't say I've ever experienced one firsthand."

"It's quite a show."

"One I wouldn't mind missing."

"Gillian..."

"Yes?"

"I'm ah...about before...I guess I didn't have to come down so hard on you."

"I didn't think before I acted. That's always a mistake."

"Not always. Anyway, I overreacted about something that wasn't that big a deal."

"Your songs are a very big deal." She liked the way he brushed his hand under her hair to her neck. He'd held her so close when the earth had shaken. There was a need in him to protect. She wondered how long it would take before he recognized it. "I know you didn't like me looking at them, but I can't be sorry I did. They were so beautiful."

"They're only... Really?"

Because the question touched her, she shifted again so that she could look down at him. How nice it was, how sweet, to discover that he, too, knew self-doubt and the need for reassurance. "Now and again, and very briefly, I've seen true sensitivity in you. A real gift for seeing things, feeling things. I like that man very much. After reading those songs, I felt closer to him."

He moved his shoulders uncomfortably. "You're making me into something I'm not again."

"No. I'm just accepting that there's more than one side of you." She kissed him softly, reaching out as much to the man he was as to the man he'd had to be.

She moved him too much, too deeply. Trace drew her away again, though he knew they'd passed the last border. "I'm going to disappoint you."

"How, when I'm willing to take you as you are?"

"I guess there's no use reminding you you're making a mistake?"

"None," she answered, just as her lips met his.

He'd never kissed her like this, softly, quietly, as if he had a lifetime to indulge himself. The passion and skill that always excited and overwhelmed her was banked. Instead, he gave her the affection she'd always fantasized about but had never expected to receive. She wondered if he realized how beautiful that gift was or how desperately she needed it now. Her sigh, as much from gratitude as pleasure, stole into the room.

He undressed her slowly, experimenting with the feelings that he'd finally let have their freedom. Strong, solid, inescapable feelings that filled him with power and serenity.

He could love and be loved, he could give and receive love, taste it, savor it, hoard it. For one day he could believe that a woman like her was meant for him, to keep, to cherish, to last.

By necessity the future had always been kept very close to the present. He could never allow himself to think in months, much less years. So even now, with her warm and willing in his arms, he refused to acknowledge the tomorrows. Today was timeless and theirs, and he would remember it.

His hands were the hands of an artist now. Skillful, yes, but sensitive. She hadn't known a man could love a woman with such restraint and still stir unbearably. His body was familiar now, so that when she undressed him she knew how to touch, where to stroke, when to linger. It was an adventure in itself to discover she could arouse him, make his body tense, his muscles bunch. It was thrilling to learn that even when aroused he could take care.

He held her differently, and though the difference was subtle, she reveled in it. Desire took on such fascinating, such miraculous angles when touched with emotion. Her name came almost musically through his lips as they glided over her. His murmurs were like quiet promises as she caressed.

He loved her. She wanted to laugh and shout it out with triumph, but she knew the words had to come from him, in his time, in his way.

Such patience. She hadn't known he had such patience in him for a woman. For her. Given it, she felt herself blossom in his hands. All that she had, all that she felt, all that she'd hoped to feel, was his for the asking.

Such generosity. He hadn't known anyone could possess such a bounty of it. He hadn't expected anyone to offer it to him with such freedom. Whatever he could give, whatever was coming to life inside him, was for her. And only her.

When they offered, and accepted, they both understood that some miracles were possible.

The light crept around the edges of the shades but did little to chase away the shadows in the room. He'd never felt so at ease with anyone. They'd slept awhile—only minutes, really—but he'd found himself refreshed and renewed. Trace rolled over on his stomach, one arm wrapped around her, and thought that the best thing to do with his energy was to make love with her again.

"Remember that shower we took the other day, when you were in a snit?"

Lazily she shifted so that she lay half over him, her cheek on his back. "I don't recall being in a snit. I do remember being justifiably annoyed."

"Whatever, the result was the same." He closed his eyes on a sigh as she began to knead the muscles at the base of his neck. "I was just thinking how nice you felt, all hot and wet, particularly when you were mad enough to spit in my eye."

"Oh? Do you have plans to make me mad again?"

"Whatever it takes. A little lower, Doc. Yeah." He sighed as her fingers moved down his spine. "That's the spot."

"I could be persuaded to take a shower." She pressed her lips to his shoulder blade, then moved them down to follow the path of her hands.

"I don't think it would take much persuasion."

"Really." She looked up at the back of his head. "Are you saying I'm easy, O'Hurley?"

"No." He grinned to himself. "I'm saying I'm good." He winced only a little when she pinched him.

"Such arrogance usually precedes a fall. Perhaps I should—" She broke off when she made a new discovery. "Trace, why do you have a beetle tattooed on your bottom?"

He opened one eye. "A scorpion."

"I beg your pardon?"

"It's a scorpion."

Willing to give him the benefit of the doubt, Gillian leaned closer. "I realize the light's a bit dim, but... No, this is definitely a beetle. A squashed beetle, at that." She gave it a quick, friendly kiss. "Trust me, I'm a scientist."

"It's a scorpion. Symbolic of a quick sting."

She pressed a hand to her mouth to muffle a chuckle. "I see. How appropriate. However, since my view is undoubtedly better than yours could be, let me assure you that your very attractive posterior is adorned with a squashed beetle.''

"It's just a little out of focus," he told her, refusing to take offense, because her hands felt so good. "The tattoo artist was drunk."

Gillian sat up, resting one hand on his hip. "Are you saying you were mad enough to trust this very sensitive area of your body to a drunk tattoo artist?"

Trace rolled over. In a move that reminded her how quick he could be, he had her beneath him. "I was drunk, too. Do you think I'd let anyone come near me with a needle if I was sober?"

"You're mad."

"Yeah. And I was twenty-two." He began to indulge in the taste of her skin. "Nursing a broken heart and a dislocated shoulder."

"Did you have your heart broken, then?" Curious, she lifted his face to hers. "Was she pretty?"

"Gorgeous," he said instantly, though he couldn't really remember. "With a body that was almost as good as her imagination." He kept his face bland as her eyes narrowed.

"Is that the truth?"

"If it's not, it should be. Anyway, I did have a dislocated shoulder."

"Aw." Gillian ran her hand up to it. "Would you like another?"

"Threats?" Delighted, Trace grinned down at her. "You know, Doc, you sound suspiciously like a jealous woman."

Now the heat came into her eyes. "I don't know what you're talking about. I'd hardly waste any healthy jealousy I might have on the likes of you."

"Are you getting justifiably annoyed?"

"And why shouldn't I, when I'm lying naked in bed with a man who's cloddish enough to tell me about another woman?"

"Good." Trace rolled off the bed. Then, ignoring her struggles, he tossed Gillian over his shoulder.

"Just what do you think you're doing?"

"Now that I've got you in a snit, I thought we'd take that shower."

Gillian caught the beetle between her thumb and fore-finger and twisted hard. "Bastard."

"I love it when you talk dirty."

He carried her laughing into the bath.

Chapter Ten

When the arrangements had been made for Trace to meet Husad's men and be driven into the mountains, Gillian was torn in two directions. She wanted Trace to get to Flynn, to see him, to come back and tell her that her brother and her little niece were well and that he'd found a safe and simple way to free them.

It was because she knew there was no safe and simple way that she wanted to tell him not to go, not to risk being killed or captured. She was well aware that if she hadn't interfered in his life Trace would have spent these past weeks basking in the Mexican sun. Whatever happened to him now was her responsibility. When she'd tried to explain her feelings to him, he'd brushed her off.

"No one's ever been responsible for me, sweetheart. It would be stupid for you to start now."

So she kept silent about her fears, knowing they were of little use to her, and of no use whatever to Trace.

When they made love, it was with a quiet madness, a restrained desperation that spoke of what neither of them had said aloud. This might be the last time. She wanted to beg him for promises, but she settled for moonlight and rough caresses. He wanted to make her a pledge, but he settled for her warmth and generosity. She could have no idea what risks were involved when he walked into the lion's den armed only with a lie. Though he knew a lie could be as lethal a weapon as any, he would have preferred the cold company of his .45.

As Cabot, he would get nowhere near Husad with a gun or a blade. As Il Gatto... But Il Gatto would have to wait. He would go to Husad's mountain headquarters, and he would come back with Flynn and Caitlin Fitzpatrick. Or he would not come back.

Shifting, he listened to Gillian's quiet breathing beside him. No nightmares, he thought, grateful. In a day, perhaps two, it would be done. Then she could go back to her life in New York, her institute, her experiments. There would be no need for nightmares once her world had been put in order again.

He stroked her hair, but lightly, wanting to touch but not to awaken. He'd never asked her about her work. To ask would have brought himself another step closer. But he tried to imagine her now, laboring over some impossibly complicated calculations, a white coat covering some neat business suit, her hair tied back or pinned up, her eyes intense with concentration.

She really believed she could change the world with knowledge and logic and science. He let the tangled silk of her hair drift between his fingers. Maybe it was good that she did, that she refused to face the hard reality that nothing ever really changed. The grimness of that fact would steal something from her, as it had from him. He wanted to remember her as she was, strong, naive, full of hope.

He didn't know how to tell her what she'd meant to him, what, if he'd been different, they might have meant to each other. So he drew his hand away and left her sleeping.

But she was awake. She'd known he was restless and lost in his own thoughts, so she'd lain quietly. There was something so tender and sweet about the way he touched her when he thought she was unaware. That was something she could hold on to the next day, when he walked out the door.

If he couldn't sleep, she thought, perhaps if she reached out and offered to hold him he would rest. But when she heard him pick up the phone, she kept her silence.

He spoke in French, which left her in the dark, then lapsed into silence. She heard him strike a match as he waited.

"This is O'Hurley, number 8372B. Patch this call through Paris to New York, code three, phase twelve."

He needed to make the call, though he knew it was against regulations when he was on assignment. Going through the Paris operation would secure it. He knew the phone wasn't bugged or tapped, and if Kendesa was tracing his calls he would know only that Cabot had called Paris. From there, the call would be scrambled.

Now he could only hope she was home.

"Hello."

"Maddy." The sound of her voice had him smiling into the shadows. "No show tonight?"

"Trace? Trace!" Her quick, infectious laugh bubbled over oceans and miles. "How are you? Where are you? I was wondering if I'd get my semiannual call. I'm so glad I did. There's so much to tell you. Are you in New York?"

"No, I'm not in the States. I'm fine. How's the toast of Broadway?"

"Terrific. I don't know what the Great White Way is going to do without me when I take a year off."

"A year? You and Valentine going traveling?"

"No... I don't know, maybe. Trace, I'm going to have a baby." Her excitement was all but sizzling the wires. "In six and a half months. In fact, they're going to be doing some tests, because it looks like I'm having more than one."

A baby. He thought of the skinny, long-legged redhead, who had always seemed to have more energy than any one person was entitled to. She'd still been a teenager when he'd seen her last. And now...a baby. He thought of Abby and her sons, the nephews he'd never seen.

"You okay?" And he wished, more intensely than he'd wished before, that he could link hands with her and see for himself.

"Never better. Oh, Trace, I wish you could make it home, even for a little while, and meet Reed. He's so terrific, so upstanding and stable. I don't know how he tolerates me. And Abby, she's going to have the baby in just a few months. You should see her. I can't believe how beautiful, how content she is, since she married Dylan. The boys are growing like weeds. Did you get the pictures she sent you?"

"Yeah." He'd gotten them, pored over the faces of his sister's sons, then destroyed them. If something happened to him, he couldn't leave behind anything that could be traced to his family. "Nice-looking boys. The little one looks like a heartbreaker."

"That's because he looks like you."

She couldn't know how the statement shook him. Trace closed his eyes a moment and brought the face in the photo back into his mind. Maddy was right, of course. Family ties might be thin, almost invisible, but they were strong.

"You hear from Chantel?"

"That's the big news." Maddy paused automatically for dramatic impact. "Big sister's getting married."

"What?" He wasn't often thrown completely off balance, but Trace nearly choked on the smoke he'd dragged into his lungs. There had been rumors, of course. There were always rumors. But he hadn't believed them. "You want to say that again?"

"I said Chantel, femme fatale, star of stage and screen, has met her match. She's getting married in just a couple weeks. We wanted to let you know, but we didn't know how to get in touch."

"Yeah. I've been—" he glanced over to where Gillian lay quiet in the bed "—tied up."

"In any case, she's really taking the plunge. It should be the glitziest wedding this side of the Windsors."

"So Chantel's getting married. I'd like to meet the guy," he said, half under his breath.

"He's perfect for her. Rough and tough and just cynical enough to keep Chantel on her toes. Trace, she's absolutely crazy about him. Seems there was a writer who'd developed an obsession about her, a dangerous one. Anyway, to keep the story short, she'd hired Quinn as a sort of bodyguard, and when the air cleared, she was making wedding plans."

"Is she all right?"

"She's fine, better than fine."

He wanted to dig deeper. He could use his contacts and sources to learn the details Maddy was leaving out. It would have to wait until he came out of the mountains—if he came out of the mountains.

"Trace, you know how much it would mean if you could come back for the wedding. It's been a long time."

"I know. You know I'd like to see you again, kid, all of you, but I'm just not suited to playing prodigal son."

"It doesn't have to be like that." She knew better than to press, but something told her she might not get another chance. "Things have changed. We've all changed. Mom misses you. She still has that little music box you sent her from Austria, and Pop..." Here she hesitated, because the ground was shakier. "Pop would give anything to see you again. He won't admit it—you know he can't—but I can see it every time your name's mentioned. Trace, every time we manage to get together, there's this hole. You could fill it."

"Mom and Pop still touring?" He asked, already knowing the answer, only to redirect the conversation.

"Yes." Maddy bit off a sigh. The son was as stubborn as the father. "They've got a gig coming up on public television. Folk dancing, traditional music. Pop's in heaven."

"I bet. Is he . . . is he okay?"

"I swear, he gets younger every year. If I had to make a bet I'd say music is the fountain of youth. He can still dance a teenager into the ground. Come see for yourself."

"We'll see how things go. Listen, tell Chantel and Abby I called. And Mom."

"I will." Maddy tightened her grip on the phone, knowing she was losing him. "Can you tell me where you'll be?"

"I'll let you know."

"Trace, I love you. We all love you."

"I know." He wanted to say more, but he knew there was nothing left. "Maddy?"

"Yes?"

"Break a leg."

He hung up the phone but didn't go back to bed for a very long time.

In the morning, Gillian watched Trace dress in Cabot's conservative European suit. She waited, nerves stretching, in silence while he deliberated over the proper tie.

What difference does it make? She wanted to shout it at him, rage it at him, while she tossed the hated, well-laundered clothes around the room. She watched him slip Cabot's little derringer into his pocket. It wouldn't do any good, she thought. He took it only because Cabot would take it. The pistol might as well have been filled with water for all the protection it would afford him.

He turned, and the man who had loved her so fiercely the night before had become André Cabot. He was sleek, well groomed and cold-eyed. She'd wanted to put off this moment, to push it back until it couldn't be pushed any longer. Now it was here, and she had to face it.

"If there is another way..." she began.

"There isn't." He answered with the same finality she'd heard when he'd spoken to his sister the night before. But then Gillian had been sure she'd heard a trace of regret. Perhaps he'd been too tired to stamp it out. But this morning he was in complete control.

"I have to ask. Is there some way you can take me with you?"

"You know there isn't."

She pressed her lips together, hating being helpless on the ground while everyone she loved walked a tightrope. "Is there some way I can contact this other agent, if things...if there's anything he should know?"

"You won't have to contact him."

She'd known that, too, and that she was dragging something out that should be done quickly. "So all I can do is wait."

"That's right." He hesitated a moment. "Gillian, I know that waiting is the hardest part."

"At least I'm allowed to pray, as well."

"It wouldn't hurt." He wished he didn't need to, but he reached out to take both of her hands. Things had changed, he realized, too much and too fast. For the first time in a dozen years, leaving was painful. "I'm going to get them out."

"And yourself." Her fingers tightened on his. "Will you promise me that, too?"

"Sure." He knew that often lies were needed. "Tell you what, once this is over, we'll take a little vacation. A couple weeks, a month, pick the spot."

"Anywhere?"

"Sure." He bent to kiss her but only brushed his lips over her forehead. He was afraid that if he held her, if he really kissed her, he wouldn't be able to turn away. But he did give himself a moment, one long moment, to memorize her face—the milky skin dashed with freckles, the dark green eyes, the mouth that could be so sweet, so passionate. "Give it some thought while I'm gone." He let her go then and picked up his briefcase. "You've got two ISS guards, Doc, but don't do any sightseeing. I shouldn't be gone more than a day or two."

"I'll be waiting."

As he walked toward the door, she struggled to keep a promise to herself. She'd sworn she wouldn't say it. But he was leaving. In a moment he'd be gone and—"Trace."

He stopped, impatience just beginning to show as he turned.

"I love you."

She saw his expression change, his eyes darken, deepen. It seemed, for a heartbeat it seemed, that he would come to her. Then his face went carefully blank. He opened the door, and left without another word.

She could have thrown herself on the bed and wept. She could have thrown all the breakables in the room and raged. It was a huge temptation to do both. Instead, Gillian stood where she was and waited for calm.

The fact that he hadn't answered her was no more than she had expected. But he was gone now, and the wheels that had been put into motion couldn't be stopped. She could pray, and would, but for now there was something else she could do. Whenever it seemed there would be no tomorrow, it was best to make plans for the next day.

She went to the phone and asked for the number Trace had called the night before. Gillian dialed it and, calling on her photographic memory, gave the person who answered the same sequence Trace had recited. Her heart beating a bit unsteadily, she waited for someone to pick up. She winced when a sleepy and irritated masculine voice did.

"Hello, I'd like to speak with Madeline O'Hurley."

There was an oath, and a feminine murmur in the distance. "Do you know what time it is?"

"No." Gillian rolled her eyes and nearly laughed. Trace was on his way to Husad, and she didn't have the least idea what time it was in New York. "I'm sorry, I'm out of the country."

"It's 4:15 a.m.," Reed said helpfully. "And my wife is trying to sleep. So am I."

"I'm really terribly sorry. I'm a friend of her brother's. I don't know if I can make the call again." And Trace would surely murder her if he found out she'd made it at all. "If I could just speak with her for a moment."

There was static, and more muttering. Then the connection became so clear that Gillian could hear the bedsprings squeak. "Hello? Is Trace all right? Has something happened?"

"No." Gillian cursed herself for not waiting. "No, Trace is fine." She hoped. "I'm Gillian Fitzpatrick. A friend."

"Is Trace in Ireland?"

"No." She nearly smiled. "Ms. O'Hurley, well, I suppose it's best to be frank. I'm in love with your brother, and I think it would do him a lot of good to come home. I thought you might help me arrange it."

Maddy gave a shout of laughter, threw one arm around her very cranky husband and decided Gillian Fitzpatrick had been sent from heaven. "Tell me what I can do."

Trace sat silently in the car as it traveled east. He had directed the driver to the warehouse where Breintz had arranged for the ISS weapons to be stored. Retrieving them had been as simple as signing a form and passing a few bills. Now they were deep in the mountains. The ride was far from smooth. In the way that Cabot had, he muttered a few complaints but exchanged no conversation. There were no questions asked, no answers given. Trace sat back and, behind tinted glasses, marked the route as carefully as if he'd drawn a map.

He'd be back.

He knew the villagers in the scattered settlements they passed would keep to themselves. They had their own way of life, and their own way of dealing with what came. A man like him, passing through their land, was only so much wind. To be noticed, tolerated, then forgotten.

Trace glanced at his watch with a slight sniff of impatience. The homing device inside it would be transmitting his location to Breintz. If his luck—and ISS technology—

held, Husad's security wouldn't detect it. If they did...he'd take that as it came.

There were times when it didn't pay to think too far ahead. It clouded the present, and it was always the instant that had to be coped with. That was why he tried not to think of Gillian, how she'd looked, what she'd said. If she meant it.

She loved him. Trace felt the emotion move through him, warm and strong and not a little frightening. She'd meant it. He'd seen it in her eyes then, and before, though he'd tried to tell himself that it was the intensity of the moment that had made her feel it, had made him want it.

When she'd said it he'd wanted to go to her, to hold her hard and tight and endlessly. He'd wanted to make promises he couldn't be sure he could keep. And, though he wasn't sure she would understand, it was because he loved her that he hadn't.

He'd never loved a woman before, so he hadn't known what a tug-of-war it could be between the selfish and the unselfish. Part of him wanted to take what she so recklessly offered. Another part of him felt it would be wrong, even sinful, for a man like him to take such pure emotion from her when he'd long since forgotten how to give it back.

Because he knew no other way at the moment, Trace decided to treat it as an assignment. He would give her what she had come to him for. Once she had her family back, he would . . . he would play it as it came.

Trace got his first sight of Husad's headquarters as the car drove over a rise. It was large, even larger than he'd expected, and built into the side of a cliff with rock carved from the mountains. Another ten miles in any direction and it would have been easily detected by air or land surveillance. But here it was isolated, almost merging into the wild desolation of the countryside. There was no land fit to farm here, no river to settle beside, no town to spread out from.

This was country for outlaws and renegades—and the hopeless.

Security seemed light, but Trace's eyes were sharp enough to spot the armed men stationed on the ridges. It was windowless and unfenced. Wise, because the reflection of glass or high-voltage wire could have been spotted from miles away. The driver signaled by punching out a code on a small box fixed to the dash. After a few seconds' delay, a wide door opened into the rock. The car drove into the mountain.

He was inside. Trace adjusted his cuff. His finger slid over and pressed on the stem of his watch to turn off the homing device. Either Breintz had his location now or he was on his own.

As he stepped out of the car, Trace took a long look around. The floor and the walls were rock. The tunnel seemed to go on endlessly and was dimly lit and cool. The door behind them had already closed, shutting out the sun and the heat. From somewhere came a low mechanical whine, telling him the air was circulated and processed. He heard, too, the sound of a door and footsteps. It was Kendesa who came to greet him.

"Again you are prompt. I trust your journey was not too unpleasant."

Trace inclined his head. "Business often causes some physical discomfort. The roads in your country are not yet as civilized as those in Europe."

"My pardon. Perhaps you would join me for a drink. I have an excellent chardonnay that should ease the memory of the journey."

"My samples?"

"Of course." Kendesa signaled. Two men seemed to come straight out of the rock wall. "They will be taken directly to the general, if you have no objection." His brow lifted at Trace's hesitation. "Surely you would not demand a receipt. We have no need to steal trifles from guests."

They both knew that the "trifles" included a TS-35. Still, his orders were to proceed with straightforward negotiations. "I would enjoy the chardonnay before meeting with the general."

"Excellent." Kendesa gave another signal, and the crate in the car's trunk was off-loaded. He gestured Trace forward. "I'm afraid a man of your taste will find our establishment crude. You will understand, of course, that we are a military operation and look not for comfort but revolution."

"I understand, though for myself I prefer comfort."

He led Trace into a small room whose walls had been paneled in light wood. The floor was carpeted, and, although the furniture was sparse, what was there was tasteful.

"We entertain rarely." Kendesa smiled as he drew the cork from the bottle. "When the general becomes more widely accepted, this will change." He poured wine into two Waterford glasses. "I confess that I have an affection for beautiful things, and the comfort and pleasure they bring."

"To profit, then," Trace said as he lifted his glass. "Because money gives the most comfort."

"I find you an interesting man, Cabot." Kendesa sipped his wine. Over the past few days he had employed the best equipment at his disposal in his search through Cabot's background. What he had found had pleased him a great deal. Such a man, and his connections, would be very useful during a period of transition.

"You've reached a level in power and wealth most men only wish for, yet you crave still more."

"I shall have still more," Trace countered.

"I believe so. You will understand that before doing business I used my resources to look into your current situation, as well as your background."

Trace merely sipped again. "Standard procedure."

"Indeed. What fascinates me, Cabot, is that you've reached this level of power while remaining almost unknown."

"I prefer subtlety to celebrity."

"Wise. There are some, even in our own organization, who criticize the general for maintaining such a high profile. Power amassed quietly is something more useful."

"The general is political. I am not." Trace continued to drink, wondering what Kendesa was fishing for.

"All of us are political, even if the politics is money. You expressed interest in Horizon."

"I did. And do."

"I have considered discussing this further with you. You are interested in the profit from Horizon. I am interested in the power."

"And the general?"

Kendesa lifted his glass again. He was nearly ready to play his cards. "Is interested in the revolution."

Unless Kendesa was playing a part, Trace sensed a slight disenchantment, and more than a little ambition. "Perhaps, with a kind of partnership, we could gain all three."

Kendesa studied Trace for a long, silent moment. "Perhaps."

The knock on the door echoed dully. "Come."

"The general is ready."

With a nod, Kendesa set down his glass. "I will take you to him myself. The general speaks no French, I'm afraid, but is quite proud of his adeptness with English. You will oblige him?''

''Certainly.'' Trace set his glass beside Kendesa's and prepared for the next step.

Gillian felt she'd waited for days, though it was only a matter of hours. She tried, unsuccessfully, to pass the time with Trace's books. Every time she started to read, she thought of him, and worried.

So she paced. And when she tired of that she sat and reminded herself of her conversation with Maddy. She would take Trace back to the States. In doing so, she would be able to give him what he'd promised her only a short time ago—a family.

For as long as she was able to hold off worry, Gillian concentrated on that. In a few days, a week at most, both she and Trace would have their families back.

And where would they go from there?

The Canary Islands? she thought, and nearly laughed out loud. She wondered what Trace would say when she told him that if he insisted on hiding from the world for the next fifty years or so she would be hiding right alongside him.

She wasn't going to lose him now, not to Husad, not to the ISS or his own stubbornness. If he wanted life in a hammock, it would be a hammock for two.

Gillian had learned a lot about herself in the past few weeks. She could do what needed to be done. She could face what needed to be faced. More, she could change what needed to be changed to find the happiness that had always remained just out of her reach.

When the fear began to edge back, she wondered what she would do if Trace didn't walk through the door again. Her life wouldn't be over. She knew you could lose what you loved and go on, but you could never go on in quite the same way. She knew there was no way to prepare herself for losing Trace. He'd opened doors in her, he'd caused the blossoming of love in her that had pushed her to open doors in him. She wouldn't lose him. Gillian promised herself that.

And went back to watching the clock.

She ordered room service only because she wanted something to do. Then she asked herself how in the world she could eat anything. She'd nearly decided to cancel the order when the knock came.

Experience had taught her caution. Even knowing she was guarded, Gillian checked the peephole for the uniformed waiter. Satisfied, she opened the door and looked disinterestedly at the tray.

"Just set it over there," she told him, gesturing because she wasn't certain he spoke English. Still, a check was a check in any language. Gillian leaned over to sign it.

She felt the prick in her arm and jerked back. The drug worked quickly, and she was staggering even as she grabbed for the table knife. The world went gray and dissolved to black before she could even think Trace's name.

Chapter Eleven

General Husad liked beautiful things, too. He liked to look at them, touch them, wear them. Still, the austerity of his headquarters pleased him. A military establishment required a certain ambience. A soldier's life could never be a soft one, or discipline was lost. He believed that, even when he dressed in silks and admired his wife's emeralds.

He was a small, spare man in his prime, with a mesmerizing voice and a glint in his eyes some took for genius and others took for madness. The title of general was self-bestowed, and, though he had indeed fought in wars, most of the medals he had pinned on his chest were self-awarded. By turns he treated his men like an indulgent father and a heartless dictator. They didn't love him, but they feared him enough to follow his orders without question.

He was dressed in a gold cloak for his meeting with Cabot. It was tied at the neck to reveal the medal-bedecked uniform beneath and the twin handguns at his hips. He had a striking face, hawkish, with silvered hair combed straight back. He photographed very well and spoke like an evangelist. His mind was slipping into a dark, violent area that even his medication no longer controlled completely.

His office wasn't sparsely furnished, as Kendesa's had been. The desk was huge, of polished oak, and dominated the room from its center. Sofas and chairs plump with pillows formed a circle around it. There were bookshelves and display cabinets. Trace studied them with what appeared to be a detached interest.

No windows, he thought, and only one door. Not likely.

There were a pair of épées crossed on the wall over an enormous aquarium in which colorful tropical fish glided in clear blue water.

"Monsieur Cabot." Husad held out a hand with the warmth and sincerity of a car salesman one step away from his monthly quota. "Welcome."

"General." Trace accepted the hand and looked into the face of the man he'd sworn to kill. The eyes were black and full of odd lights. Madness. Could anyone stand this close to it and not smell it?

"I hope you didn't find the journey too inconvenient."

"Not at all."

"If you would be pleased to sit."

Trace took a chair and waited while the general stood with his hands folded behind his back. Kendesa stood silently at the door. For some moments, Husad paced, the sound of his highly polished boots absorbed by the carpet.

"The revolution needs both allies and arms," he began. "We wage a holy battle for the people, a battle that requires us to destroy the unworthy and the unbeliever. In Europe and the Middle East we have often been successful in bringing destruction to those who oppose us." He turned to Trace, head high, eyes blazing. "It is not enough. We have our duty, a sacred duty, to overthrow the oppressive governments of the world. Many will die in righteousness and sacrifice before we succeed. And we will succeed."

Trace sat calmly, noting that, as reported, Husad had a stirring voice, a strong presence. But even though he went on in the same vein for ten minutes, he basically said nothing. Trace noted, as well, that once the speech was over he glanced toward Kendesa. For approval? he wondered. For guidance?

"Your mission, General, if you will pardon me, interests me only as it concerns my associates and myself. I am not a patriot or a soldier, but a man of business." Trace folded his hands and continued. "You require arms, and I can supply them, for a price."

"Your price is high," the general said as he walked to his desk.

"My price includes the risk factor for securing, storing and delivering the merchandise. This same price can be quoted to others."

Husad reached down and came up with the TS-35. Even as Trace tensed, he heard Kendesa make a quick, surprised movement behind him.

"I find this weapon of particular interest."

The TS-35 was slim and amazingly lightweight. Even on a forced march, a soldier could carry it as easily as his food rations. The clips were slimmer than the average pack of cigarettes. Husad balanced its spearlike shape in his hands, then brought it up to sight it. In the middle of Trace's forehead.

If it was loaded, and Trace was certain that it was, the projectile would obliterate him where he sat, then go on to kill Kendesa and anyone unlucky enough to be standing in its path for the next fifty yards.

"The Americans talk and talk of peace while they make such brilliant weapons." Husad was speaking almost dreamily now. "We are considered madmen because we talk of war. Such a weapon was made for a man of war. And the war is holy, the war is righteous, the war is food and drink."

Trace felt the sweat roll cold down his back. To die here, now, would be foolish, pitiful. "With all respect, General Husad, the weapon isn't yours until it's paid for."

The finger hovered on the trigger a moment, flexed, then retreated. With a charming smile, Husad lowered the gun. "Of course. We are warriors, but we are honest. We will take your shipment, Monsieur Cabot, and we ask, in the name of friendship, that you lower your price by half a million francs."

Trace's hands were damp as he reached for a cigarette. For survival's sake he wanted to agree and be done with it and get on with what he had come to do. But the man Cabot would never have agreed so easily. Nor would Husad, or Kendesa, expect it.

"In the name of expediency, General, we will lower the price by a quarter of a million, payment on delivery."

The weapon lay on Husad's desk now, and he stroked it as he might have a small child, or a pet. Again Trace saw his gaze shift briefly to Kendesa. "The papers will be drawn up. You will be driven back to Sefrou. In three days you will make the delivery, personally."

"It will be my pleasure." Trace rose.

"I am told you have an interest in our guest." Husad smiled. His teeth shone, and his eyes. "Personal interest?"

"Business is always personal to me, General."

"Perhaps you would be interested in observing the doctor. Kendesa will arrange it."

"Of course, General." Kendesa opened the door. Trace saw him give both Husad and the weapon an uneasy look before they walked back into the corridor.

"The general amuses himself in odd ways," Trace commented as they walked.

"Were you afraid, Monsieur Cabot?"

"I have, as you have not, observed the power of that weapon. You may choose to die for your cause, Kendesa. I do not. My associates might find it unpalatable to continue to do business with one so unstable."

"The general is under some stress."

Trace crushed out his cigarette on the stone floor and decided to take the risk. "I am said to be observant. Who is it that wields the hammer, Kendesa? Who is it that I am actually doing business with?"

Kendesa paused. As was his habit, he wore a Western suit, without frills or jewelry. The decision came easily, because he had considered it for some time. If Cabot didn't continue to satisfy him, it would be a simple matter to arrange his disposal. "As is often the case, the one with the title is but a figurehead. The general's mental condition has become frail over the past year. It has become my duty to assume more responsibility." He waited to be certain Trace understood. "Does this change your position?"

Not the general, Trace thought, but Kendesa. Kendesa had ordered Charlie's death, Fitzpatrick's kidnapping. So he would deal with Kendesa rather than a half-mad puppet. "It satisfies me," Trace replied.

"Excellent." For the general's usefulness was almost at an end. Once Fitzpatrick had completed his task, Kendesa would take full power. And how much sweeter it would be with the backing of Cabot's organization, and the wealth that went with it.

Kendesa waved aside two armed guards. Taking a key from his pocket, he unlocked a door.

No research-and-development lab could have been better equipped. The lighting was brilliant, every surface was spotless. Trace spotted two surveillance cameras before he turned his attention to Gillian's brother.

It was the man from the snapshot, but he'd grown thinner, older. Strain had dug lines in his face and bruised the skin around his eyes. He was clean-shaven, but his hair, darker and deeper than Gillian's, was unkempt. His white lab coat hung loosely over jeans and a plain blue shirt.

Flynn pushed away from the microscope and stood. The hatred in his eyes brought Trace a wave of relief. He hadn't given up or given in. He was hanging on, and not by a thread, but by his teeth. If the man had enough strength to hate, he had enough strength to escape.

"Dr. Fitzpatrick, your work goes well today?"

"I haven't seen my daughter in two days."

"We discussed incentive, Doctor."

Flynn's hand closed into a fist. He had withstood their torture. He was all but certain Kendesa had known he would withstand it. It was only the threat that they would take his Caitlin into that dark little room that kept him in the lab.

"I'm here." His Irish brogue had barbs in it. "I'm working. I was promised that she wouldn't be harmed and that I would see her daily if I cooperated."

"I'm afraid the general feels you work too slowly. When there is progress, we will bring your daughter to you. In the meantime, I will introduce you to Monsieur Cabot. He is interested in your work."

Flynn turned dark, hate-filled eyes on Trace. "Go to hell."

Trace wanted to congratulate him, but he only nodded stiffly. "Your work here will put your name in the history books, Dr. Fitzpatrick." Trace looked around, obstensibly interested in the lab, while he searched for another exit. "Fascinating. My organization feels the profit from your serum will be enormous."

"Your money will do you little good once a madman has destroyed the world."

Trace smiled. So he understood. He kept his voice mild. "Your serum will ensure power and profit for those clever enough to earn it. There is progress?" he asked Kendesa.

"It is slow." This time Kendesa smiled and watched Trace carefully. "The missing link is Fitzpatrick's sister. She has in her possession certain notes, certain knowledge that will expedite the completion of this work. She'll be joining you, Doctor."

Trace felt the air stop pumping into his lungs. Before he could speak, Flynn was rushing forward.

"Gillian? What have you done with her?"

Kendesa had his gun out quickly. "Calm yourself, Doctor. She is unharmed." He turned a curious smile on Trace. "Were you aware, *monsieur*, that you traveled with the good doctor's sister?"

"I?" He could play it two ways. But if he went with instinct and attacked, Flynn Fitzpatrick would be dead. "I'm afraid you're mistaken."

"The woman you brought to Casablanca was Dr. Gillian Fitzpatrick."

"The woman I brought to Casablanca was a little American tart I picked up in Paris. Attractive, amusing and dull-witted."

"More sharp-witted than you know, *monsieur*. You have been used."

So that was it. For once Trace blessed the ISS for the strength and depth of his cover. "You're mistaken." There was a low edge of fury to his voice.

"No, I regret it is you who are mistaken. The woman purposely sought you out, hoping you would bring her closer to us and her brother. I assume she played her part well."

"Very well. If you're correct."

"Quite correct. A short time ago she was in Mexico, where she sought out and enlisted the help of a certain ISS agent. We can assume it was he who instructed her on what course to take. Do you know the name Il Gatto, Cabot?"

Trace drew out a cigarette, making sure his hand didn't appear quite steady. "I know it."

"He seeks revenge on the general, and uses you and the woman to gain it."

"Who is he?"

"I regret I do not yet have that information." Anger broke through the sophisticated calm briefly. "The general was unfortunately hasty in executing three men who might have been able to identify him. But the woman knows, and will tell us. In time."

"Where is she?" Trace blew out a stream of smoke. "I do not tolerate being a woman's pawn."

"On her way here, if not here already. You are welcome to speak with her when you return. Once we have her notes, and she has identified Il Gatto, I may consider it a gesture of goodwill to give her to you."

"Bastard." Flynn raised his fist and would have struck if Trace hadn't moved more quickly. Grabbing Flynn's arm, he twisted it up behind his back and held him close, their faces an inch apart.

"Your whore of a sister owes me." Flynn bared his teeth but was helpless to strike back. "I'll take my payment from her, and from you, Doctor." He shoved him aside. "I've seen enough," Trace said curtly, and strode toward the door.

"Let me see Caitlin. Let me see my daughter, you son of a bitch," Flynn cried.

"Perhaps tomorrow, Doctor," Kendesa said calmly. "Perhaps then I shall reunite your family." In the same unhurried manner, he opened the door and locked it behind him. It gave him some pleasure to see the smooth, sleek André Cabot with his feathers ruffled.

"There is no need for embarrassment, my friend. The woman, under the guidance of Il Gatto, was a formidable enemy."

Trace turned on him. In an instant he had Kendesa against the wall. Even as the guards' guns clicked into place he had the key from Kendesa's pocket palmed in his hand. "I will not be made a fool. The woman is unharmed?"

Kendesa waved the guards aside as Trace's grip relaxed. "We did not want her damaged."

"Good." A muscle twitched in his cheek. "Very good. When I return in three days, I want her. Get the information you need, Kendesa. Get the information and then turn the woman over to me. The price of the shipment can be reduced another quarter of a million francs, between us."

Kendesa lifted a brow. "The price of your pride is high."

"Before I am through, she will wish, with a full heart, that you had killed her." Trace straightened his jacket and seemed to bring himself under control. "I assume the child is still alive."

"She is kept on the second level. Mild tranquilizers keep her quiet. They are full of passion, these Irish."

"Indeed." Trace saw the car and driver waiting where he'd left them. "I will report to my associates. If the papers are in order, we will finish our current business."

"Cabot." Kendesa rested a hand on the door of the car. "Does Il Gatto disturb you?"

Trace looked directly into Kendesa's eyes. "I feel he would have little interest in me, and a great deal more in you. I should watch my back, *mon ami*. Cats strike quickly."

Trace settled in the back seat and for the first time in years began to pray.

He would waste precious time traveling back to Sefrou, contacting Breintz and gathering the weapons. As the driver started down the mountain, Trace considered putting him out of commission and going back. But how far would he get alone, with a miserable peashooter of a .45?

Straining against his own impotence, he looked at his watch. Automatically he reactivated the homing device, but he was more interested in the time. He could be back, fully armed, by dark.

She'd be all right. She was strong. She was braver than she should be. He would come back for her and get her out, no matter what had to be done, no matter what had to be sacrificed.

But the cold sweat he was in reminded him what it was to fear for more than your own life.

When the tire blew out, he was thrown against the side of the car. Swearing, he straightened. Instinct had him reaching in his pocket as he stepped from the car. The driver got out, turned toward the damaged wheel, then dropped like a stone.

Trace drew out his pistol. Smelling ambush. Even as he whirled, Breintz rose from a rock. "Your mind's elsewhere, old friend. If I'd wanted you dead, you'd be dead."

Trace pocketed the pistol. "They've got Gillian."

"I know. One of her guards lived long enough to contact me." Breintz dropped agilely from the rock. "My orders are to give you twelve hours to get the Fitzpatricks out. If you're unsuccessful, Hammer's headquarters is to be destroyed."

"Give me your weapon."

"One rifle?" Breintz lifted a brow. "Such conceit."

"Twelve hours doesn't give me a hell of a lot of time. Give me the rifle."

"For once Il Gatto is not using his head." Breintz bent down to examine the driver's clothes. "Could it be the woman is more than an assignment?" Breintz drew off the driver's braided headdress and settled it over his hair. "An adequate fit."

Trace schooled his breathing until his head cleared. "You drive. We can take out the guards at the gate and use their weapons. The layout's simple enough. We get Fitzpatrick, I find Gillian and the kid."

"Agreed." Breintz gestured for him to follow. With the ease of a goat, he climbed over the rocks. Trace saw the case he'd purchased from Bakir. Breintz only smiled. "I have worked with you before." Breintz handed Trace a grenade launcher. "And this is my country. I say modestly that my contacts here are excellent."

Trace yanked off Cabot's raw-silk jacket and threw it in the dirt. He slipped the strap of the weapon over his shoulder and reached for another. "I'd forgotten how good you were."

"Old friend—" Breintz was quietly taping clips together "—I am even better now."

Trace strapped on an ammo belt. "We have to wait until dark."

Breintz sat cross-legged. "It will come soon enough."

"You don't have orders to go in with me."

"No." Breintz closed his eyes and began to drift into meditation. "Charles Forrester was a good man."

"Thanks."

Wishing he could find the same kind of serenity, Trace sat beside him. And waited for sundown.

Gillian awoke slowly, with her head throbbing and her mind fuzzy. Once or twice she nearly found consciousness, only to go into the grayness again. She heard weeping, quiet and heartfelt, and wondered if it was her.

She felt warmth against her side, then again warmth stroking along her arm. Instinctively she reached out for it.

"Aunt Gillian, please wake up. Please, Aunt Gillian, I'm so scared."

It was like the nightmare. Gillian felt her skin go clammy and fought it off. Just a dream, she told herself, but Caitlin's pleas were coming clearer and clearer. Opening her eyes, she saw her.

"I thought you were dead." Caitlin, eyes puffy and red, buried her face in Gillian's hair. "They dropped you on the bed and you lay so still I thought you were dead."

"Baby." She pushed herself up and nearly passed out again. The drug had been strong and had left her with a raging headache and traces of nausea. Unsure what was real, she reached out and touched Caitlin's face. "Oh, baby. It's you. It's really you." Gathering the child close, she rocked her. "Oh, Caitlin, little darling, go ahead and cry. Poor little lamb, how frightened you must have been, all alone like this. I'm here now."

"Are you going to take us home?"

Where was home? And where were they? As she looked around the dim room, Gillian remembered the waiter, the prick of the hypodermic. Closing her eyes, she cursed herself for her stupidity. Did they have Trace, too? Oh, God, did they have him, too?

"Can we go home now? Please, I want to go home."

"Soon," Gillian murmured. "As soon as I can. Caitlin, can you dry your eyes and talk to me?"

With sniffles and nods, Caitlin burrowed closer. "You won't go away?"

"No. No, I won't leave you." They'd have to kill her first, she promised herself as she kept Caitlin close. "Where's your da?"

"They keep him downstairs, in a laboratory."

"Is he all right? Be brave now, darling. Is your da all right?"

"He looks kind of sick. I can't remember when they let me see him last." She swiped her hand over her wet cheeks. "He cried once."

"It's all right. It's going to be all right. There's a—" She cut herself off as she remembered how carefully Trace had searched their hotel rooms for microphones. Someone could be listening to them even now. She couldn't mention his name or give her niece the comfort of knowing they had help. "There's sure to be a way out," she said instead. "We just have to be patient. We're together now." Then she lifted a finger to her lips, signaling to the child to be silent. As quietly as she could, she searched the room.

She knew it was more luck than skill that led her to it. When she found the mike, her first instinct was to smash it. Even that small sign of defiance would have been satisfying. But she made herself think coolly. Leaving the mike in place, she climbed back onto the narrow bed.

"I met a man in Mexico," she began, knowing whoever was listening would already be aware of that. "He said he'd help. He has a funny name, Caitlin. Il Gatto. It means 'cat'."

"Does he look like a cat?"

"No." Gillian smiled to herself. "But he thinks like one. When I don't contact him tomorrow," she said, "he'll come after us."

"And take us home?"

"Yes, darling. Do you know where we are?"

"It's like a big cave with lots of tunnels."

"I see." Gillian lifted Caitlin's eyelids and examined her pupils. Drugs. The fury rose and nearly overpowered her. "Do you ever go outside?"

"No. There aren't any windows."

Caitlin cringed as the door opened and a man with a rifle over his shoulder carried in a tray. He set it on the edge of the bed, gestured to it, then walked out again.

"I bit him once," Caitlin said, with some of her old spirit.

"Good for you."

"He smacked me."

"He won't smack you again." Gillian looked at the tray. There was rice and some cubed meat with two glasses of milk. She sniffed at it. "Have you been eating well?"

"The food doesn't taste good, but I get hungry. Whenever I eat, I get sleepy."

"You need to eat, darling." But she shook her head as she lifted the tray. "It helps keep up your strength." Gillian dumped the contents of both plates under the bed. "And you need to sleep, as well." Looking around for a likely place, she poured the milk on a pile of dirty linen in the corner. Caitlin watched her with wide eyes. "Come on, baby, try to eat a little more."

When Caitlin pressed a hand to her mouth and giggled, Gillian nearly wept from the sight of it.

"That's it. Now drink your milk." Grinning with her, Gillian climbed into bed again.

A trace of mischief lit Caitlin's eyes. "I don't like milk."

"It's good for your bones. You wouldn't want soft bones, would you?" Gillian cuddled with her. Putting her mouth against the child's ear, she whispered. "They put something in the food to make you sleep. You have to pretend to sleep so they don't find out we didn't eat it. Do just what I say. If one of the men comes back, lie very still so they don't know we've fooled them."

Caitlin nodded. "Don't go away, Aunt Gillian."

"No, I won't go away."

Gillian cradled the child in her arms. In the dark, she stared at the ceiling and planned.

Sunset came with brilliance. The mountains went pink with it, and the sand gold. In the last of the light, Breintz changed into the driver's clothes after fixing the tire while Trace loaded weapons on the floor of the car.

They worked in silence now. Everything had been said. As the sun dipped below the high peaks, Trace stretched out on the floor in the back and Breintz climbed behind the wheel. They headed east for the last time.

Breintz began to whistle tunelessly as they approached. As Trace had, he noted the sentries on the ridges above the building. Following Trace's directions, he punched out the code and waited for the door to lift up.

As he stopped the car inside, he lowered his head to conceal as much of his face as possible. A guard approached as the door closed behind him.

"You made good time," he said, just before Breintz brought an elbow to his throat. Trace was out of the car and leading the way to the lab.

They pulled up short some twenty feet later. Two more guards were dealt with in utter silence. Trace knew they would have to move quickly once they broke into the lab. There the cameras would give them away. Trace shrank back out of sight as Breintz moved forward, weaving slightly.

"A cigarette," he demanded in Arabic, keeping his voice a bit slurred. "What good is wine without tobacco?"

As one of the guards broke into a grin, Trace and Breintz moved quickly. Not a shot was fired.

"You still have a light touch," Breintz commented as Trace slipped the key into the lock.

"And yours has improved." Taking a deep breath, Trace opened the door. "Keep working," he said in a low voice to Flynn the moment he spotted him. "Keep as much of your back as possible to the cameras."

Despite the order, Flynn set down his tongs and test tube. "You." There was a look in his eyes that told Trace he'd been pushed almost to his limit.

"For God's sake, if you want to get your daughter out, keep working. I don't want surveillance to see anything unusual until the last minute."

"Push it along," Breintz said mildly as he kept a lookout.

"Pick up the damn test tube, do something scientific. I'm ISS."

Flynn picked up the tube, but in a grip that threatened to shatter it. "You're a pig."

"Maybe, but I'm here to get you and the kid—and your idiot sister—out of here. Keep working. Do you want to see a goddamn badge?" Trace cast a look at the first camera. "Just do what I say, do it slow, and do it right."

Something in his tone made Flynn obey, but the strain was still evident. "I thought you were French."

"I'm as Irish as you are, Fitzpatrick," Trace said reassuringly, and grinned. "And, by the saints," he said, dropping into the easy brogue of his alter ego, Colin, "we'll be gettin' out and blowin' this place to hell."

Maybe it was simple desperation, but Flynn responded. "When we do, the first bottle's on me."

"You're on. Now move as far as you can to the left, the edge of camera range. Go after those papers."

Flynn set down the tube and obeyed. With his back to the cameras, he looked over the papers as if he were checking his equations. "How did you find us?"

"Your sister had a lot to do with it. If you've got half the guts she does, we're going to make it. Now keep reading. Something doesn't check out. Take out your pencil like you're going to make notes. I'm going to blow the camera out. When I do, you run. Breintz'll take you out while I go up for the kid and Gillian. Now!"

Trace blew the camera out with a single blast. When Flynn passed through the door, both agents had their weapons ready. "Give me twenty minutes," Trace said to Breintz.

"I'm not going without Caitlin."

"I'll get her." Trace shoved Flynn in Breintz's direction. "You're the key. If they get their hands on you again, none of us are going to make it."

"She's my child." Weariness and despair had frozen into icy determination. "I won't leave her behind."

"You're her brother, all right," Trace muttered. And time was running out. He shoved a rifle into Flynn's hands. "Can you use it?"

Flynn felt a ray of hope bloom like a sunrise. "With pleasure."

"Say a prayer to whatever gods work best," Trace told Breintz.

"I already have."

Gillian heard the door open and lay as silent and still as Caitlin. The child had truly fallen asleep, a natural sleep. Gillian gripped the pitiful weapon in her hand. During the hour she'd lain in the dark, she'd tried to accept that Trace was gone. They'd discovered the deception, killed him and kidnapped her.

She wanted to mourn for him, to grieve, to rage. But first she would have her revenge, and her family's freedom.

With her eyes half open, she saw the man bend over her. Gillian held her breath and swung. The edge of the plate caught him full force on the bridge of the nose. She heard the grinding break, saw the spurt of blood. While he was blinded by it, she lifted the other plate and struck again. He staggered but grabbed at her arm as he went. Though her arm twisted painfully, she remembered what her neighbor in New York had told her.

Go for the eyes.

This time he yelped. The butt of his gun slammed into her side as he tried to bring it into place. And then she was fighting for her life.

It was through a red wave of fear and fury that she heard Caitlin begin to whimper. As she had in the nightmare. At the sound of it, Gillian fought like a madwoman. She gripped the rifle. So did he. It exploded with the most terrible sound she'd ever heard.

Then she was standing, holding it, and the man, whose face she had never seen, was at her feet.

"Aunt Gillian!" Caitlin climbed out of bed to grasp Gillian's legs. "Is he dead? The bad man, is he dead?"

"I think—I don't know." She swayed, as though the drug had taken over again. "I don't know. We have to go. We have to go now."

Then she heard the gunfire, close and coming closer. Shoving the child behind her, Gillian lifted the rifle again. Her hands were slick with sweat as she prepared to protect her own.

They'd found the first guard faster than Trace had counted on. The alarm was out, and if it hadn't been for luck and a brutal frontal attack they would have been cornered. They'd reached the second level.

"I'll hold them here." Breintz took his position behind a column at the top of the stairs. "Find the woman and the child."

Trace switched to the grenade launcher and sent three over the rail. "Keep down," he ordered Flynn, and began to move. He broke open a half-dozen doors, then saw the one that was already open. With his back pressed against the wall, he gripped the gun in both hands and took two deep breaths before swinging into the opening, prepared to fire. Gillian's bullet grazed his left shoulder. He was too shocked to feel the sting.

"Good God, woman."

"Trace!" With the gun lowered, she sprang forward. "Oh, Trace, I thought you were dead."

"Damn near." He brushed his fingers over his sleeve, disgusted when they came away red.

"Flynn." With a sob, she fell against him.

"Da!" Caitlin flew across the room and was scooped up by her father.

"Family reunions later," Trace told them. "Let's move. Breintz!" Trace sent another few rounds into the first level to cover the agent. "Get them out. I'll keep everyone busy." He unhooked the Uzi he'd taken off one of the guards. "Fifteen minutes," he said between his teeth. "Send it up in fifteen minutes."

"I would prefer to see you again."

"Yeah." Trace swiped sweat from under his eyes. He dashed back toward the stairs, sending bullets flying, before Gillian realized what he was doing.

"No! No, he can't!"

But he could. Gillian knew that he had to face his destiny, just as she did. "I'm sorry, Flynn." She kissed him quickly. "I have to stay with him. Go quickly." Then she was racing behind Trace.

He set off a series of explosions that not only cleared the stairs but nearly obliterated them. He was halfway down when he heard the noise at his back. For the second time, he turned on Gillian.

"What in the name of God—?"

"You know they have a better chance if we separate. I'm staying with you. That was the deal."

It was too late to send her back. If he'd had even seconds to spare, he would have shouted at her. Instead, he grabbed her arm and hauled her along with him.

They'd caused considerable damage, Trace saw with satisfaction. And more confusion. The general was out, waving and firing the TS-35. As he furthered the damage to his headquarters and added to the casualty toll among his own men, he ordered them to stand and fight the army of invaders. The unexpected attack appeared to have cut the bonds on his last hold on sanity. Trace lifted his gun. The general fell before he pressed the trigger.

"Fool." Kendesa stood over the gold-cloaked body. "Your time has passed." Bending, he retrieved the American-made weapon. "What you have cost us." He whirled to shout at the scattering soldiers. "To the front entrance, idiots!" he ordered. "Bar the front entrance!"

Too late, Trace thought grimly as he stepped out from cover. "You've lost, Kendesa. And the fool is you for believing that the woman duped me when it was I who duped you."

"Cabot."

"When it suits me."

Kendesa's expression changed. "Il Gatto, at last."

"Definitely at last. Our business is finished, Kendesa, and this is personal."

Perhaps he would have killed him where he stood. He'd been prepared to. But before it could be put to the test, the general raised his handgun. "Traitor." He wheezed as he fired. Kendesa staggered back, but didn't fall. Again Trace aimed.

This time, heaven interfered.

The ground shook, violently. Trace's first thought was that Breintz had set the charges early. He grabbed Gillian's hand and started to run. Another tremor had them both ramming into the rock wall.

"Earthquake," Trace said as he fought for breath. "A real one. The whole place is going to go."

"They got out, didn't they?"

"They had time." It was all the hope he could give her.

They raced down one passage, only to have it cave in in front of them. Gillian heard screams as the dust blinded her. Without pausing for breath, Trace pulled her down another. "There's got to be more than one way out. We won't make it to the front." Again he went with instinct and headed for the general's quarters. "He'd have an escape route," he said as he blasted the lock off the door. Pulling Gillian inside, he went for the obvious. "Look for a button, a mechanism," he shouted as he searched the bookcase. He could hear stone falling from great heights. Something was burning, and the fire was close. With both hands, he shoved aside books. Then he found it. The panel slid out.

The corridor beyond was narrow and vibrated from the tremors underground. But it was unguarded. Praying his luck was still holding, he shoved her through. In seconds they were out in the night.

Men ran and shouted, scattering. Behind them the building was splitting apart, huge chucks of rock tumbling down with a noise that seemed impossible. Then the noise grew greater with the first explosion. Without bothering with cover, Trace ran. No one came after them.

It seemed to Gillian that they ran for miles. He never let her stop to rest, and she didn't ask to. Then, like a shadow, Breintz rose from a rock.

"So we do meet again."

"Looks like." Trace dragged Gillian over the rocks to the makeshift camp.

"The gods made it unnecessary for me to complete our plan." With his usual calm, Breintz handed Trace night-vision glasses. Lifting them, Trace focused in the direction they had come from.

"Not much left."

"And Kendesa?"

"The general took care of him." Trace lowered the glasses again. "If not, your gods did. Hammer's smashed." He handed the glasses back. "Looks like a promotion for you."

"And you."

"I'm finished." He sat with his back to a rock and watched Gillian gather her family to her.

"I owe you." Flynn sat with his daughter curled on his lap and his sister close against his side.

"Just doing a job."

"In any case, I owe you. You have a name?"

Trace accepted the bottle Breintz handed him. The long swig he took had a kick he could have lived on for a week. "O'Hurley."

"Thank you, O'Hurley, for my daughter."

Caitlin reached up to whisper in her father's ear. Then, at his murmur, she rose and walked to Trace. "My da says you saved us."

"Sort of." She was thinner than in the snapshot, and her eyes were too big in her pale face. Unable to resist, Trace reached up and tugged on one of her tangled red locks. "It's all done now."

"Can I hug you?"

Nonplussed, he shifted his shoulders. "Yeah, sure."

She cuddled against him and, with the resilience of childhood, giggled. "You smell," she said, not unkindly. "I guess I smell, too."

"Some."

As she pressed a wet kiss to his cheek, he held her, and his eyes drifted to Gillian.

"Just little pieces," she murmured to him. "All we can change are little pieces. But it's worth it." Because she was afraid she would weep, she rose to walk a little way into the shadows. She heard him come up behind her.

"I know you want to know how I got there and what happened, but I can't talk about it now."

"All right. It's all right." He started to reach for her hair, then dropped his hand again. "We have to get going. There'll be a plane in Sefrou to fly us to Madrid. The ISS will take care of you."

"I thought they'd killed you." It was anger, rather than tears, that sparkled her eyes as she turned. "I thought you were dead, and all you can talk about is planes and the ISS?"

Trace touched the blood drying on his shoulder. "The only hit I took was from you."

"Oh, God, I'd forgotten." She came to him quickly. "I might have killed you."

"Not with that aim."

"You're wrong." She wiped the back of her hand over her mouth. "I killed a man. With my own hands." She looked down at them now and shuddered. "I didn't even see his face, but I killed him."

"And you think you can't live with that." He cupped her chin in his hand so that she would look at him. Her face was filthy, and there was blood on it from a scrape along her cheekbone. "You can, Gillian. You can live with a lot of things. Believe me, I know."

"Trace, would you do something for me? One more thing?"

"Maybe."

Still cautious, she thought, and almost laughed. "If it wouldn't put you out too much, would you hold me? I don't want to cry, and if you hold me I won't."

"Come here," he murmured, and wrapped his arms around her. It was over, he thought, and she was safe. Maybe, just maybe, they had some time. "Cry if you want. It doesn't hurt anything."

He was warm and hard against her, and the night was quiet again. "I don't need to now."

Chapter Twelve

After everything we've been through, I don't understand how you can be nervous over this.''

"Don't be ridiculous. I'm not nervous." Trace yanked at the knot of his tie again. As far as he was concerned, Cabot was dead, and the ties should have gone with him. "I don't know why in the hell I let you talk me into this."

Enormously pleased with herself, Gillian sat in the rented car as they drove away from the Los Angeles airport. "You gave me your word we could go anywhere I wanted after things were settled again. And where I wanted to go was your sister's wedding."

"A shabby trick, Doc, after I saved your life."

It was precisely because of that that she was determined to save his, or at least a small part of it. "A man's word is his bond," she said solemnly, then laughed when he swore at her. "Oh, Trace, don't be cranky. It's a beautiful day, and I don't think I've ever been happier in my life. Did you see how wonderful Flynn and Caitlin looked when we left them? I can hardly believe it's all over, really over."

He relented enough to put a hand over hers. "It's over. Your brother and the kid can go back to Ireland and put all this behind them. With Husad and Kendesa gone and Hammer's headquarters destroyed, they've got nothing to worry about."

"Addison wasn't pleased about the Horizon project being destroyed, or Flynn's refusal to try to duplicate it."

Trace gave a short laugh. Maybe he'd been wrong about scientists—or at least some of them. Fitzpatrick had stood toe-to-toe with Addison, turning aside offers, pleas, bribes and threats. Gillian had taken the same stand, saying nothing about her memory and leaving Addison and the ISS with a handful of doctored notes. For better or worse, Horizon was finished.

"Addison wasn't pleased about much. He grumbled for an hour over losing a crate of weapons, including a TS-35."

"I think he was more displeased to be losing one of his best agents."

Trace lifted a brow. "I don't think he'd put it that way."

"But he did, to me." She ran a hand down the skirt of her dress. She'd fallen in love with the rich green silk. It was a bit more elaborate than her usual style, but, after all, this was Chantel O'Hurley's wedding. "He was hoping I could convince you to stay 'on board,' as he put it."

It was hard not to feel a nasty little streak of satisfaction at that. "What did you tell him?"

"That he was mad as a hatter. Oh, look how tall the palms are. In New York it's probably cold and sleeting."

"I guess you miss it?"

"Miss what?" She turned to look at him. "New York? Oh, I haven't really thought about it. I suppose everyone at Random-Frye thinks I've dropped off the edge of the earth." She sighed, content. "In some ways I think I have."

"I guess Arthur Steward wonders."

"Dear old Arthur," Gillian said with a smile. "I suppose he might, at the odd moment." It didn't surprise or even annoy her that he knew about Arthur. After all, she knew about his squashed beetle. "I'll have to send him a postcard."

"You'll be back in a couple of days."

"I don't know. I haven't decided." She wasn't going back to New York, or anywhere else, without him. He just didn't know it yet. "What about you? Are you winging straight off to the islands?"

Why was it she could make him so uncomfortable when she smiled that way? It was as if she could see what he was thinking. Or trying not to think. "I've got some business to take care of in Chicago first." He paused for a moment, because he hadn't taken it all in yet. "For some reason, Charlie left me his house."

"I see." She smiled again, brilliantly. "So it seems you have a home after all."

"I don't know anything about real estate," he mumbled. They were in Beverly Hills now with its mansions and trimmed hedges. This was the kind of place his father had always dreamed of. The O'Hurleys had come up in the world, he thought. Or some of them had. He yanked at his tie again. "Listen, Doc, this is a dumb idea. We can head back to the airport, take a flight to New Zealand. It's beautiful there."

And at the other end of the world. Gillian resisted the urge to lecture or comfort. "A promise is a promise," she said simply.

"I don't want to spoil this for Chantel, or the rest of them."

"Of course you don't. That's why you're going."

"You don't understand, Gillian." And he'd never been able to bring himself to explain it before. "My father's never forgiven me for leaving. He never understood why I had to. He wanted—I guess he needed for me to be a part of the dream he had. The O'Hurley Family, in big, bold lights. Broadway, Vegas, Carnegie Hall."

She was silent for a long moment. Then she spoke quietly, without looking at him. "My father never forgave me, never understood me. He wanted me to be one thing, and I was always another. Did your father love you, Trace?"

"Sure he did, it was just—"

"My father never loved me."

"Gillian—"

"No, listen to me. There's a difference between love and obligation, between true affection and expectation. He didn't love me, and I can accept that. But what I can't accept is that I never made peace with him. Now it's too late." She looked at him now, and though her eyes were dry they shone with emotion. "Don't make that same mistake, Trace. I promise you, you'll regret it."

He could think of nothing to say, no argument to give. He was here because he'd promised, but more, because he'd wanted to come. The ideas, or maybe he should call them dreams, that had begun to form couldn't be brought to fruition until he'd resolved his life. He couldn't do that until he'd closed the rift with his family. With his father.

"This could be the biggest mistake you've ever made," he said as he pulled up to the gates guarding Chantel's estate.

"I'll risk it."

"You're a stubborn woman, Doc."

"I know." She touched his face. "I've got as much on the line as you do."

He wanted to ask her to explain, but a guard knocked smartly on his window. "You're early, sir," he said when Trace rolled down the window. "May I see your invitation?"

She hadn't thought of that, Gillian realized with a start. Before she could speak, Trace pulled out a badge. "McAllister, Special Security."

The ID looked official, because it was. The guard studied it, compared the laminated photo to Trace, then nodded. "Go right in, sir," he said, nearly snapping a salute.

Trace tooled through the gates and started up the long drive.

"McAllister?"

Trace slipped the ID back in his pocket. "Old habits die hard. Good God, what a place." The house was huge and white and elegant. The grounds were trimmed and rolling. He thought of the crowded hotel rooms they'd shared, the meals his father had cooked on hot plates, the airless dressing rooms, the audiences that snarled as often as they applauded. And the laughter. And the music.

"It's beautiful," Gillian murmured. "Like a picture."

"She always said she'd do it." The pride came through, deeper than he'd expected. "The little brat pulled it off."

"Spoken like a true brother," Gillian said with a laugh. She was helped from the car by a man in uniform, and was suddenly every bit as nervous as Trace. Maybe she should have made him come alone. She was hardly prepared to meet royalty, even the Hollywood variety. And his family might resent... As he came to her, she reached out a hand. "Trace, maybe I shouldn't."

The front door burst open and nearly cracked on its hinges. A woman with a wild mop of red curls and an exquisite dress of sapphire blue raced down the stairs. With something close to a war cry, she launched herself into Trace's arms.

"You're here! You're really here!" With her arms in a stranglehold around his neck and her mouth smothering his, Trace could do little more than absorb the scent and feel. "I knew you'd come. I didn't believe it, but I knew. And here you are."

"Maddy." Because he needed to catch his breath as much as he wanted to look at her, Trace drew her back by the shoulders. There were tears streaming down her face, but she was grinning. And the grin was exactly as he remembered. "Hi."

"Hi yourself." She pulled the handkerchief out of his pocket, blew her nose hard, then laughed. "Chantel will kill me if my nose is red." She blew again. "How do I look?"

"Terrible, but there's so little you can do with that face." With the laughter, they were close again. He held her and wished he could believe it would be so easy with everyone. "Maddy, I love you."

"I know, you jerk." Her breath hitched on a sob. "Stay this time?"

"Yeah." He brushed his cheek against her hair. "I'll stay this time." Looking over her head, he watched Gillian.

"I can't wait to show you off." Maddy drew back beaming, then glanced at Gillian. "Hi."

"Maddy, this is Gillian Fitzpatrick."

Still sniffling, Maddy turned. "I'm so glad to meet you." Gillian found herself enclosed in the same exuberant hug. "In fact, I'm thrilled." She drew away far enough to wink, then squeezed Gillian again. "You look wonderful, both of you, just wonderful." She slipped an arm around each of them and started up the stairs. "I can't wait for you to meet Reed. Oh, here he is now."

Coming down the hall was a leanly built man with hair shades darker than Trace's and more conservatively cut. He looked as if he'd been born in the tux. So this was Reed Valentine of Valentine Records. Rich, well-bred and straight-line. Thinking of his free-spirited, unconventional sister, Trace decided he could have come up with no one less suited to her.

"Reed, it's Trace." Maddy gave Trace another quick kiss, then dashed to her husband. "I told you he'd be here."

"So you did." Reed slipped a protective arm around Maddy and sized up the brother even as the brother sized up the husband. "Maddy's been looking forward to seeing you again." With his arm still around Maddy, he offered a hand. Trace took it. It wasn't as smooth as he'd expected.

"Congratulations."

"Thank you."

"Oh, don't be stuffy, Reed. We have to kill the fatted calf, at least."

Reed saw the expression on Trace's face and smiled. "I have a feeling Trace might prefer a drink." He turned a smile of considerable charm on Gillian. "Hello."

"Oh, I'm sorry," Maddy began. "This is Gillian. She's with Trace. We should go in and sit down, and I'll find everyone. Things are a little confused."

To prove it, two boys raced down the hall, one in oblivious and desperate pursuit of the other. "I'm going to tell Mom."

"I'm going to tell her first."

"Whoa!" Maddy grabbed an arm each before they could come to blows. "Slow down. You'll have those cute little tuxedos filthy before we can start the wedding."

"He said I looked like a geek," the smaller of the two said.

"He kicked me," the older said righteously.

"I *tried* to kick him, only I missed." He looked across at his brother, hoping he'd have another chance.

"Kicking's not allowed. And, Chris, you do not look like a geek. In fact, you look very handsome. Now, can you behave long enough to meet your uncle?"

"What uncle?" Ben, the oldest, looked up suspiciously.

"The only one you haven't met. Trace, this is Ben, and this is Chris. Abby's boys."

He wasn't sure whether he should shake hands, crouch down or wave from a distance. Before he could make up his mind, Chris stepped forward to give him a good study.

"You're the one who went away. Mom said you've been to Japan."

So crouching down seemed natural. "Yeah, I've been there."

"We studied about it in school. They eat raw fish there."

"Sometimes." Good God, he thought, he could see himself in the boy, just as he saw Abby's solemn eyes in the brother.

"Did *you*?" Chris wanted to know.

"Sure I did."

Chris made a face. He couldn't have been more pleased. "That's gross. Dad—that's Dylan—took us fishing, but I wouldn't clean them."

"I did," Ben said, tired of being left out. He shouldered Chris out of the way to get a good look for himself. "I liked the spaceship model you sent me. It was neat."

"I'm glad you liked it." Trace wanted to ruffle the boy's hair, but figured it was too soon.

"He only lets me play with it if I beg and beg," Chris put in.

"That's because you're a geek."

"Am not!"

Ben started to launch into a full-scale exchange of insults, then clammed up when he recognized the sound of footsteps.

"Trouble?" Dylan said mildly as he stepped into the hall.

"Dad, we've got another uncle, and he's here." Delighted to be in charge, Chris grabbed Trace's hand and dragged him forward. "This is Uncle Trace. This is my dad. We changed our name to Crosby and everything."

So this was the brother no one knew very much about. Dylan's writer's instincts were humming. "Glad you could make it. Abby's always showing the boys where you've been on Ben's globe. You get around."

"Some." Trace was pleased enough to meet the brother-in-law, but he was wary of the journalist.

"He eats raw fish," Chris supplied. "Hey, Mom, guess who's here?"

Abby came from the direction of the kitchen, her dancer's legs still graceful beneath the deep rose dress that draped over the child she carried. Her dark-blond hair swung loosely at her shoulders. "The caterers want me to tell certain greedy little fingers to keep out of the canapés.

I wonder who they might mean." Her brow was lifted as she smiled at her husband. Then, looking past him, she saw Trace.

"Oh." Her eyes, always expressive, filled as she opened her arms. "Oh, Trace."

"Mom's crying," Ben murmured as he watched his mother being held by this man he'd only heard about.

"Because she's happy," Dylan told him, placing a hand on his shoulder. "Imagine if you didn't see Chris for a long, long time." Ben considered it, and a gleam came into his eyes. "Monster." With a laugh, Dylan ruffled his hair.

"It's such a surprise. Such a terrific surprise."

Trace brushed a tear from her cheek. "Maddy already stole my handkerchief."

"It doesn't matter. How did you get here? Where did you come from? I've so many questions. Give me another hug."

"This is Gillian," Maddy announced, though Gillian had done her best to stay in the background. "She brought him." At Trace's lifted brow, Maddy grinned. "I mean, he brought her."

"Whichever way, hello." Though she sensed some intrigue, it could wait. Abby kissed both of Gillian's cheeks. "I'm glad you're here, both of you. And I can't wait to see Chantel's face."

"Why wait?" With a laugh, Maddy hooked an arm through Trace's. "She's upstairs making herself more beautiful."

"Nothing changes," Trace commented.

"Not much. Come on. Gillian, you, too. Chantel will want to meet you."

"Maybe I should—"

"Don't be silly." Abby cut off her protest and took her hand. "This is a once-in-a-lifetime."

"Dylan and I will . . . check on Quinn," Reed said.

"Thanks." Maddy threw him a smile as she climbed the stairs.

"I wonder how Pop's going to react," Dylan murmured.

"That's something I don't want to miss. Come on, boys, let's see how the bridegroom is holding up."

With her usual flair for the dramatic, Maddy rapped on Chantel's door.

"I don't want to see anyone unless they have a bottle of champagne."

"This is better." Maddy opened the door and stuck her head inside. "Abby and I brought you a wedding present."

"At the moment, I'd prefer the champagne. I'm a nervous wreck."

"This'll take your mind off it." With a flourish, Maddy pushed the door wide.

Chantel sat at her dressing table in a long white robe, her crown of pale-blond hair done up in intricate coils. She saw Trace in the mirror and turned very slowly.

"Well, well," she said in her dark, alluring voice. "Look what the cat dragged in." She rose to look at him.

She was every bit as beautiful as he remembered. Perhaps more. And was undoubtedly every bit as hard a nut to crack. "You look pretty good, kid."

"I know." She tilted her head. "You don't look too bad. A little rough around the edges, maybe."

He stuck his hands in his pockets. "Nice house."

"We like it." Then she let out a long breath. "Bastard. There goes my makeup." He met her halfway and swung her in one long circle. "I'm so glad you're here, and I hate you for making me cry so I look like a hag for my wedding."

"A hag?" He drew her away. "Fat chance."

"Trace." She brushed the hair from his forehead. "We always knew the day would come, but you couldn't have picked a better one. God, don't you even have a handkerchief?"

"Maddy took it."

"Figures." She used the heel of her hand.

"This is Gillian." Maddy all but shoved her into the room.

"Oh?" Always cautious, Chantel lifted a brow. "How do you do?"

"I don't want to disturb you." Chantel's brow lifted a little higher at the accent, and a smile came into her eyes. "I think I should go down or—"

"She's with Trace," Abby put in.

"Is she really?" In the way of triplets, the sisters communicated the rest. "Well, isn't that nice? Excellent taste, Trace." She took both of Gillian's hands. "Sorry I can't say as much for yours, but champagne is definitely in order."

"I'll get it."

"For heaven's sake, Maddy, I'll have one of the servants bring it. You can't go traipsing up and down the stairs in your condition. Take everyone into the sitting room down the hall. Quinn's barred from this wing, so I'm not risking any bad luck. I'll be there as soon as I fix my face again." She put a hand on Trace's arm. "Stay, please."

"Sure." He shot a look at Gillian, but she was already being washed away in the wave of his sisters.

"We missed you," she said when they were alone. "Is everything all right?"

"Yeah, why?"

With her hands in his, Chantel sat with him on the bed. "I guess I always figured you'd come home in absolute triumph or absolute destitution."

He had to laugh. "Sorry, it's neither."

"I won't ask what you've been doing, but I have to ask if you're staying."

"I don't know." He thought of Gillian. "I wish I did."

"All right. You're here today. I hate to be sloppy, but I can't tell you how much it means to me."

"You start crying again, you will look like a hag."

"I know. You always were a pain in the—"

"Chantel, Reed said you needed me. I've been trying to keep your father from fighting with the—" Molly paused halfway into the room.

He'd thought he'd prepared himself to see her again. She looked older, but not old. Changed, but somehow constant. She'd scolded him and comforted him, walloped him and soothed him. Whatever was needed. He felt twelve years old as he stood and looked at her.

"Mom."

She didn't want to burst into tears. That would be a foolish thing before she'd said so much as a word. With the strength that had gotten her through years on the road, she took a deep breath. "Let me look at you." He was thin, but he always had been. Like his father. So like his father. "It's good to have you back." She took the next step and folded him in her arms. "Oh, Tracey, how good it is to have you back."

She smelled the same. She seemed smaller now, more delicate, but she smelled the same. He buried his face in her hair and let himself feel. "I missed you. Mom, I'm sorry."

"No regrets." She said it almost fiercely as she held on. "There's to be no regrets. And no questions." She drew away to smile at him. "At least not now. I'm going to dance with my son at my daughter's wedding." She held out a hand for Chantel. Some prayers *were* answered.

"Molly! In the name of all that's holy, where did you run off to? Those so-called musicians don't know a single Irish tune."

Molly felt Trace stiffen. "Don't repeat mistakes," she said with a sternness he remembered well.

"What's the matter with that girl, hiring a bunch of idiots? Molly, where the devil are you?"

He bounced into the room the way he bounced through life. Sure of himself and on the edge of a dance. It was rare for Frank O'Hurley's feet to falter, but they did when he saw his son.

"I have to see about champagne," Chantel said quickly. "Mom, there's someone I want you to meet. Come let me introduce you."

Molly stopped at the door and looked into her husband's eyes. "I've loved you all my life," she said quietly. "And will no matter what foolish thing you do. Don't disappoint me, Frank."

Frank cleared his throat as the door shut behind him. A man shouldn't feel awkward with his own son. But he couldn't help it. "We didn't know you were coming."

"I didn't know myself."

"Still footloose and fancy-free, are you, Trace?"

His spine stiffened. "So it seems."

"That's what you always wanted." It wasn't what he wanted to say, but the words came out before he could stop them.

"You never knew what I wanted." Damn, why did it have to be a repeat performance? "You never wanted to know. What you wanted was for me to be you, and I couldn't be."

"That's not true. I never wanted you to be anyone but yourself."

"As long as it fit your standards." Trace started to walk out, but then he remembered what Gillian had said. He had to make peace, or at least try. He stopped, still feet away from his father, and dragged a hand through his hair. "I can't apologize, I won't apologize, for being who I am, or for doing anything I've done. But I am sorry I've disappointed you."

"Wait a minute." Frank held up a hand. A moment before he'd been afraid he would lose Trace again, and he hadn't been sure he would be able to get him back. He'd had years to regret. "Who said I was disappointed? I never said I was disappointed. What I was was angry, and hurt, but you never disappointed me. I won't have you saying it."

"What do you want me to say?"

"You had your say once, twelve years ago. Now I'll have mine." His chin was jutted out. He, too, wore a tux, but on him it looked like a stage costume. Trace would have bet his last nickel there were taps on the bottoms of his shoes. He hoped there were.

"All right, but before you do, I want you to know I didn't come to spoil Chantel's wedding. If we can't do anything else, I'd like to call a truce for one day."

The calm strength surprised Frank. His boy had grown up. Pride and regret pulled him in opposite directions. "It's not a war I want with you, Tracey. It never was." Frank pushed a hand through his hair in a gesture that surprised Trace because it mirrored one of his own habits "I-I needed you." He stumbled on the words, then cleared his throat. "You were my first, and I needed you to be proud of me, to look up to me like I had all the answers. And when you wanted to find your own, I didn't want to listen. Knowing I was a failure to you—"

"No." Appalled, Trace took the first step forward. "You never were, you couldn't be."

"You sent your mother money."

"Because I wasn't around to give anything else."

The old wound remained, gnawing. "I never gave you— any of you—the things I promised."

"We never needed things, Pop."

But Frank shook his head. "A man's meant to provide for his family, to pass some legacy on to his son. God knows I never gave your mother half of what she deserved. The promises were too big. When you left, saying what you said, I had to be bitter. Because if I stopped being bitter, I couldn't have stood knowing I wasn't the father you wanted, or being without you."

"You've always been the father I wanted. I didn't think . . ." Trace let out a long breath, but it didn't steady his voice. "I didn't think you wanted me back."

"There's not a day that's gone by I haven't wanted you back, but I didn't know how to tell you. Hell, didn't know where you were most of the time. I drove you away, Tracey, I know that. Now you've come back a man and I've lost all those years."

"There are plenty more. For both of us."

Frank put his hands on his son's broad shoulders. "When you leave, I don't want it to be in anger. And I want you to know that just by looking at you here, I'm proud of what you've made yourself."

"I love you, Pop." For the first time in twelve years, he embraced his father. "I want to stay." He closed his eyes because the words brought such tremendous relief. "I need you. I need all of you. It's taken me too long to figure that out." He drew away. "I want my father back."

"Ah, Tracey, I've missed having you." Frank reached for his own handkerchief and blew smartly. "Damn girl ought to keep a bottle in here."

"We'll find one. Pop." Trace looked into his father's damp blue eyes. "I've always been proud of you. What you gave me was the best. I just had to see what I could do with it on my own."

"This time, my boy, we kill the fatted calf." He put his arm around Trace's shoulder. "And we'll have that drink, you and me. When this hoopla of your sister's is over, I might even risk your mother's temper and get a little drunk. A man's entitled to celebrate when he's given a son."

"I'm buying."

Frank's damp eyes sparkled. "That's my boy. Made a bundle, did you? And you saw all those places you wanted to see?"

"More than I wanted to see," Trace said and smiled. "I even sang for my supper a time or two."

"Of course you did." Fresh pride burst through him. "You're an O'Hurley, aren't you?" He gave Trace a slap on the back. "Always had a better voice than you had feet, but that's no matter. I expect you've got stories to tell." He winked as they started out. "Start with the women."

That hadn't changed, either. Though he hadn't expected it, it made him glad. "It might take a while."

"We've got time." He had his son back. "Plenty of it."

They were halfway down the stairs when Trace saw another tuxedoed figure. "I'll check it out," the man said in a phone with his back to the stairs.

"Quinn, my boy." Frank's call could have brought down the roof. "I want you to meet my son, Trace."

Quinn turned. He and Trace stared at each other. The shock of recognition came, but it didn't show. "Nice to meet you." Quinn held out a hand. "I'm sure Chantel's thrilled you're here."

"It's interesting meeting all my in-laws in one fell swoop."

"We need a drink," Frank announced. "Guests'll be trooping in before we know it." And he was going to show off his family. All his family.

"Pour me a double." Trace patted his father's shoulder. "I'll be right with you."

"We'll make it a quick one for now. I still have to straighten out those musicians."

"Small world," Quinn commented when they were alone.

Trace shook his head, studying the man who had once, in his early days with the ISS, been his partner. "It's been a while."

"Afghanistan was what—eight, ten years ago?"

"That's the ballpark. So you're going to marry Chantel."

"Come hell or high water."

"Does she know what you do?"

"I don't do it anymore." Quinn pulled out his cigarettes and offered one. "I've got my own security business. You?"

"Recently retired." Trace pulled out matches. "I'll be damned."

"You know, I'm amazed I didn't put it together, O'Hurley."

"We weren't using names in that operation, not real ones."

"Yeah, but the thing is, you look more like her than either of her sisters."

Trace blew out a long stream of smoke and laughed. "If you don't want to sleep on the couch for the next six months, I wouldn't mention that to her."

The O'Hurleys overwhelmed her. Gillian had never met anyone like them. She found herself sitting with the family as Chantel was married in the warm California winter under a white silk canopy while some five hundred guests looked on. There was champagne by the bucket, flowers by the truckload, and tears enough to swim in.

For hours she was caught up in the whirlwind they created until, head spinning, she sought out a quiet spot to let it all settle. She wasn't sure it was quite proper for her to slip into the parlor, but the music was muted here. And she could put her feet up.

"Sneaking out?"

With a gasp, she pressed a hand to her heart. "You scared the life out of me." She relaxed again as Trace came to sit beside her. "You shouldn't creep up behind a person."

"I've been doing it for years." He stretched his own legs out. "Feet hurt?" he asked as he looked at her discarded shoes.

"I feel like I've danced my toes off. Doesn't your father ever slow down?"

"Not that I've ever noticed." God, it was good to be back.

Gillian snuggled back against the pillows. "He likes me."

"Of course he does. You're Irish. Then there's the fact that you can do a fairly adequate jig."

"Fairly adequate?" She sat up straight again. "I'll have you know, O'Hurley, your father said I could go on the road with him and your mother anytime I wanted."

"Packing your trunk?"

She sat back again with a sigh. "I don't think I could keep up with either of them. They're all wonderful. Every one of them. Thank you for bringing me."

"I think I've figured out who brought whom." He lifted her hand and kissed her palm, leaving her speechless. "Thank you, Gillian."

"I love you. I just wanted you to be happy."

When he let her hand go again, she curled her fingers into the palm he'd kissed. "You said that before." Rising, he walked to the window. From there he could see the tables ladened with food and wine and hundreds of people milling around and dancing.

"That I wanted you to be happy?"

"That you loved me."

"Did I?" Very casual, she studied her nails. "Isn't that interesting? As I recall, you didn't have much of a reaction then, either."

"I had things on my mind."

"Oh, yes, saving my brother and Caitlin. We haven't quite finished there." She reached in her purse and drew out a piece of paper. Standing, she offered it to him. "The hundred thousand we agreed on. I had my lawyers send the check." When he didn't move, she walked over and pushed it into his hand. "It's certified. I promise it won't bounce."

He wanted to jam the check down her pretty throat. "Fine."

"Our business is over, then. You've got your retirement fund, a house, your family." She turned away, knowing she was very close to murder. "So where do you go from here, Trace? Straight to the islands?"

"Maybe." He crumpled the check and jammed it in his pocket. "I've been thinking."

"Now *there's* good news."

"Watch your mouth. Better yet, just shut up." He took her by the shoulders and kissed her hard. As he hadn't, Gillian thought, in much too long.

The door opened. Abby took one step in and stopped. "Oh, excuse me. Sorry." Just as quickly, she was gone again.

Trace swore lightly. "Maybe you *are* in love with me. And maybe you're plain stupid."

"Maybe." This time she swore, too, and made his brow lift. "Maybe I'd like to know how you feel."

"We're not talking about how I feel."

"Oh, I see."

Before she could move away he had her close again. It was amazing how quickly panic could come to someone who'd lived his life one step ahead of danger. "Don't turn away from me."

She gave him a straight, level look. "I'm not the one who's doing the turning, Trace."

She had him there. And, damn it, his palms were damp again. "Listen, I don't know how attached you are to New York, to that place you work. I could sell the house in Chicago if it didn't suit."

She felt the gurgle of laughter—or triumph—but swallowed it cautiously. "Didn't suit what?"

"Didn't suit, damn it. Gillian, I want—"

This time Maddy burst through the door and halfway into the room. "Oh, hi." At the expression on Trace's face, she rolled her eyes. "You didn't see me," she said as she began to back out. "I never came in. I was never here. Now I'm gone." And she was.

"Some things never change," Trace muttered. "I never in my life had a minute's privacy with those three around."

"Trace." Gillian put a hand on his cheek and shifted his face back toward hers. "Are you asking me to marry you?"

"I'd like to muddle through this in my own way, if you don't mind."

"Of course." Very solemn, she sat on the window seat. "Please go on."

Did she think one of her long, quiet looks was going to make it easy for him? He could write down how he felt, he could put it to music. The words would come then. But now, just now, he was fresh out.

"Gillian, I think you're making a big mistake, but if you're set on it, we could try it. I've got some ideas about what to do with myself now that the ISS is history." His hands were in his pockets again, because he didn't know what else to do with them. "Maybe I could pitch some of my songs—but that's not really the point," he went on before she could speak. "The point is whether or not you could handle—that you'd be willing to— You know, you really have no business getting tangled up with me."

"This time you shut up."

"Wait a minute—"

"Just shut up and come over here." He scowled, but crossed over to her. "Sit," she said, then gestured to the seat beside her. She waited until he sat down, then took his hands. "Now, I'll tell you exactly what the point is. I love you, Trace, with all my heart, and I want nothing more than to spend my life with you. It doesn't matter where. The house in Chicago is special, I know, and there are laboratories in the Midwest. What I have to know is that you'd be content. I won't start the rest of my life by holding you down."

There was no one else like her. And there would never be anyone else for him. He wished he had the right words just now, something soft and sweet. One day, he thought, they might come easily.

"I told you when we first met that I was tired. That's the truth. I don't need to climb mountains anymore, Gillian. I already know what's at the top. I'll probably be a lousy husband, but I'll give you the best I've got."

"I know that." She took his face in her hands and kissed him lightly. "Why do you want to marry me, Trace?"

"I love you." It was a great deal easier to say than he had thought. "I love you, Gillian, and I've waited a hell of a long time to make a home."

She rested her head on his shoulder. "We'll make one together."

*   *   *   *   *

Silhouette Special Edition

Now appearing
in a special return engagement, Nora Roberts's
bestselling 1988 miniseries featuring

THE O'HURLEYS!
Nora Roberts

Book 1   THE LAST HONEST WOMAN   *Abby's Story*
Book 2   DANCE TO THE PIPER   *Maddy's Story*
Book 3   SKIN DEEP   *Chantel's Story*

And making his debut in a brand-new title, a very special
leading man . . . Trace O'Hurley!

Book 4   WITHOUT A TRACE   *Trace's Tale*

In 1988, Nora Roberts introduced THE O'HURLEYS!—a close-knit
family of entertainers whose early travels spanned the country. The
beautiful triplet sisters and their mysterious brother each experience
the triumphant joy and passion only true love can bring, in four books
you will remember long after the last pages are turned.

Don't miss this captivating miniseries—a special collector's edition
available now wherever paperbacks are sold.

OHUR-1A

Double your reading pleasure this fall with two Award of Excellence titles written by two of your favorite authors.

Available in September

DUNCAN'S BRIDE
by Linda Howard
Silhouette Intimate Moments #349

Mail-order bride Madelyn Patterson was nothing like what Reese Duncan expected—and everything he needed.

Available in October

THE COWBOY'S LADY
by Debbie Macomber
Silhouette Special Edition #626

The Montana cowboy wanted a little lady at his beck and call—the "lady" in question saw things differently....

These titles have been selected to receive a special laurel—the Award of Excellence. Look for the distinctive emblem on the cover. It lets you know there's something truly wonderful inside!

Take 4 bestselling love stories FREE

Plus get a FREE surprise gift!

Win 1 of 10 Romantic Vacations and Earn Valuable Travel Coupons Worth up to $1,000!

Inside every Harlequin or Silhouette book during September, October and November, you will find a PASSPORT TO ROMANCE that could take you around the world.

By sending us the official entry form available at your favorite retail store, you will automatically be entered in the PASSPORT TO ROMANCE sweepstakes, which could win you a star-studded London Show Tour, a Carribean Cruise, a fabulous tour of France, a sun-drenched visit to Hawaii, a Mediterranean Cruise or a wander through Britain's historical castles. The more entry forms you send in, the better your chances of winning!

In addition to your chances of winning a fabulous vacation for two, valuable travel discounts on hotels, cruises, car rentals and restaurants can be yours by submitting an offer certificate (available at retail stores) properly completed with proofs-of-purchase from any specially marked PASSPORT TO ROMANCE Harlequin® or Silhouette® book. The more proofs-of-purchase you collect, the higher the value of travel coupons received!

For details on your PASSPORT TO ROMANCE, look for information at your favorite retail store or send a self-addressed stamped envelope to:

PASSPORT TO ROMANCE
P.O. Box 621
Fort Erie, Ontario L2A 5X3

ONE PROOF-OF-PURCHASE

3-CSSE-2

To collect your free coupon booklet you must include the necessary number of proofs-of-purchase with a properly completed offer certificate available in retail stores or from the above address.